BLOOD CRAFT

BLACK MAGIC OUTLAW
BOOK SEVEN

Domino Finn

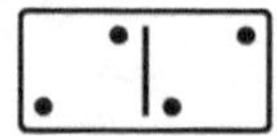

Published by Blood & Treasure, Los Angeles
First Edition

Cover by James T. Egan of Bookfly Design LLC.

Print ISBN: 978-1-946-00807-7

DominoFinn.com

Magic is Real

Not only that, it's all around you. Energies, events, encounters. Dark places filled with mythic creatures every bit as dangerous as their legends.

Opening your eyes to this reality isn't easy. Silvans are tricky. Vampires operate in the shadows. Even wizards greedily hoard their secrets.

What you need is an outlaw. Someone with nothing left to lose. A tour guide to the supernatural underground who packs enough grit and spellcraft to handle anything in your way.

What you need is Cisco Suarez, a hard-talking, hard-fighting, hard-luck hero.

Welcome to the exciting world of Black Magic Outlaw. It isn't always easy, but it's always a blast.

Previously in Black Magic Outlaw

The name's Cisco Suarez, and I'm a necromancer. It's all fun and games till you wake up dead in a dumpster, but I broke out of my zombie curse, got revenge on the people who did this to me, and took my life back.

Now I've gone legit. Got myself a new car, a swanky penthouse, even my own coffee shop. I also picked up some trouble with the local vampire clan, the Obsidian March. I killed their boss and made a tenuous alliance with Clan Beaumont for protection. If only my troubles ended there.

A serial killer named Manifesto introduced himself to Miami by killing animists. I had to put him down, but only after he tricked me into revealing my shadow magic on prime-time news. My identity's still a secret but the word is out. I'm the talk of the town and the FBI is gunning hard for the mysterious Shadow Man.

Which brings us to now...

BLACK MAGIC OUTLAW

Chapter 1

I leaned against the creaky fence as the sun went down on *Calle Ocho*. The Little Havana street was famous in its own right, though maybe notorious was a better word. Pedestrian on the surface, a little run-down as far as tourist attractions went—the strip's real reputation emerged only with the night.

Working ladies did laps on the sidewalk, swaying hips and waving arms on display for passing traffic. This was near the Palmetto Expressway, the kind of hood with security bars on storefront windows and motels advertising heart-shaped Jacuzzis. Overhead, the neon of the Cielo Motel painted everything a peppy shade of aqua.

Yup, just another day in paradise.

But it wasn't all bad, especially when it came to authentic Miami cuisine. Case in point was the food I was briskly finishing off. Cubans are so crazy about eating pig they put it in their signature sandwich twice. And in case the meat itself wasn't enough, the only proper way to cook the local bread was with a healthy dose of pork lard. I downed the last bite of ham, pork, and Swiss cheese in pressed bread and focused on the work at hand.

Miami was still reeling in the wake of a serial killer. Manifesto had captured the nation's attention. He'd been a cipher, someone sent to expose the magic in the streets, to punish its practitioners, but Manifesto had just been a man. He was dead and the police didn't have much.

But I had more. I had the lunatic's journal. Crazed accounts of initiation by a celestial fleet of black sisters. Manifesto treated his curse reverentially, as if the angels themselves had opened his eyes to the truth. I didn't know much about angels but I knew these didn't fit the bill. And buried in page after rambling page, the only location Manifesto mentioned by name was the Cielo Motel.

There was something else I had that the police didn't. I was an animist, and a particularly skilled one by this point. On any given day there was a good chance I was the best hand at spellcraft in the city, which added a few tools to my belt. As the last of twilight receded and the long shadow of night yawned over Miami, the power within me thrummed.

The Cielo was a tough motel to stake out from a distance. Since its clientele preferred to do business under the cover of darkness, the parking lot was behind the building. The rooms didn't have ample windows and the curtains were almost always drawn anyway. And that's where my business was.

You see, Manifesto had mentioned a room. I didn't know which one, but I'd spent last night renting out several by the hour with no luck. If I did this long enough, it was only a matter of time till I found the right one.

I closed my eyes and reached out. A desiccated pigeon on the back roof blinked and cocked its head. I looked through its eyes and scoped out the parking lot. Aside from a strung-out man in loose pants rummaging through a dumpster and piling treasures into a black garbage bag, there was nothing to see.

My phone rang.

I casually opened my eyes and wiped crusty fingers on my jeans before pulling out my burner. It was my friend Evan. "Yeah?" I answered.

"I got something for you," he said, acting outside his capacity as a police lieutenant. "Something better than the brute force approach you're so keen on."

"If it ain't broke, don't fix it."

"Your clock might not be broken, Cisco, but it runs a little slow. There's nothing wrong with speeding things up a bit."

I nodded to myself. It was a given that Evan would gloat over his new find. I just hoped it was worth the suffering.

"One of Manifesto's last credit card receipts," he said, "before he went dark, was two hundred and forty dollars at your motel."

After the serial killer had been anointed, as he would call it, he became a lot harder to track. He'd emptied his bank account and cut up his plastic. But if this was where it had all started for him, he wouldn't have had the wherewithal to hide his tracks yet. This clue strengthened the significance of my hunt for the motel room.

"The other credit card charges are recurring payments," continued Evan, "so nothing notable. But this is the one we wanted."

"Is there a room number?" I asked.

"No, but two-forty seems a bit pricey for the area, don't you think? I took the liberty of checking out the Cielo's website and found their executive suite runs eighty bucks an hour. You extend that to three hours and you have our charge. Seems Nathan Bartlett Jones was a man of stamina."

"Unless he was the type to cuddle. Listen, we don't know what happened in that room, but I'd lay odds on the black sisters using him more than he used them."

"The point is, I called the motel and inquired about the executive rooms. They only have six of them."

I blinked, impressed. "You mean I'm not destined to see cloudy hot-tub water for nights on end?"

"You're welcome," laughed Evan as he hung up the phone.

I slipped the burner into my pocket, took a last sip of Materva, and tossed the can in the trash.

"It's go time," I said to my silent partner. "Stay out of sight."

My cowboy boots clattered across the street as I held up my hand to approaching headlights. I hit the far sidewalk and made a bee line for the office. Luckily there was a different manager than last night so he wasn't suspicious of my repeat business. I paid cash for one hour in the first executive suite. Without looking up from his porn mag, the manager slid a clipboard my way. I used the grungy pen to sign in as "Buck Wild" and searched the counter for hand sanitizer. No such luck.

I scooped up the key and marched through the breezeway to the back. The dumpster diver was gone. Vending machines lined the base of the building, not only offering sodas and snacks but condoms and lubricants as well. Classy joint. I turned up the stairwell along the side of the building and made my way for executive suite 204.

I paused just before my hand touched the doorknob. Frowning, I slipped the metal key into my back pocket. The door was already open. I glanced up and down the empty hall and over the balcony into the quiet parking lot. Was this a troubling development or piss-poor property management? I cracked my fingers. The dog collar on my wrist wriggled in anticipation, and I pushed the door open with the tip of my alligator boot.

Wow, executive was right.

A patterned quilt of purple and brown covered the king-size bed. A mirror accompanied it on the ceiling. The heart-shaped Jacuzzi was lined with red rose petals, a nice touch for the executive but not nearly the only upgrade. Beside the leather contraption that looked more like gym equipment than a chair, there was a full-blown stage and stripper pole. Colored lights adorned the walls with dizzying splendor. And for some reason, the bathroom had a see-through glass wall and door. I supposed there was no reason to miss the show while dropping the kids off at the pool.

The room was more gaudy than glamorous, but one

thing it didn't overdo was its square footage. With the lit bathroom interior fully visible, I could see the whole place, and there clearly weren't any intruders.

I pushed the door closed and cleared my throat. So this was where Manifesto's angels had sexed him up. He claimed he was birthed in blood and granted numerous pleasures of the flesh. It wasn't an uncommon thing for Nether beings to do. Legends throughout histories and cultures are rife with mystical female seducers preying on man's impure urges.

Nathan Jones, however, didn't find himself in the hospital with lost time. He didn't go missing or turn up a day later face-down in an Everglades swamp. Whatever happened to him changed him. Gave him a purpose, magic resistance, protection by mystical black owls, and a cause he was willing to die for.

First order of business was turning off all the glaring recessed "show" lights. I flipped switches for the bed and stage, but lots of LEDs remained. I found additional switches for the lit plexiglass stage, the mirror lights, and the bathroom. There were still tracking lights on the carpet and the glowing base of the bed, but as far as I could tell those were on for good. We wouldn't want people to trip while caught up in the throes of passion.

With the room adequately dark, I let the shadow flow from my pupils and flush my irises black. As I had done with all the rooms before, I paced the suite searching for forensic evidence of a ritual. Something—anything—that suggested powerful magic had passed through this place.

The bathroom was clean. The stage too. Pools of water

can sometimes be tough, especially with repeated cleaning, but the real disappointment was the bed. Beds were where the magic happened, metaphorically and literally, and while there may have been traces of the supernatural, it was impossible to examine what was only a faint suggestion. The room was dry.

I chewed my lip. Eighty bucks down the drain. I could complain about the room and try to swap for another one, but that trick wouldn't fly five more times. No, in situations like this it was best to grease the wheels with cash and hope for as few questions as possible.

I blew air from my lips and leaned my head back, ready to move on, and then I saw it. A slithering blackness in the ceiling mirror. It wasn't a glow like I'd expected, but it was definitely a mass of leftover Intrinsics. Magic. I squinted more power into my eyes and studied the anomaly.

This wasn't shadow magic, even if it appeared similar on the surface. It was dark, lingering like a stain, and just as hard to penetrate, except this one would take more than Tide with Bleach to unravel.

My first thought was a rabbit hole to the Nether, but that wasn't right. This wasn't grounded in a thin barrier of the Earthly Steppe. Neither the drywall nor the bed were enchanted; the mirror itself was. Reflective surfaces were portals to the Murk and sometimes worse places. Something had passed through here, anything from oozing spellcraft to perhaps even a being of some sort.

I cocked my head and scratched my chin, wondering about the best way to deal with this. It could take days to dissect, and I'd rather pay the vandalism bill than indefinite hourly rates. Which meant the mirror had to go.

I zipped open my belt pouch and produced a bronze knife. While not suited to hunting or fighting, it was a damn handy utility tool. I hopped onto the bouncing bed and stuck the knife into the silicone seam between the mirror and the drywall.

I took my time. While a large enough chunk of cracked mirror might have worked fine, I preferred the entire piece. I sliced through the sealant and tested the fixture lightly at various points. As I rounded the second corner, an alert shot into my mind.

I shut my eyes. The eyes of the pigeon illuminated a backdrop of black sky. An owl swooped into the foreground unerringly fast. Pointed talons reached out and the vision went black. I jerked my head away in momentary pain.

The black owls were here.

Chapter 2

I ran to the door. Screw Intrinsics, the owls were the most direct link I had to Manifesto's handlers. For all I knew, they could be the black sisters. The Nether was full of shape-shifters.

I flew outside, boots skidding on concrete, sawed-off in my lowered hand. It was loaded with regular birdshot to do as little collateral damage as possible. Once again I was greeted by ghostly emptiness. It was why I'd chosen so early in the evening to conduct my searches—less chance I'd run into working stiffs getting stiffed.

The motel was only two stories high. I was on the second level, but I couldn't see above the overhanging roof of the breezeway. I hurried around the bend of the U-shaped floor plan to get a side view.

Not a bird in the sky. Certainly no acid-filled predators clawing at my face. Not my pigeon either. I slowed and frowned. Without eyes in the sky, the owl could be anywhere. Then again, I had the feeling it wasn't a danger.

We were both here doing the same thing: snooping.

I returned my shotgun to the shadow and leaned on the metal railing with a sigh. The owls were proving to be experts at taking out my avian minions, and anything bigger would be difficult to utilize in the city. But I had a more troubling worry. How did they know I was here? Was utilizing zombies giving my position away?

There was another possibility. This site was important to Manifesto's angels, for some reason, so the owls were keeping an eye on things.

A door in one of the budget rooms downstairs slammed open. The same man I'd seen digging through the trash before sprinted out, only this time he was in his tighty-whities. Well, "tight" was an overstatement. This dude had lost so much weight to his meth habit that his underwear swung loosely around his skinny legs.

From my side vantage, I watched him with ease from above. He first sprinted to the vending machines, then the opposite direction where he finally landed at the ice machine. He hurriedly flipped it open, dug down, and unloaded the full metal scoop into the front of his drawers.

Ladies and gentlemen, say hello to Florida Man.

I cracked a smile as he dumped a second scoop to fill his loose underwear and relaxed. There wasn't enough hand sanitizer in the world to purify that ice scoop. I idly watched as the man twitched erratically as he paced the hall and paused, paced and paused.

My grin faded when I heard crying from the open motel door.

My senses perked. It was that feeling you get when you're being watched. Nobody else was walking the halls, upstairs or down, and I had a clear view of the seven cars in the parking lot. The black sky was likewise clear.

I walked to the end of my wing and started down the stairs as Florida Man's concentric pacing neared his room. Stray cubes of ice escaped his underwear and tumbled to the floor, but he didn't seem to notice. The bulk of it was cooling his junk.

Back on ground level, I approached slowly so as not to startle the man. Hell, he didn't even see me yet. As I came in line with the open room, a crying woman on the floor turned her head to me.

"My daughter..." she sobbed, mouth drenched in mucus.

Florida Man stiffened as he noticed me. His bare feet quickly stomped back to the room. "Woman, you be quiet!" He raised his fist.

I closed the distance in a blink and grabbed his arm from behind. He was all of a hundred pounds so it was easy. "That would be a REALLY bad move."

The addict tried to twist his arm away but might as well have been chained to a radiator. I hissed in frustration and shoved him to the floor of his room.

"My daughter," cried the woman again.

She was huddled on the floor too, leaning against the spartan nightstand. Drugs and wads of cash lay on top. There was no child in sight.

I turned to the door. Outside, a light flickered within one of the parked cars. With the interior lit, I noticed for the first time how darkly tinted the front windshield was. Florida Man was a familiar.

That meant vampires. The Obsidian March was here.

I stomped outside, reaching into shadow and pulling out my shotgun. As I marched, the car started and the headlights sprayed my face. I planted my boot to jump into action, and then a huge explosion rocked my back.

The force plastered me to the asphalt. Clusters of fire rained down. One chunk hit the hood of the car as it pulled away. I rolled over and saw the remains of executive suite 204 turned inside out by the detonation. The blast was upstairs and hadn't hit me head on, and the collateral damage had been minimal. On the other hand, my forensics were utterly obliterated.

I grunted and hopped to my feet as the car disappeared down the driveway. I sprinted around the building to keep it in sight, but it was too far ahead by the time I rounded the corner. I cursed myself for chasing it directly instead of using the walkway to cut it off at the sidewalk. As the car approached *Calle Ocho* I raised my shotgun and aimed a desperate shot.

Two red orbs appeared at the end of the alley in the path of the escaping car. A ghostly Spaniard in full conquistador armor materialized. The wraith drew a rapier and waited.

The vampire swerved slightly, trying to go around the obstacle, but there wasn't enough clearance. The car accelerated instead, ready to blindly rush into the busy street.

The car passed through the ghostly Spaniard. It shot into

the street across two lanes of traffic, miraculously not hitting anyone until it slammed into a streetlight on the opposite sidewalk. The horn blared and cut out.

I blinked. There was no sign of the wraith. I pulled my finger off the trigger and hurried after them. The car was stationary, and oncoming traffic had slowed after the accident. I moved around the car and blocked the exit as the driver's door opened.

The vampire leaned back behind the deflating airbag. He was in human form, clutching a punctured neck with trimmed black fingernails. While the air moving through his neck made an unsettling sound, there wasn't a drop of blood in the dried-up husk.

"The truce..." he croaked.

I pointed the gun his way but knew the birdshot would do less damage than he'd already incurred. "I don't answer to vampires," I spat. "What are you doing here?"

The wraith materialized in the passenger seat beside him, bleached skull staring hard, ghostly side-sword resting against his gut.

"I wasn't trying to kill you," said the vamp through pained teeth.

My eyes darted to the back seat. A little girl about my daughter's age lay tied up with a burlap sack over her head. My stomach turned.

"Your blade's too low," I growled. "You need to get them in the heart."

The vamp's eyes widened. "We have a truce!"

The Spaniard's rapier stabbed the fiend through. He

jerked and popped like an overfilled balloon. This time there was plenty of blood, a spray of it all over the windshield.

I scowled and turned to the burning debris on the hood. The smoke coming from the Cielo. The throng of stopped cars watching the show.

"Damn." I opened the back door and pulled the girl out, setting her on the sidewalk and removing her hood and bindings. "You're safe. Stay here for the cops."

The sirens started in the distance. I stood and checked the car, but the Spaniard was already gone. Nothing left to accomplish here, I turned and fled down an alley, hurrying to my car two blocks away.

Chapter 3

I gunned the Firebird and hit the highway. Despite being dark, it was still early in the evening and I caught the end of rush-hour traffic. That wasn't a bad thing. As I sat on 836 ready to jump onto I-95 and get out of the area, I had a lot of time to think things over.

Manifesto was a dead serial killer who'd been murdering animists and making their talents public. He'd been cursed by something or someone, but operated as a loner, aside from the interference of a stray owl.

The Obsidian March, on the other hand, were an organization of upirs, Nether vampire clans involved in drugs, human trafficking, and more. Given the Manifesto aftermath, they were keeping a lower profile lately, but there were more and more of them, always present, under the surface. Just like cockroaches.

And while there was the odd upir, like Beaumont, who came across as a rational being, the majority of them were dangerous due to their complete indifference towards human life.

Beyond the face of it, I didn't see how the two groups were linked.

There was the obvious reality that both Manifesto and the vampires operated out of the Cielo. They'd both been at odds with me recently. But they had completely different motivations.

The vampires were just filling a void in the criminal underworld. No more explanation was necessary. They'd obviously known about Manifesto, but I doubted he knew about them. He was opposed to what he called the "other kind." Supernaturals. It was a group he dumped spellcasters like me into as well.

That also brought into question the owls, what they were, and why they were helping him on his holy mission.

The only thing I had was their motives. They operated in secrecy to not only hunt down and kill animists, but to expose their existence to the public at large. It was a threat even to the Society, about as organized a group of businesslike wizards I'd ever seen.

So, if Manifesto had been an attack on *their* organization, killing a few randos until they showed up and walked into his crosshairs, then I was doing their dirty work for them by chasing this down.

But there was the very real possibility that, like me, they were just in the wrong place at the wrong time.

Ugh, the more I pondered it, the more my mind went in circles. I wasn't getting anywhere with this thought exercise. Thinking was overrated.

Besides, traffic on I-95 was clearing up. I avoided the toll lane since I didn't want a SunPass record of my route and gassed the Firebird north. I dialed Milena and put the phone on speaker.

"Hey slugger," she answered, slightly out of breath. "Didn't expect you so soon."

"Yeah, I decided to play hooky and cut out of work early to go on a hot date."

She chuckled. "Anyone I know?"

"What about that redhead with all the piercings at your club?"

"*Sucio!*" she chided. "Besides, you wouldn't like her. She's only a C cup."

"Fine," I said laboriously. "Then are you free tonight?"

"You know it, Shadow Man. But I'm still at the gym for a bit."

That's what I liked about Milena. She took things as they came and had fun. No hang-ups about stripping, or dating a necromancer with a secret identity. After a youth of tragedy, she just wanted to live. We were a lot alike, except I hadn't figured out how to relax yet.

I checked the car's clock. "I thought your class was over? And don't call me that."

"Class is done but we have free access to the gym for another hour."

"Sweet. I could use the alibi. See you soon."

I hated to drop in unexpectedly, but Milena was good for it. We were closer than we'd ever been, almost always sleeping over at each other's places. You might call it my first official relationship since the one that killed me over a decade ago.

And I wasn't kidding about the alibi either. Showing up in public on the other side of the city would throw suspicion on any eyewitness accounts at the Cielo. The stars were aligned, too. My silver muscle car made great time in a trafficky city, and I even got lucky with Midtown parking and snagged a spot as someone pulled out.

I walked a block down the newly developed area rife with shiny signs and storefronts. Even the sidewalk was new. The windows to the gym showed only a few people still going at it, in solo or in pairs. The sign posted on the door reported a last hour of business as they wound down.

I slipped in discreetly and found Milena battering a heavy bag with her shin. She wore short shorts and a sports tank. Her hair was tied back, which was a cute look for her.

She halted a kick midair as she saw me, straightened, and wiped her face with a towel. "You're not supposed to see me like this. I'm not ready yet."

I grabbed her in an overbearing hug and kissed her cheek. "I like you sweaty." I pulled away and nodded at the punching bag. "This guy bothering you?"

She slapped me away. "I like working this way. The solitude helps me think."

"MMA helps you think..."

She shrugged. "A few girls at the club do it to protect themselves from creeps, but the last gym they showed me wasn't real fighting. More like Pilates."

I nodded. "And you're pretty serious about it?"

"Ever since being chased around the beach by a garbage demon, you could say that."

"It wasn't a demon, it was a poltergeist. They're—" I stopped, realizing the explanation wasn't necessary. I instead pivoted to a "Point taken." The explanation got me thinking about her friends at the strip club. "What happened to that one girl you worked with? The one who likes to flash and kiss people?"

She snorted. "No such luck for you. Brenda moved to Vegas. And you're gonna make me jealous if you keep talking about redheads."

"Heh," I said, squirming slightly. "I was just wondering about your friends."

She hiked a shoulder and pounded the bag. "We're in a transient business. It's hard to keep lasting relationships."

I could relate, as much as I aimed to change that.

"You'd like this new girl I'm hanging out with," she said. "She's a charmer."

"Why do you say that?"

"She's always hanging around rich guys."

"What am I," I said with wounded pride, "chopped liver?"

"Not at all." She laughed and patted my chest. "You're a perfectly acceptable sugar daddy."

I nodded. "That's better."

An older woman with close-cropped hair and lean muscles emerged from the back area. Her eyes immediately zeroed in on me and she came over. "Nice to see new blood," she said, smiling at me. "You just dropped in?"

"I've been here a little while," I lied, still working on my cover.

Milena pulled me over. "This is Cisco." She turned to me. "Amy's the instructor here."

We shook hands. "You a fighter?" she asked.

"Oh, well, I've gotten into fights, if that's what you mean. But not so much..." I pointed to the punching bag.

"Not so much technique," finished Milena. "You could describe his fighting style as ham-fisted."

"Works for me," I said.

She went on. "Arbitrary. Unwieldy. Desperate."

"I think she gets it." I turned to the instructor. "It's not that I don't respect technique, mind you. I just get by how I can."

Amy laughed good-naturedly, but her body language told a different story as she squared up with me. "You care to put on some gloves and hit the mat?" She raised her fists playfully.

"No thanks," I hurried. "I know when I'm outmatched."

They laughed again. Amy punched my arm for good measure, and I don't think she was holding back. I held back a wince as she waved and headed to another class member.

"She's scary," I whispered.

"Don't tell me you don't like strong women now."

I squeezed her into me so our faces were close. "I love them. But you're strong enough for one night. What do you say we get outta here and head to that cool pizza joint down the street?"

"What is it with guys and pizza?"

"I'm but a simple man, without an explanation for the intricacies of the universe. And I like bacon."

"Going for the trifecta after your Cuban sandwich?"

"How'd you know?"

She chuckled. "Pizza sounds good, actually. Give me a minute to take a shower."

"Do they allow pairs?"

She tossed the sweaty towel into my face.

"I'll wait right here," I peeped.

I watched her until she disappeared. Three blessings for whoever invented short shorts. Alone for a minute, I glanced over the spartan gym and noticed Amy eyeing me while flexing, like some kind of animal kingdom display.

On second thought, I decided to wait outside.

Chapter 4

I woke up the next morning naked and without a blanket. Milena snuggled beside me wrapped like a burrito. She was also lying on my left arm. I ignored the tingly sensation of my limb slowly withering from blood deprivation and smiled at her ceiling.

I remembered how surprised I was when I first laid eyes on her fancy Midtown condo. I'd just woken up from my ten-year nightmare and a lot had changed in the world. Hell, a lot had changed over the last year. Milena was no longer my baby sister's cute friend. She was with me now.

Of course, as they always did, the bad thoughts intruded on the good. My parents weren't alive to see this. Even worse, I didn't deserve it. I would've traded places with my sister Seleste in a second if I could. It didn't seem right. She was in the ground and I was newly rich and happy. The guilt was woven into me.

Which was why I admired Milena so much. Seleste had been the hot one. Milena used to be a bit chubby and overlooked growing up. After the tragedy, she fell pretty hard, even dipping into drugs and crime. She never went back to being an A student, but she got her act together, focused on bettering herself, getting in shape.

Eventually, she started getting noticed by guys. Becoming a dancer was her way of embracing her sexuality. It was a liberating way for her to reclaim her power. That's why she partied and lived life a day at a time. It wasn't because she didn't appreciate anything meaningful, it was because she realized what was.

The notification light on my phone blinked. I stretched toward the nightstand but was still pinned to the bed by Milena. I tried to slide my arm out gently, but everyone knows the maneuver's impossible to pull off. She stirred as I grabbed my phone and checked the text message.

Nice, my service order was ready for pickup.

Milena yawned. "That's not your other girlfriend, is it?"

"A man would be crazy to cheat on you."

She was too tired to appreciate the compliment. "More vampire business?"

"Nah."

She propped herself on her elbows and turned to me. "Can zombies text?"

I turned off the phone display. "I doubt they have the aptitude. Plus, the screen would get all smudgy."

Milena's eyes went wide as she saw the clock. "Crap. I have to get up for work."

"Work? What's work?"

She scoffed playfully. "Some of us have high mortgages

to pay off. And it's just a mandatory meeting. One hour tops."

She tried to jump out of bed but was wrapped up tight. She slowly rolled over the edge. I caught her first and unrolled the sheet. She was naked too. We kissed.

"You don't need to keep paying for the condo," I said.

She clicked her teeth. "Cisco, I don't want your money."

It wasn't what I'd meant, but it got me thinking. "It's not too much to ask. My ill-gotten gains are from the guy who screwed up both our lives. You deserve a piece of it." I swallowed, worried I was giving away too much. "Just think, no more mandatory meetings."

"My work's fun. I get to pick shifts and sleep in. Besides, I'm already using you for pizza."

"Fine, I promise to take you somewhere nicer tonight."

"You better."

"And don't pretend you're also not using me for my strapping endurance."

She hooked her legs around me and put her arms around my neck. "We'll just see about that."

I drove through Downtown on the way home. It was a nice day with a beaming sun and cool breeze, so I had the T-top open. When I parked curbside, I leaned back in the seat and almost forgot about the nasty business from the night before.

Almost.

A call from Evan came through. Considering the tip he gave me the last time we spoke, I was surprised this call hadn't come sooner. As much as I wanted to enjoy the morning, I answered the phone to tackle this head on.

"Did you need to blow up the room?" came his exasperated voice.

I breathed calmly. "It wasn't me."

"What is it with you and explosions? There could've been casualties."

"IT WASN'T ME."

He hissed. "That excuse is getting tired. With so much publicity on you these days, you should be lying low. Going on vacation or something. It's a good thing places like that don't have a lot of cameras."

"I counted on that," I answered coolly. "And I saved a little girl, didn't I? The explosion had nothing to do with me."

"It's not you, Cisco, but it's the way you do things. Brash and in-your-face. Do you really think if you weren't cavorting around the Cielo the last couple of nights, things would've played out the same?"

"I—" I huffed in annoyance. "Look, the people who cursed Manifesto did it there. They left behind some evidence."

He finished the thought. "And with you sniffing around,

they took measures to destroy it. That about sum it up?"

I didn't say anything. Sure, my actions had forced their hand, but I refused to take back saving that girl. The Obsidian March was a criminal enterprise currently being investigated by Evan's district-spanning police unit. They were the only cops who knew what they were really up against. But their methods were still very much by the book, involving paper trails and methodical investigations.

I couldn't wait for all the legal ducks to line up in a row.

Before I opened my mouth to speak, Evan changed the subject. "Listen, I'm calling 'cause we've got a related development. Quentin Capshaw's back in Miami, and he claims to know who the Shadow Man is."

I blinked. Capshaw was a two-bit hypnotist doing the show circuit. He might've been Manifesto's next victim if I hadn't intervened.

"He's a hack," was all I said.

"Regardless, that's now two of your messes I'll be cleaning up today."

I grimaced. "Thanks, Evan. I owe you, bro."

"Swing by the house later so we can coordinate."

"Will do."

I hung up. Evan wasn't pissed at me, per se. He was venting about the extra work I'd caused him, but he believed in what I was doing. He was a part of it, at times. He hated the vamps more than me, hated me associating with any of them. In the end, we did things differently.

But he was a solid friend and would do what it took to protect me. With his wife and daughter being animists as well, there was no escaping our world.

I exited the car and slammed the door, eager to recapture my carefree mood. The swanky jewelry store didn't have much of a facade—in fact it was gated like Fort Knox—but after passing through walls of security I was greeted with rows of expensive bling.

I flashed the woman behind the counter a smile but knew it came off more annoyed than pleasant. I mumbled about the text message for my service order and she brought over a new jewelry box. Her grin was infectious enough to start with, but when she opened the box I smiled for real.

My mother's old wedding ring, resized for Milena.

It was silver, of course, not gold. Old habits die hard for a necromancer, right? But this was probably all my mother could afford at the time. She always showed off how pretty the silver was, pure as her love for my father. Looking at it now, with all the years of tarnish polished away, it was a sight.

Of course, I didn't dump the ring at the fanciest jeweler in the city for a size adjustment and polish. My mother's fake diamond had long ago fallen off. I had it replaced with a sapphire, blue so deep it bordered on indigo. I'd caught Milena eyeing something like it before and hoped to surprise her. It was a bonus when I'd been told the gem symbolized new love and trust.

"It is enrapturing," said the woman with a dazzle in her eye.

With the final product in my hands, the whole thing hit me. How fast all this was. But I'd lost ten years of my life to the darkness already. Milena was about as special as anyone was to me. She understood me and I understood her, the forever optimist. It was past time I took a page from her book and enjoyed whatever life I had left to the fullest.

Which meant there was no reason to delay things on account of propriety. Hadn't I just promised to take her someplace nice tonight?

"Today's the day," I announced with a grin.

"I would say good luck," joked the simpering woman, "but you won't need it with that rock."

I gave her a wink and pocketed the box on the way to the car.

Chapter 5

I was re-energized, no doubt about it. The tunes were in full force as I rumbled down the Brickell strip. When I turned into my condo parking lot, a thin girl with black fingernails loitered in front of the building twirling blonde pigtails.

I sighed. I'd seen enough vampires for a while. I didn't make eye contact, which was awkward with the top open. Once inside the garage, I gassed the engine so all anybody could hear was the V8 echoing against the walls.

The garage elevator only went as high as the lobby. It was a nice open common room with a fountain and a piano, but it wasn't my front door. It was one of those annoying details you don't think about when you first buy a place.

Luckily, I'd found a workaround to the problem, a base of operations of sorts right here on the ground floor. Instead of heading to the tenant elevators, I marched across the lobby to the attached storefront now leased to me. With an entrance on the street and an additional one directly into my lobby, it was perfect.

I pulled open the glass door to Outlaw Coffee & Colada and slipped behind the marble counter alongside a young redhead in a dark blouse and skinny jeans. I didn't make them wear uniforms. I crossed my arms as Darcy finished up a latte.

"Seen the news?" she asked with an innocent lilt.

"It wasn't me."

I took in the shop. Brisk business, not too packed or overwhelming. More importantly, no trouble in sight. It was a good place.

And Darcy? She was my Padawan, of sorts. A runaway and loner at heart, she'd found common cause with our crew. As a powerful telekinetic, it was nice having her on our side. For now, she took to the barista thing surprisingly well. I think she liked the normalcy of it.

"Kasper around?" I asked.

After handing the coffee to a customer, she turned to me and snickered. "Kasper's more like a coffee mascot. He dances around the sidelines, but doesn't actually do the work. I think he's upstairs. The man doesn't keep normal hours."

I smiled. "He never did."

I grabbed a rag and wiped a spot on the counter, which led to me discovering a few stray sugar packets to clean up. The normalcy *was* good, I couldn't deny that, but it wasn't for me. I wasn't built for this mundane stuff. A couple weeks go by and I'm itching for something to take on.

That said, the coffee shop was necessary cover. I was a public figure now, with a tall tale about returning from

South America with coffee connections and a fledgling business. After a decade off the grid, it handily explained my sudden reappearance with lots of money, even if I was still a person of interest to the FBI.

They couldn't touch me 'cause Cisco Suarez was legit.

A skinny dude in his twenties frowned at a menu card. He'd been sitting at the bar a few minutes and didn't look any less confused than when he'd arrived.

"You need help with something?" I asked.

"I'm just waiting on a friend." He pulled his head away from the menu. "Oh, are you the owner?"

It caught me off guard, since none of us had uniforms, but it must have been my ratty clothes. I nodded.

"Do you have any suggestions? What's a... cafe..." He pointed at the menu.

I smiled. "You're not from around here, are you?"

"Um..."

"How long've you been in Miami?"

The young man gave a resigned shrug. "Only a few hours."

"I thought so," I chuckled. I manned the coffee machine and brewed a new shot into a small metal cup. "It's a *cafecito*," I said, pronouncing the second C like an S. "And it's only the best way to drink an espresso. Since you're new here, I won't accept any excuses not to try this ambrosia of the gods." I spooned sugar into another metal cup, poured the first few drops of coffee in, and mixed vigorously. I combined the resulting crema and coffee into a ceramic demitasse cup and slid it over. "That'll be sure to wake you up. On the house."

"Wow, thanks."

"Welcome to the Magic City."

He stared at the shot with hesitation, watching the sugary frothy swirl. My eyes drifted to the wall of windows along the sidewalk. Tutti was lounging around the storefront smoking a cigarette.

"So much for normalcy," I grumbled.

"What's that?" asked the guy, holding the demitasse before his mouth, pre-sip.

"Nothing. Enjoy."

I walked out from behind the bar. Tutti was a member of the Obsidian March, newly converted to the home team by an ally of sorts. This was another added convenience of having a street-level base of operations. I could take walk-ins without inviting the unsavories up to my home.

For her part, Tutti was unsavory unless you were into the trashy look. She was skinny and wore skirts that showed off long legs, but anyone with experience saw more trouble than she was worth.

I pushed outside. "You're smoking up my patio."

She unapologetically blinked purple lashes and flicked some ashes into the wind, all while keeping her eyes on my shop. "Lots of Nether activity these days, don't ya think?"

I frowned. "I don't like being stalked. What do you want?"

"Beaumont wants you to pass by sometime this morning."

"You couldn't come in and say that?"

The sprightly girl turned to me. "I was enjoying a smoke. Besides, he asked me not to be pushy."

It was strange. Leverett Beaumont was my aforementioned vampire friend. Probably better to call him a tenuous ally. Evan didn't like me dealing with him, but he was the boss of Brickell. With us both living in his territory, as long as we stayed friends we were protected from supernatural home invasions. At least from anyone who respected the power structure. And believe me, the Obsidian March respected the power structure. That alone was worth the cost of admission.

Beaumont was a mob tough guy recently growing in power, in no small part due to me, and he was so far staying true to his gentleman facade.

"If I agree to pass by, will you find another smoking hole?"

She squeezed the butt into a table. "I didn't know it bothered you so much. But no worries. My job here is done." She strolled up to me in that demure yet dangerous fashion vampires were famous for, eyes up, lips pouting toward mine as she caressed my arm. "The Nether's always more than it seems, Cisco."

I clenched my jaw. Did she know I was investigating the black sisters? Beaumont was using her as a connection within the Obsidian March, but I wondered if her old loyalties had died with the old boss. The one I had killed. Before I could get a good enough look into her eyes, she turned and strolled away.

I shoved back inside, feeling a bit like a ping-pong ball in the middle of a hectic rally. The guy visiting Miami confronted me.

"That was great!" he exclaimed. "Where has that been all my life? I owe you a gift in return."

I waved an arm. "Not necessary. I—"

"I insist," he said, offering me a fanciful envelope.

I arched an eyebrow and took it, wondering what the deal was. He couldn't have prepared this so fast. It wasn't a standard envelope like you'd buy with a card, but was hand-cut and folded, like an art project. It was sealed with dried green wax with a symbol of a branch, pine needles with a berry. On the flip side was glittery gold script that read "Cisco Suarez."

"Wait a minute."

I turned but the door to the street was folding closed. A few people passed on the sidewalk but the guy was gone.

I returned to the bar and sat in the stranger's seat as Darcy was picking up his empty cup. "What's that?"

"I'm not sure," I said. "Did you notice anything strange with that guy?"

"Nope, all we said to each other was hi."

She watched me break the seal and unfold the paper. Inside was a thin piece of tree bark with printed text.

> *You are cordially invited to the royal wedding of*
> *Principesse Ceelandra of the Juniper Circle*
> *and Champion Throok of Amethyst.*

I lowered my forehead to the counter. "He was a silvan." Suddenly Tutti's warning about Nether activity made sense.

"Really?" asked Darcy, a bit too loudly. She moved close and whispered. "You mean, from..." She pointed down.

"That's the place."

Silvans were legendary aberrations of the human race, most famously featured in Greek mythology but with parallels all over the world. Ceela was a satyr, part girl and part horse. Throok was a minotaur. I could only imagine the rest of the gang attending that wedding.

Darcy took the invitation and read it over. "Shen says their glamours are impossible to crack."

Pretty much all silvans used glamour to appear human while on the Earthly Steppe. It was taxing to them and there were some exceptions, but the point was, when they wanted to appear human, it was almost impossible to detect otherwise. A scan of the Intrinsics wouldn't even turn up trace magic. I wondered how Tutti had known, but then she was from the Nether herself. Maybe she had a sense for such things.

"This is really cool," piped Darcy. "It says you need to bring a gift."

I eyed the suggestive line of text.

> *Bring a token from your world in exchange for a token from ours.*

"Yeah, silvans are big on symbolic trades."

"And this is really late notice for a wedding. It's in three days! They couldn't give you a bigger heads up? A save-the-date at least?"

"I'm not going."

"Of course you're going," she said. "I can be your plus one."

I snatched the card from her hands. "I don't need a date."

"You can't take Milena. She doesn't know magic."

"It doesn't matter 'cause I'm not going."

"Whatever." She took the dirty cup over to the sink.

I grumbled to myself again. An invitation to the Nether was coincidental timing considering my investigation. Part of me wanted to enjoy the party and catch up with old friends. Ceela and Throok were all right. Another part of me wondered if the silvans could help me with my search for the black sisters.

Ping-pong ball was right. A smile cracked my lips.

Chapter 6

Just down Brickell Avenue was a steakhouse blending modern cooking styles with traditional jazzy flair. Carbon was a hip spot that dominated all of Miami's best-of lists, and it was difficult to snag reservations. Which meant it wasn't exactly my type of place even if I did enjoy a good cut of dry-aged beef.

Despite only opening for dinner, Carbon was accessible to certain associates doing business with Beaumont. Like my coffee shop, he used the joint as his convenient base of operations. I guess I learned from the best. I entered the dazzling space and ignored the few workers handling deliveries. The man himself sat in a raised booth in the back.

The sophisticated Frenchman owned a third of the high-end shops in the neighborhood. He was an old-school restaurateur who wore white tuxedo jackets and anachronistically gelled his brown hair to the side. I didn't let his looks disarm me. He was the head of the Beaumont clan, independent of the Obsidian March, but an upir all the same.

"Cisco," he said in a pleased voice as I slid into the booth. Before I realized someone was behind me, the man placed a glass on the table and poured me champagne.

"You celebrating?" I asked.

"Always." He sipped from his glass while I ignored mine. "Riddle me this. You end the menace of a serial killer but nearly get exposed as the infamous Shadow Man. In the same fell swoop, you take out Miami's Obsidian March boss, practically ending all pretenses of war. A victory worth celebrating. Except, precisely when it's in everyone's interests not to cause a stir, a tough guy takes out a low-level trafficker at the Cielo Motel."

I shrugged. "The March has lots of enemies."

"Indeed." He sipped again. "This particular enemy was wearing red alligator boots."

I frowned at my glass.

"We're in the middle of a cease-fire, Cisco. The police, the FBI, the media—it's all anybody can do to keep them back."

"That vamp must've missed the memo about operating in Greater Miami. I had to set him straight."

"With fire."

"That was his. Technically, the ghostly sword through his chest wasn't mine either." Beaumont squirmed slightly at the mention and my eyes darkened. "Consenting adults are one thing. The Obsidian March can't take any more kids on my watch. I won't compromise on that."

Leverett Beaumont studied the swirling bubbly in his

glass. "They're a shortsighted bunch, I agree. But there are a lot of them. I can only keep them out of Brickell if they trust I have a handle on matters."

I nodded to acknowledge the point. I didn't care about my condo, so much. Besides usually having a friend or two around, the place was warded up the wazoo. But my friends, Evan and Emily, my daughter Fran and their kid John, I had to keep them safe. Evan was my best friend with his own protection: he was a moralistic police lieutenant. He understood but didn't like the compromises that had to be made. Me? I ran in sketchy crowds. I even liked them, to an extent, as long as everybody played nice.

"Another street war will spill onto our doorsteps. And I worry about the media more than the March. You were a public figure as a kidnapping victim. If you keep turning up tied to mysterious events, theories of you being the Shadow Man will be impossible to quell."

"Your concern is touching." My voice was laced with sarcasm.

Beaumont snorted lightly. "You're no help to my organization if you're compromised."

It was no secret the underworld boss wanted me as part of his empire. A powerful animist like me would help solidify the Nether fiend's grip in this steppe. It would give him a level of respectability that could no doubt lead to other connections, like my friends in the Society.

But I was my own man. The only pledge we'd made was to help each other keep the Obsidian March in check. They were a growing menace and I couldn't kill all of them, so it was down to backroom politics. Meanwhile, Clan Beaumont did things as peaceably as possible. They drank blood from animals and blood banks. While undeniably gross, it wasn't evil.

My phone buzzed and I checked the message.

> **Milena:** *Besitos.*

I messaged, "Back at ya."

I cleared my throat, hating to ask Beaumont for anything and knowing favors weren't free. "So what if I need to know what the Obsidian March knows?"

He arched an eyebrow. "That punk you killed didn't know anything. He was a peon, and a dumb one at that."

"Not true. He was there to destroy a mirror I needed for evidence."

"The two are not mutually exclusive." He beckoned with his hand and a waiter a few tables away disappeared into the back. In a moment he came back with Tutti in tow. She looked annoyed until she slid in the booth next to her new boss and kissed him on the cheek. Beaumont's eyes didn't leave me. "Tell him about the Cielo."

She pulled back from his cold reception and crossed her arms. "Can't a girl have some fun around here?" A mischievous grin spread over her face and her foot rubbed up my thigh.

It didn't escape me that those toes of hers could probably sprout claws. I pushed her foot away and she frowned.

"Fine," she huffed. "Benny was the loser you killed. He

was there 'cause you were snooping around the night before. And no one topside told him to do it."

My eyes narrowed. "Who did?"

"It wasn't through the chain of command."

"How would you know?" I asked. "Are you even part of that chain anymore?"

She sneered. "I have lots of friends in important places, okay? And they still trust me." She leaned over to Beaumont and caressed his gelled hair. "I just tell them I'm keeping an eye on the Frenchman here."

Leverett grabbed her hand but didn't jerk it away. There was a moment of tenderness there. "She wouldn't be a part of my organization if she didn't bring anything to the table, Cisco. If you don't trust her, trust me. Her information is good. It's the same reason the March won't be retaliating against you."

Tutti's hand dropped to Beaumont's lap and she grinned. "Benny was working on the side for someone in the Nether. His business, his payback. Got it?"

I did. In the structured world of criminal enterprises, going off on your own could bring the wrong kind of heat down on the whole organization. Getting killed for doing something stupid was good old-fashioned comeuppance.

Another text came in.

Milena: Guess who's going to a smoking-hot boat party tomorrow? WE ARE!!! My friend Jem is dating a guy with a yacht!

I replied back, "Jem? Like the 80s cartoon? Stripper names are outta hand these days."

Beaumont set his glass down. "Is there an emergency?"

"Sorry," I said, clearing my throat. "Important, pressing matters."

"I didn't realize I rated so low on your list of priorities."

"There's kind of a lot going on now."

I put the phone away and took a long breath. I didn't trust Beaumont. I was smart enough for that much. But he worked with the March. While we both hated them, he was the one intimately familiar with their operations. Opening up to him was a risk, but it was a measured one.

"Can we..." I started as delicately as possible, "can we speak alone?" After a beat I nodded toward Tutti.

She smacked her lips. "Come on! You ask what I know then kick me out when it's time to share? I can help."

"Help as much as you like, but you still tried to kill me once or twice."

"You still got your panties in a bunch over that? I—"

Beaumont lifted a hand to halt the debate. Tutti bit her lip and listened. "Thank you for your contribution, dear. If you're needed again, I'll call on you."

She glowered but that was the extent of her objection. She took his hand softly and lowered it to his lap. "You sure?"

"It's proper courtesy."

She flashed angry eyes at me. "Have it your way. But eventually you're gonna learn some respect." The vampire stormed away from the table and left the restaurant completely.

"Sorry," I said, not sure why I was apologizing. "I just wanted to keep this next part between us."

His voice was crisp and unfettered. "I understand."

I swallowed. Any second thoughts I had about revealing my investigations were thrown out the window after that performance. It was full speed ahead now.

"What do you know about black owls?"

He blinked. "Owls?"

"Black owls from the Nether. Manifesto was cursed with"—I waved my hand over my face—"owl eyes. And the couple times I was close to him they came to his defense. There was one at the Cielo."

The upir's face was still but his eyes were alight. This was interesting information to him. Possibly new.

"What are they?" I asked. "Shape-changers? Upir pets?"

"The Obsidian March doesn't employ black owls."

"Come on, they've gotta be familiars or something. They have acid for blood."

He repeated my description flatly. "Black owls with acid blood."

"Yes. Are you seriously telling me that doesn't ring a bell with you? Out of everything that might be in the Nether. Could they be harpies or something?"

Beaumont shook his head. "I've never heard of black owls. You're sure it wasn't spellcraft of some sort? A construct?"

"No, I know magic. I still have a feather from one of them. They exist, I know that much, maybe somewhere deep in the Margins, way past the reach of the marches."

He sighed. "If there was a link, you killed him. I can tell you this isn't the Obsidian March. Not in Miami. Their Florida leadership is still in flux."

"Thanks in no part to your maneuvering."

He bowed his head. "It's a fluid situation." The crime boss toyed with his glass but set it aside in distaste. "This new development is concerning. I wish you had told me earlier."

"There wasn't much to tell. All I had to go on were the crazed words of a serial killer. I know this much: There's something down there that's shoving trouble up here, and they're going to a lot of trouble to remain anonymous."

The usually assertive vampire chewed his lip. "The information my Obsidian March consort relayed holds up. Upirs may be incidentally involved here and there, pressure applied or bribes made as needed, but we can't know who's involved without catching them in the act. However, that ties into why I asked you here today."

I paused a beat. "It wasn't about the Cielo?"

"In part, but I'm not your parole officer, Cisco. There's something more pressing. My spies have come across whispers of people looking for you. Silvans."

"Yeah," I said, "I got a wedding invitation from the Juniper Circle."

His eyes went wide. "They simply invited you?"

"Sure." I pulled out the card and flashed it at him.

"It's an obvious trap."

"What? No way. I know Ceela and Throok. They're

good kids."

Beaumont leaned forward with an air of urgency. "Don't trust them. Silvans are capricious and cruel."

"Any better than the so-called fiends?" I snickered. "I might remind you how many times the Obsidian March tried to kill me."

"You don't understand. The information I have concerns you being hunted by a silvan assassin. An expert at their craft."

My cheek twitched. If there was a silvan that wanted me dead, it could explain the black owls. The vampire marches lived far from the silvan circles. It was possible the upirs had limited knowledge of silvan tricks and creatures.

At the same time, both groups hated each other with irrational venom. The silvans dominated the Nether and forced fiends like the vampires topside. They were biased against each other, which meant I had to take Beaumont's opinions with a grain of salt.

Ceela and Throok couldn't possibly want me dead. I was the one who'd enabled them to run away together, to get the Circle of Bone to back off from absconding with the bride. It was why I was a human getting a Nether invitation.

But then, could that same act in royal meddling have put me in someone's crosshairs?

"They might be able to help me with a link to the owls," I said.

"Which is fine and good if it's the March going after you. If it's the silvans, you'll be walking to your own gallows."

Chapter 7

I pushed the up button on the lobby elevator just as a text came in. It was Evan. He was home and wanted to talk. The metal door slid open. I stepped aside as a couple unloaded and sighed.

Was it too much to ask to relax on my couch for a second?

I did a one-eighty to the garage elevator. Ten minutes later I pulled into Evan's driveway. He had a nice Spanish-style house of two stories. Great place for a family. I didn't begrudge him the turn of events in our lives, married to my ex-girlfriend, raising my daughter as his own. He was the rock that protected the ladies in my life when I hadn't been around.

"Cisco!"

The door opened to my ten-year-old excited to see me. Of course, she only knew me as a friend of the family.

I dropped to my knees and gave her a hug. "How are you doing?"

She snorted. "Better than you. I think you're in trouble."

Evan waited at the back of the entryway with crossed arms and a smirk. I nodded. "You think I'm gonna be grounded?"

"No," said Fran, "but you might get disappeared to a government black site."

I mussed her hair and stood up. "They're so cute at this age."

Evan shook my hand. "Good to see you in one piece. I wonder how long that's gonna last."

Fran giggled. "Cisco's bulletproof, Dad."

I arched an eye her way and put up finger guns. As she copied the gesture, an ethereal shadow rose from the corner. It crept behind her and reached for her wavy brown hair.

Without looking, Fran aimed one of her guns over her shoulder. The shadow manifestation disappeared and she laughed. "Too easy, Cisco."

I surrendered my hands to the air. Evan rolled his eyes. "Enough with the lessons, Jedi master. Let's talk." He led me toward the living room but didn't sit on the couch. "So you say this Quentin guy is a hack?"

"He was good enough to tickle my mind a second, but he's clueless."

"Is he part of this wizard guild of yours?"

"I'm not part of the Society, and Quentin's not that good."

Evan's hands went to his hips. "So how could he possibly know who the Shadow Man is?"

"He doesn't," I assured him. "I met him once. No names

were involved. He doesn't know a thing about anything."

"But what if he does?"

"You're on Reddit," cut in Fran. She held her phone up to me and showed a Google Maps satellite view of the Cielo Motel. It was marked with labels showing the destroyed room and the site of the car accident.

"Eh," said Evan dismissively, "the usual internet sleuths. There aren't enough specifics to incriminate you."

Fran wandered to the sofa, staring at her phone, and sat down.

"Anyway," he continued, "I have some facts. The City of Miami is providing resources to the FBI. Although I only spoke to the mayor about it, Special Agent Rita Bell heard I was digging into it. Rather than risk her operation being exposed, she called to give me a heads up."

"Let me guess: She also gave you a warning."

He nodded. "She's running an op, post-Manifesto closure. Apparently Quentin Capshaw has piqued a lot of ears, including the FBI's."

"He's working with them? Why bother coming to Miami?"

"I don't know, but this city is ground zero, and he's coming out in a way that best promotes his image. He's holding a live press conference tomorrow morning."

I dropped my jaw. "The bastard is on a publicity tour."

"Sounds like it. And why would the man put his reputation on the line like this if he doesn't know anything?" He grumbled. "Emily was wondering why that secret society didn't put a stop to this."

I winced and rubbed my mouth. "They're afraid of being outed more than anything else. I'm not part of the organization, so if I'm on the chopping block, they have no reason to intervene. They know I won't lead the authorities to them."

He scoffed. "So you'll protect them but they won't protect you?"

"That's about the sum of it."

I paced to the other side of the room. The Society had helped me enough by sorting out my financials. As with Beaumont, I didn't want to commit to playing for someone's team, so I was fine with them staying out of the picture. This wasn't their problem, it was mine.

"Damn. Tomorrow morning doesn't give us a lot of time to get to him."

"No it doesn't," agreed Evan.

"Can't you pick him up? You could be running an investigation too."

"No can do. The FBI owns this one. They cleared it with the chief, the mayor. It's a done deal. It's the whole reason Rita called me."

I scowled. "She warned you off it."

"Bingo. The City of Miami is to assist them if, and only if, they request it. I already offered, but Rita didn't bite."

Emily strolled into the room, all casual afternoon glamour. She hugged me and we kissed cheeks. "You're still in one piece," she noted.

"Evan already did that bit."

"Ah," she said with a nod. She picked at my tank top.

"When was the last time you changed your shirt?"

I pushed her away. "You guys talk about these things when I'm not around?"

"No," they both said.

"Yes," corrected Fran from the background. "Check out these guys." She got up and spun her phone around to us again.

Video of men wearing gray camouflage was cut together. They unloaded pickup trucks in some backwoods compound somewhere in the Everglades. A closeup of one of the crates showed it filled with rifles.

"What are we looking at?" I asked.

Evan grunted. "There's been word of local militias stockpiling weapons in the wake of the Manifesto fiasco. Not everyone thought he was a monster."

"What? He went around slaughtering innocent people."

"He was killing the 'other kind,' " stressed Evan. "He was warning the general populace of the dangers of magic."

"Are you serious with this?"

He threw his hands up. "Hey, it's them, not me. But I can understand it. It's not much different than telling everyone we have a problem with human-trafficking vampires."

"But they're not human."

"I get it, brother."

Emily cut in. "You're such a hothead, Cisco. It's not about humanity. You know better than that. It's about powerlessness. Spellcraft is the unknown. It's an enemy they have no defenses against."

I nodded bitterly. A large chunk of the population thought Manifesto was a kook. Another chunk ran with the conspiracy theories out of genuine excitement, like UFO enthusiasts or Bigfoot chasers. But a small portion of them took the possibility of animists so seriously that they were afraid of them. And fear requires action.

"Fran..." I started in warning.

"I know, Cisco. No one knows about what I can do. I'm not going around bragging about it."

Emily nodded. "We know how to keep secrets. No one's messing with my baby."

I huffed. That was the good news. "So I've got street necromancers still mad at me after the way the powder horn thing played out." I ticked my fingers down the list. "I've got the FBI on my ass. The Obsidian March wants me dead. Oh, and I just found out the silvans might too."

Evan grinned. "Don't forget Capshaw about to out you tomorrow morning."

"One thing at a time." All five of my fingers were ticked. I cursed. "You know, I was really hoping I could spring the question tonight."

Emily almost tackled me. "How could I forget?!? You HAVE to show me the ring."

I pulled the box from my pocket and showed it off as they crowded around. Emily ogled the sapphire. "I'm so happy you and Milena are getting together for good."

Fran shrugged and said, "I don't understand the fascination with material possessions."

Evan chuckled. "You will, honey."

I watched their eyes on the ring. On me. This was my family, and we were ready to welcome a new member. We were all stoked about it.

For once my aggravation at putting off normalcy wasn't faked. I stared at the ring along with them, thinking today was no longer the day. But hey, it could wait till tomorrow. Sexy boat parties are romantic too, right?

Chapter 8

Greater Miami is dotted with a patchwork of incorporated borders, with the city of Opa-Locka being one such four-mile stretch. The place was about as corrupt as they came. The city manager pled guilty to extortion a few years ago, and the new one wasn't much better. The county had since taken over the community's water management, and they were trying to do the same against an ineffective and dwindling local police force.

I hadn't spent a lot of time in Opa-Locka. I mostly just knew it for the flea market and executive airport. The latter was famous as a launching point for the Bay of Pigs invasion. The rest? Not so notable. Half of it was a claustrophobic warehouse district and the other half run-down residences.

Instead of fine dining with Milena, this was where I found myself this brisk night. I was here because Quentin Capshaw was here, holed up somewhere seedy.

My car was another city over, blocks away. I'd learned

my lesson from the Cielo. Given the sensitive matter at hand, I was in full incognito mode. Black hoodie, black jeans, black sneakers. I looked like I was up to no good. Ironically, in this neighborhood, I blended right in.

With Shadow Man speculation in full gear, I couldn't be too careful. It was Quentin, after all, who was supposedly going to out me. His claim had credibility, but I didn't believe it. My encounter with him had been brief, and if I needed to I would play off any meeting as part of being a supernatural consultant for Miami PD. Still, I had to find out what he was going to say before he said it.

Headlights lit the area. I ducked behind a wall of cinder blocks as an Opa-Locka police car drove past. It was the third time. Too much for regular patrols. I stared at graffiti of a red crescent moon as I waited for the lights to fade.

I returned my attention to the warehouse where Quentin was holed up. Two news vans were parked across the street.

My gaze shot behind me as I felt a presence. No one was there. I relaxed and turned back to my stake out.

"Nice of you to join the fun," I muttered.

The Spaniard materialized at my side. "This is not the matter you should be attending to. The netherling owls threaten the sanctity of this domain."

"This is related to Manifesto. Kinda."

"This is about your reputation. Nothing more."

"Easy to dismiss as a dead guy. The living need to pay attention to their rep. Sometimes it's the only thing keeping them alive."

As we watched, a camera man exited one of the vans and

hurried to a dark alley to take a leak.

"This is a waste of time," urged the wraith.

"I have plenty. I've been invited to a silvan wedding. I can investigate the owls then."

The Spaniard's eyes burned a hole in the city. "Wild folk," he spat. "They bring nothing but death. It would be unwise to heed their invitation."

"You too? Listen, the silvans are my friends. It's the Nether fiends we should be worried about."

"I make no distinction."

I clenched my jaw. I sometimes wondered if the classifications had merit or were just a case of the haves and have-nots. Still, silvans may have toyed with the human race, but they didn't have a penchant for drinking human blood.

"I've hit a dead end up here. The best way to find the source of the owls is to go under."

The ghost cocked his head. "And what of your silvan assassin?"

"You heard that?" I studied him a moment. "Hey, you weren't watching this morning when Milena sat on my—"

"I care not for your exploits, brujo. I'm here to atone for my own sins."

I shifted uncomfortably. I wasn't really sure what the Spaniard's deal was now that he was free of the Horn, but he'd never spoken like that before. And while I often wondered what sins he'd specifically committed, I was pretty sure I didn't want to find out.

After an involuntary shiver, I zipped the hoodie up over

my chest and quickly changed the subject. "I don't like this. Quentin should be somewhere swanky. He stays in high-profile hotels. He should be flush after his recent talk-show circuit."

Evan had come through with the location and other specifics. Quentin Capshaw had agreed to talk to the FBI, but only after making a public announcement. The hypnotist and his beefed-up security crew had flown into Opa-Locka earlier today. Special Agent Bell would pick him up after the press conference.

But if he was staying here, he was afraid of something.

When the street was clear, we made a wide circle around the block toward the back of the building. Peeking around the corner revealed a parked police cruiser with a single officer inside.

Damn. Evan had also given me the heads up about the cops. Opa-Locka had their own police force, unswayed by Miami PD, perhaps even with a chip on their shoulders against them. They wouldn't do me any favors.

The more I considered it, the more it seemed the underfunded cops were on the take, hired for a little overtime by Quentin Capshaw himself. Personal police protection explained the location.

I grumbled and reversed direction, dedicating fifteen minutes to getting back to my starting spot and continuing around to the opposite side. The span of warehouses grew more jumbled, closed in by trailer trucks and stacks of empty palettes.

"Brujo," warned the Spaniard.

"I see them," I muttered, passing a larger crescent moon tag on the asphalt. The route wasn't ideal, but there were only so many approaches to Quentin's hidey-hole. We hurried down a narrow alley, sticking to shadow, and my mood sank as I heard the voices. I angled to the edge of the building and peeked around.

Seven people holding quarts congregated around a charcoal grill. But this was far worse than a malt liquor cookout.

Brownish smoke billowed from the grill with the distinct odor of sulfur. It was a tribute of some sort. The hoodies were decked out with tokens and fetishes and other instruments of spellcraft.

"Occultists," noted the wraith. "Who are they?"

I chewed my lip. "I don't know them. Nigerians, maybe. I've run into Igbo and Yoruba cliques before, but they're not very big. Their magic community's splintered. They shouldn't be a problem."

The hoodies perked up and waved across the alley. Another group of five approached, mostly women this time. More Nigerians, I thought, but they had different markings, most prominently a sword. Several held wands with tassels of oxtail.

Just my luck. This was some kind of underworld gang meetup.

"Brujo!" came a sharp growl at my back, but it wasn't the Spaniard. I spun to three men with blue moons painted on their foreheads. The one who'd yelled was a wide man with a bald head and lots of scars running up his arms. The other two gangs sprang to alert and approached.

"Great," I muttered. "Three of you now." I raised my hands to calm him and spaced myself from the wall in case I needed room to maneuver. Footsteps collected at my back.

"You should not be here," he growled in a commanding voice. "You have broken with *Omenala*."

I didn't know what *Omenala* was, but I knew I wasn't popular on the street these days, especially among the death dealers. Judging by the bones some of these hoodies wore, I had definitely overstepped my bounds.

"Guys, guys," I soothed. "We're not in the neighborhood for you. You go your way, we go ours."

The man looked around, full of pomp. "There's a good price on your head."

"You really don't want to go there. All of you against the two of us... It won't be as easy as you think."

He arched a brow. "The two of who?"

"The two of—" I turned and noticed the Spaniard had disappeared.

Crap.

Chapter 9

The Spaniard didn't like being seen. Maybe it was because his proper life ended five hundred years ago. Because he no longer belonged in this world. Maybe it was because the sight of desiccated bones was horrifying to humans. But hey, I was the one who'd freed him from his slumber. He didn't much care what I thought. Besides, we were family.

Which is why it didn't surprise me one bit when he vanished. He'd fought at my side before, but he wasn't my familiar or spell construct, waiting on my command. Ever since being on his own, the wraith had been more aloof. He had his own agenda and ideas. And as he had said, I shouldn't be in Opa-Locka.

But I wasn't the type to overly dwell on who was right or wrong. I just took things as they came and, if need be, powered right on through.

"Despite what you may think," I said flatly, "this is a total coincidence. I didn't mean to step onto anyone's turf. I'm just avoiding a couple of squad cars."

"The police won't help you," said the woman with the oxtail wand at my back.

"I'd rather not get them involved. I'm trying to keep things quiet."

The bald man cut in. "Stealing our lives was not enough for you?"

Which led to the other reason the Spaniard disappeared. While under the control of Connor Hatch, the wraith had abused his powers to subjugate the necromancer populace of the city. Showing his face was bound to escalate things.

"I fought and killed the jinn who did that to you," I said.

"You flaunt your power for all to see," accused the woman.

I ducked as a bottle flew past and popped on the distant concrete. I glared at the hood behind me to prevent any more projectiles. Tassels on Yoruba wands bristled defensively.

I could've brandished my spellcraft, shown a little display of force to remind them who they were dealing with, but I was afraid once I did all hell would break loose. I counted fourteen animists in the huddle around me. Even against a bunch of scrubs, magic was a wild card. I couldn't be sure what they were capable of.

"Ozo Ebu," called one of the blue mooners, "say the word and I will strike."

Ozo Ebu was the wide man at the head of that gang. I didn't know him, but I knew ozo to be an Igbo honorific. Instead of stripes on a sleeve, the bald man's face had ceremonial scrapes across his forehead and right cheek.

Permanent scars signifying his importance. He took his role as leader seriously.

He spoke in a basso voice. "Men have been killed for breaking taboo. It is the old way. You deserve no less, Shadow Man."

I grimaced. "The identity of any alleged shadow vigilantes is unfounded speculation. We don't want to start any rumors."

"Don't worry. Your secret is safe."

I chewed my lip and eyed the crowd. "Really?"

"Of course," he answered with a chuckle. "We're being paid for our discretion."

He lunged. As large hands closed around me, I dissolved into shadow. But something was off. It wasn't that easy. I attempted to sidestep and his fingers painfully raked my sides.

I peeled out of his grip and solidified. He spun to me, fingertips still glowing with purple threads of my ripped magic.

More bottles flew. As I ducked to avoid a close call, a machete swung overhead. I met the strike with the tattooed flesh on my forearm. The turquoise flash knocked a bent blade from his grip. As the man's face followed the tumbling weapon, I pumped some shadow into my other fist and sent a haymaker into his temple. He rammed several of his friends on the way to the ground.

The alley exploded with incantations and frenetic action. I slid through the shadow to escape their circle. Some of them were familiar enough with my tricks to easily track me.

That was fine. Escape wasn't my goal here. I just needed them all where I could see them.

Two pistols flashed. The Helm of Awe tattoo on my left palm flared to life and a rounded energy barrier absorbed the incoming bullets. Two masses of shadow from beneath upended the gunmen.

As the crowd converged, I reached into my belt pack and tossed plastic eggs of powder at my feet. As the delirium-inducing dust clouded around, I raised the cloth mask over my nose and mouth to purify my air. Fists and blades struck me from multiple sides.

My skin had been strengthened with zombie rituals, but I wasn't invincible. What's more, once a few hands grabbed me, I could no longer easily dive into the darkness.

My fist flew forward. I sent my elbow behind me. I leaned into those holding me from behind and kicked my boots up to stagger some more. Each of my blows was reinforced with shadow magic, packing enough punch to do serious damage.

The woman came forward with a copper sword. I guess it wasn't just symbolic. As the blade came in, I spun around and brought the man at my back to stop it. He cried out and released me. With one of his hands still on my shoulder, I turned to shadow and dove aside, dragging him with me. When we came back, he was so disoriented a headbutt knocked him out cold.

I turned with a growl. A few of them were down, but it was at the expense of angering the rest. Oxtail wands jerked spasmodically and zaps of lightning and wind bit my flesh. I spawned another shield but it failed to catch the spellcraft. I was working on another strategy when my leg was clamped tight. An orange python with white eyes flexed around my leg.

Ozo Ebu bore down on me, my mobility limited as the snake tightened around my knee. When I attempted to dive into the shadow, I jerked back to the physical world. That damned python was a double whammy.

Ebu grabbed me in a bear hug. "I've got you now," he cried, spittle in my face.

I stretched back and rammed my head forward as hard as I could. When I connected, I saw stars. Ozo Ebu growled in delight, blue moon on his head glowing faintly.

"Yes," he taunted, "squirm for me."

He squeezed and my ribs strained. Punches battered my back. My arms were down at my sides but I forced them forward, meeting between us. I spawned a ball of shadow between my hands, simultaneously building it up and forcing it down. The blows kept coming. I almost lost the construct as a bottle smashed my head, but my focus held.

Finally, I had the bundle of spellcraft ready to blow. I spread my hands and released the pent-up energy. A bomb went off between us.

The alley shook and everyone went flying. I tumbled head over heels and ground to a skidding stop atop a woman with a sword. She tried to weakly lift it but I snatched it and knocked the pommel into her forehead. Other animists reeled on the ground after the blast. The orange python wriggled on the cement, head blown off.

I gritted my teeth. That had been loud. The police—hell, all of Opa-Locka—would've heard that.

Several gang members least affected by the explosion hopped to their feet and recovered weapons. Ozo Ebu groaned as one of his men helped him sit up. The man's belly welled with a black bruise.

Just as I'd thought. He was a tough one, which was all the better. The last thing I wanted was to kill any of them. I took the blast admirably as well, but being at ground zero wasn't a cakewalk. I felt seventy years old as I pushed to my boots.

"As I was saying," I growled with conviction, "I'm passing through. I doubt there'll be anymore objections?"

Ozo Ebu's eyes were ice cold but he didn't make a sound. The woman was unconscious, and I didn't even know who the leader of the crescent moon gang was. I nodded and took a painful step.

All around me, various handguns cocked. Animists stepped from the shadows with white skulls painted over their faces. Sickly green smoke crawled over the alley floor.

"Ha, ha, ha," came Ebu's triumphant voice. "It's not just us, you see? You're finished now."

I clenched my jaw as I slowly spun to see just how outnumbered I truly was. A new gang had arrived at the meeting, and this wasn't your garden-variety street outfit. This was the largest group of necromancers in Miami.

Ebu's smug smile came into view. "I believe you are familiar with our friends, the Bone Saints."

Chapter 10

Despite being grounded, the Nigerian gangs had a boost of confidence. The Bone Saints were Haitians, voodoo bokors from a different diaspora, but necromancers tended to know each other. And boy did I know the Bone Saints.

I turned expectantly to the green smoke and a precise voice rewarded me. "You are far from home, Suarez." Jean-Louis Chevalier stepped around the corner and approached.

He was painted up more elaborately than the other Bone Saints. Rows of teeth were painted over his lips, his eyes and nose darkened to resemble hollow cavities. Tattoos shimmered a faint green on his chest and arms, and he wore an intricate silver gauntlet that ended in pointed fingers.

"I could say the same about you," I returned, careful not to appear in pain. "I thought you stayed in Little Haiti."

"It is a time of expansion," he said coyly. "The war is ended. The cartel is gone." He frowned. "The Obsidian March has been more prevalent."

"A temporary hitch."

He nodded and surveyed the regrouping animists. "It's disappointing to see you struggling against so few."

Despite having fought off fourteen people, Chevalier had more at his immediate disposal.

"This?" I snorted. "This was just a brotherly disagreement."

"You've broken *Omenala*," charged Ebu.

I noted the positions of every Bone Saint I could. Several had automatic weapons, and I recalled them sometimes using enchanted rounds. I would need to take them out first.

Chevalier sighed loudly. "What are you doing here, Suarez?"

"Maybe I wanted to see an old friend."

"You are no friend of ours." He spat on the ground. "When you raid Obsidian March safe houses in Wynwood, where do you think the vampires flee to?"

My cheek twitched. Little Haiti was just north of those stomping grounds. "They're keeping everyone busy, Chevalier. We all have the same problem."

"Our problems are very different," countered the gang boss. "You have a price on your head. Several, in fact."

"So I hear."

Chevalier turned to the Nigerians. "He's also protected by Beaumont."

"He's not in Brickell," spat Ebu. "This is *our* turf."

The bokor nodded. "Also true, Suarez, which brings me back to my original question. I want a serious answer this time. What are you doing here?"

"I don't answer to the Bone Saints. Or to the... Igbo and

Yoruba. But I'll tell you because we're *friends*." I said the word without apology and stepped closer. "Quentin Capshaw is in that building down there and he's spreading rumors about the Shadow Man."

The Haitian's eyes fluttered. "You're a fool. Quentin doesn't know anything. It's a trap."

"I know about the police on his payroll."

"The police are more blind than you are. Think about the private airport. The controlled jurisdiction away from your City of Miami friends. Quentin's a braggart, designed to roust the Shadow Man from hiding, and you took the bait."

"Why are you telling him this?" demanded Ozo Ebu.

"Because no one needs the heat this brings."

Ebu scowled. "You are guests here, too," he warned.

Wait a minute. I was starting to get the feeling Chevalier wasn't just here for the meeting. Obviously he'd been close by with his membership, but...

The Spaniard's red eyes fixed on me from behind a parked loading truck. The sly devil had gone for help.

The sound of helicopter blades bouncing around the distant skyline wiped the smile off my face.

"Are you listening, Suarez? The feds are setting up a perimeter. They may be closing in on you as we speak."

I took a step backward. Although there was an airport nearby, the sound of the helicopter peculiarly stood out, especially as it rumbled closer.

Special Agent Bell didn't trust Evan and the Miami cops. She'd been eyeing me as a suspect even before the Shadow

Man video went public. Had she really orchestrated this whole thing just to lure me in?

A glance around the alley revealed the Bone Saints holding their weapons down. The Spaniard was gone again. I nodded at Chevalier in thanks and turned down a narrow path.

"Why save him?" bemoaned Ozo Ebu. "After what he did?"

Jean-Louis Chevalier beckoned his gang to retreat with a silver finger. "Perhaps, Ozo, it's because he is the only one who can save this city."

I raced down the grimy walkway and out onto the next street. To my left, toward Quentin's building, was another patrolling squad car. I took off in the opposite direction, toward the airport.

The drone of the helicopter grew louder. It was definitely coming my way. I sprinted full speed down the street in a bid to get out of the area. I couldn't outrun the chopper, of course, but I could make it so it never found me.

Cars turned the corner up ahead and I ducked into a side street. In the distance, a police siren chirped. I cut through an industrial lot with several junked cars, then down another block.

My phone buzzed. I slipped behind a locked shed and checked the screen. The ID was blocked. I hissed, ripped open the phone, and pulled the battery. My shoes stomped the phone to hell and I looked around desperately. I slid the plastic parts under the door to the shed so it was safely inside. Then I broke around the corner and hauled ass.

The ground vibrated as the helicopter passed overhead. A spotlight bisected the street. I skidded and turned before being lit up. Red and blue lights flashed in the distance. The perimeter was active now and they weren't even trying to hide it.

As I raced away, headlights twirled ahead. I couldn't hear the engines very well but several cars were closing in. I hugged a warehouse wall and hurried the opposite way.

Stupid, this was stupid. Maybe there'd come a day when I had a long hard talk with Quentin about this, but for now I was stupid to be anywhere near him. Rita Bell had played us all to perfection, even going so far as to give Evan the heads up not to interfere with her case. The lady really had a hard-on for me.

A spotlight lit me up against the wall, the spinning helicopter rotors blowing at my jacket. I turned my face away and scrunched the hood tight so it wouldn't fly open.

A megaphone crackled. "Surrender or we will open fire."

I sneered. The powerful bath of light would all but kill my shadow magic. I looked up and down the street. Cars approaching on both sides. Across the street was a scrap-metal yard. It was messy and tangled from the ground, but not a whole lot obstructed the view from above. Past the junkyard was a parking lot with a bordering line of trees.

"I repeat," ordered the chopper. "Lie down with your hands behind your back and surrender."

I ground my teeth hard. A black Ford Explorer accelerated toward the curb. I didn't have a lot of moves but

—

Automatic fire ripped into the sky. The helicopter pitched, taking evasive action. My eyes shot to the distance but I couldn't find the source of the shots. As the spotlight veered off me, I leapt into action.

I jumped past the Explorer's headlights and dove into shadow for a boost across the street. The SUV stopped and agents unloaded with rifles. Another jump through shadow pulled me through the chain-link fence, with the officers on my tail stymied by the high razor wire.

I hurried through the metal yard as the helicopter made another pass. Whoever had suppressed them was gone. I made it around two scrap heaps before the spotlight blared over me again.

Damn, I couldn't shake them. My only chance was getting to the protected airspace of the airport. If I was lucky, the feds weren't cleared for operation there.

More gunfire cracked. Dirt exploded and metal sparked as these particular rounds were aimed my way. The feds weren't kidding about shooting.

At the end of the scrap yard I jumped through the fence and into the section of swale bordering the parking lot, under the canopy of unkempt trees. The branches shook wildly as the chopper hovered overhead, but the spotlight lost sight of me. I was hidden in here.

It was a temporary respite. There simply weren't lot of places I could go. I followed the property north toward the airport and the helicopter made a wide berth around the cover.

A caravan of FBI vehicles swerved around the block and

entered the open parking lot. With my command of the shadow, I'd made faster time than they'd estimated. The vehicles came to a stop behind me as agents unloaded.

Unfortunately, several barking canine units hopped out. This was going south fast.

"Shadow charmer!" came a sharp call. A woman dressed in black waved at me from up ahead. She was across the multilane street at the end of the parking lot. Unfortunately, my tree cover ended at the fence line.

I waited a beat as the dogs rustled behind me. I wasn't ignoring them, I was worried about exposing myself to the helicopter again. There wasn't a lot of cover ahead. Then again, it was closer to restricted airspace.

Even more concerning was the woman herself. She was hunched against a locked-up muffler shop, in the shadows. I considered using my shadow vision to get a better look but headlights sweeping by changed my mind. I couldn't afford to be blinded right now.

"Now or never!" urged the woman with a wave of her hand.

"Screw it," I muttered.

Loping dogs came at my back. I melted through the fence and made a run for it. The canines leapt but couldn't scale the chain link. Instead they belted out forlorn howls to alert their handlers.

At this time of night, I crossed the multi-lane highway with ease. I was almost on the other side when the spotlight found me again. The helicopter swooped around to pursue.

I reached the muffler shop where an Asian woman with a

black pony tail and tattoo sleeves waited.

"You blew my cover," I said.

She turned without replying and gunned it across the property. A stretch of dirt too large and too open to sneak across. The helicopter slowed overhead.

"This is your last warning," announced the megaphone.

Light flashed from a shed ahead. A controlled burst of fire flew past the air support. The spotlight swiveled as the chopper once again took evasive action.

So it was them who had helped me before. I gunned it after the woman with preternatural speed and got a better look at the muscled man with the rifle. He had long black hair hanging over shirtless shoulders, taking cover behind a metal structure beside a patch of trees and several parked cars in the lot of a water-processing facility. The path north to the airport was intersected by a wide canal.

The two of us reached cover as the chopper circled around. Already, headlights were pulling out of the parking lot and onto the highway to cut us off.

"We're trapped," I said. "There's no way we can get out of sight by car or boat."

The woman smirked. "We're going deeper than that."

I followed them into a wild bramble of overgrown weeds on the edge of the canal, half expecting a submarine. Instead, the woman slipped down a muddy hole in the ground.

I paused and locked eyes with the man. His gun was pointed up, black fingernail over the trigger.

"You're vampires," was all I said.

He wore no expression. "Take it or leave it."

As the helicopter bore overhead, I cursed and slid into the hole.

Chapter 11

Most people live their whole lives without seeing real magic. Even those that get a glimpse of the hidden secrets all around us have no idea of the scale of it. The Earthly Steppe is the world we know, but there are elemental steppes above and below. The Aether, the world of jinns, is made of ethereal fire and air. And the Nether, well, it's basically a cross between the Island of Misfit Toys and a sewer. Born of water and earth, it houses most of the mixed animal crossbreeds of legend.

And vampires. You can't forget the vampires.

I hopped to my feet in the darkened tunnel of dirt. Roots hung loose from the ceiling above. Noticeably absent were the blaring sirens and drone of the helicopter. The darkness extended in either direction with the only indication of the other world a hazy beam of light shining from a cavity in the ceiling.

Rabbit holes weren't easy to find but they were all over the place. It was how supernatural creatures snuck into our world, and how they managed to consistently stay out of sight when necessary.

The beam of light was interrupted as the muscled man came through and landed on his feet beside the woman. We were clear of the feds. Without a grasp of magic, they wouldn't be able to follow in our footsteps. Unfortunately, I had now essentially trapped myself with two very capable-looking vampires.

"Who are you?" I demanded, holding my shotgun to the man's face.

The Asian woman twisted her lips coyly. "Is that how you say thank you?"

She spoke with a thick accent and was playful, unconcerned with my weapon. Sharpened eyes oozed confidence, which made her twice as hot as she already was. Both arms were tatted with sleeves and a hint of hardened abs showed over tight pants.

"Put the gun down," said the man, M27 resting on his shoulder. "I'm Lago. We're Clan Beaumont."

I lowered the sawed off slightly. Lago had wavy dark hair coming down the chest of a boxer. His dirty beard and enigmatic eyes looked like they had something to hide. A black Samoan tattoo draped over his right pec, shoulder, and arm. Which must've been the inspiration for the shirtless look.

"How can I be sure?" I asked.

"Can you ever?" pondered the woman.

I frowned and considered the pair a moment. A decision had to be made one way or the other and it wasn't like I could call Beaumont himself. Besides my burner being smashed to bits, the Nether wasn't equipped with cell towers.

"You didn't kill anyone," I realized.

Lago blinked stoically. "What's that?"

"Topside. You fired at the police chopper twice but didn't actually kill anyone. You weren't trying to."

He grunted. "Unnecessary collateral damage."

"Good enough for me." I dropped my shotgun into shadow and turned to the girl. "And you are?"

"Does it matter?" She crossed her arms and leaned against the dirt wall, eyeing me.

Lago embraced her and said, "This is Trinh. She likes to be difficult. And she never answers a direct question."

"Answers are boring." They took in each other's grins before kissing passionately.

"Oh neat," I grumbled. "A power couple."

Trinh disengaged in annoyance. "Jealousy isn't becoming. Let's get a move on." She started hiking down one of two dark corridors.

Which was pretty much what most of the Nether consisted of. Winding underground tunnels cut from rock and earth by who knows what or when. It was almost impossible to know where to go unless you grew up within the labyrinth, and even then you'd only know your home territory.

Making matters more complicated, the Nether Steppe didn't map to Earth in a one-to-one fashion. Physical space worked differently here. Any leftover bearing of the cardinal directions was utterly useless, as was common sense. We could walk fifty feet, climb up a different rabbit hole, and find ourselves in the Greek Islands.

Which was actually pretty cool. A person could make a lot of money by mapping the place out.

For now, as Lago started after Trinh, there was no way to know which direction I was supposed to be going or where we'd end up. Since it didn't entirely matter, I wordlessly followed, choosing instead to keep an eye on their mannerisms.

Trinh was about as cocksure as they came. Young, smoking hot, and without a spare second for anyone. She was all business. Sexy, ornery business.

Her muscled partner matched some of her traits. You had to possess a certain amount of confidence when your battle dress didn't include a shirt. But Lago so far lacked Trinh's flair. He was plainspoken and direct. Which meant he would be easier to get answers from.

Trinh wasn't heavily armed. She wore a pistol at the small of her back, opting to keep her hips free for a knife on each side. I took her for the type who enjoyed getting up close and personal. Lago was the heavy gunner, lugging an automatic weapon and a belt with a side arm and spare magazines.

I followed them a good ten minutes without saying a word, just getting a feel for their movements and, well, whether or not they intended to eat me. At this point I figured if they were gonna make a move, it would wait until we reached our destination, where they might be backed up with greater numbers. I leaked some shadow into my eyes to keep a vigilant watch of the dark tunnels and pulled alongside Lago.

"You guys aren't the most chatty bunch," I said to break the ice. "You one of those couples that prefer to enjoy each other's silence?"

The vampire's mouth crooked. "We've known each other a long time."

I scratched the back of my head. "You know, I've been meaning to ask about that but haven't had the time. How long do you guys live, anyway?"

"Long enough."

"I get it," I said with a nod. "You're not really supposed to talk about it. But I'm a friend, right?"

He turned to me deadpan as he walked.

"Fine, friends might be a bit much, but allies, right? At least according to you."

He grunted. "I grew up in the sixties, but I'm fairly young."

Trinh spun around from her lead position. "Don't think that makes us weak."

"It's nothing like that," I assured her. "It's just I have questions." When they didn't respond, we walked another several paces in silence. "So you guys get your food from blood banks? What are we talking, once a week?"

"Something like that," said Lago. "We drink from different sources. Human blood is more of a delicacy."

Which would make sense. Upirs were from the Nether, where humans didn't naturally live. We wouldn't be the standard food source. And I knew firsthand that Beaumont enjoyed wine and champagne.

"So like, do you sometimes say screw it and pop into a drive-thru for a breakfast sandwich?"

Trinh no longer tried to hide her annoyance. "Enough with the questions. Take them up with the chief. He's the one who wants an *animist* in the ranks."

"Trinh..." warned Lago gently.

I quit the interrogation and chewed my lip. They were referring to Leverett Beaumont, no doubt. The head of Clan Beaumont, independent of the Obsidian March in the Nether and a fledgling crime organization topside. But the exchange revealed a few important details.

One, Clan Beaumont specifically wanted an animist. That was me.

Two, they weren't supposed to talk about it.

And three, the venom in Trinh's voice when she spoke the word animist revealed her true feelings about my kind.

The feeling wasn't uncommon among vampires. Generally, the few we interacted with were sneaking around the Earthly Steppe, going about their business in secret. Animists were some of the only humans who knew about them. More importantly, they were also among the few who had the ability to do something about the threat.

I had very emphatically exercised this ability in the past.

But still, something about Trinh's voice made me wonder if her feelings were more personal.

"Fair enough," I finally said after an awkward silence, "but I do have the right to know one thing. Opa-Locka isn't

Beaumont's territory. I didn't tell him I was going after Capshaw."

"Is there a question in there, shadow charmer?"

I steeled against her icy voice. "Is Beaumont keeping tabs on me?"

She chuckled and marched ahead. Lago gave me a single nod. "Be grateful he is. We saved your ass tonight."

"I don't need saving."

"Whatever you say, tough guy. The fact is you're under our clan's protection. It's what you agreed to, until Beaumont tells us otherwise. We're just following our marching orders."

I didn't waste my breath with a snappy comeback. He was dead on. If I needed to take this up with anyone, it was the big man himself.

The problem was, I did happily accept his protection. My condo, and more importantly, Evan's house, where Fran lived. As long as I didn't sell my soul in a devil's bargain, I couldn't deny the value in that protection.

What I hadn't bargained for and didn't especially appreciate was the idea of having babysitters. If Clan Beaumont was onto my little side project tonight, had they also been present at the Cielo Motel? Did they always have eyes on me, even when I stayed over at Milena's place?

My face soured. This was gonna get rectified.

We walked for another hour before the foul spirits dissipated. We'd passed a few rabbit holes here and there; one knotted between thick tree branches, another nestled behind vines. The passageways weren't familiar and I was a little surprised we hadn't encountered anything else. But then, I'd previously visited the silvan portions of the underground. Upirs and the distant marches had their own turf, and the two didn't often mingle.

Trinh and Lago stopped in a spot where webbed bands of light danced on their faces. Above them, in the dirt ceiling, was a perfectly round hole filled with water. The pale light refracted through it.

"This is you," said Lago, nodding upward. "It's as close as we can get."

I arched an eyebrow. "Why are you laughing?"

"It's a little wet," smirked Trinh.

Her partner extended his hand. "We'll need your keys. Someone will pick up your car."

I snorted. "No one gets to drive my Firebird."

"None of us should be anywhere near North Miami tonight. That includes your car for the FBI to find."

Trinh crossed her arms. "It isn't the most inconspicuous thing in the world."

I cursed. They were right. Again. I'd had the foresight to park outside the general area which had ended up outside the perimeter, but it would only take a lucky glance to see my car relatively close to their trap. It might already be too late.

"Fine."

I begrudgingly removed the key from my *Knight Rider* key chain and handed it over. While I was at it, I unzipped the black hoodie and tossed it on the ground with my sneakers. I found the canister of powder in my belt pouch, sprinkled it generously over the clothes, and dropped a lit match on top. The flames incinerated the evidence, leaving me in a tank top, black jeans, and dirty socks.

"You two coming?" I asked.

"Our job ends here," said Lago.

Trinh rolled her eyes. "It's been fun."

Chapter 12

I breached the surface of the water and coughed. A little wet was an understatement: I floated near the shore of Biscayne Bay. As I navigated over the base layer of ascending limestone, I recognized Brickell Point.

This was the meeting point of the Miami River and the Bay, where fresh water from the Everglades cut through Downtown Miami and spilled into the ocean. As I hugged the concrete embankment of the river walk, I was greeted with a wide brick path lined with palm trees. Beyond was a rare field of green in what was almost yet another swanky condominium site. Now it was a public park right next to a swanky condominium site. In the middle of the night, a few loiterers locked their gazes on me as I climbed onto the river walk.

Just going for a swim on a brisk night.

I ignored the gawkers and trudged past, dripping wet, cutting through the grass. The park itself was just a small field. A historic landmark, actually. A ring of stone encompassed the famous Miami Circle, which was nothing more than a patch of ground. Safely buried underneath was the real attraction, the limestone foundation for what was once an indigenous building. It wasn't much to look at but it was the oldest such evidence on the East Coast, somewhere in the neighborhood of two thousand years.

Of course, nobody knows what the site was used for, but with my particular expertise I could take a guess. As I passed, I could feel the Intrinsics oozing from it. Even this far gone, the leftovers of countless rituals was intense.

Back on the wide highway of Brickell Avenue, I still had several blocks to walk in my socks. I approached a string of electric scooters parked on the sidewalk but grumbled as I reached into my pocket. Without my phone I couldn't rent a ride. Oh well, it was probably better not to look like a tourist anyway. I sighed and marched down the street to my building.

Luckily the lobby was empty and the person at the front desk had stepped away. I slinked into the elevator and hit the button for my private penthouse. As I rested against the back wall, the Spaniard blinked in at my side.

"Vampires," he muttered. It was only one word, but there was a whole conversation behind it.

I rubbed my temples. "I know."

"Your authorities are close to you."

"*I know.*"

This time it was me who'd said few words with a lot behind them.

"You know," I pointed out, "there is a security camera in this elevator."

"Is that so?" The wraith turned to the shaded lens in the corner wall. "I've discovered I cannot be recorded. Perhaps only the living eye can see me, when I allow it."

"So it's settled. I just look like a crazy person talking to myself."

After tonight, I wished I could get myself some of that ghost magic. It would make avoiding the FBI easier. But at least the shadow helped obscure my identity. Better for them to chase the Shadow Man than Cisco Suarez.

The elevator dinged and the door slid open to my personal hallway. There weren't any cameras here, but I didn't say another word till we were through my front door.

"Tonight just cemented it in my head. I need to lie low, away from prying eyes. The feds are too close and I don't like the vampires watching me. I'm gonna accept that wedding invitation."

The ghostly conquistador growled. "The Nether is their domain."

I spun on him. "Not silvan territory. The marches steer clear of the silvan circles. I'll be attending as an honored guest."

"You'll be vulnerable there. You'll be—"

He paused and turned his head. I followed his glowing stare to Kasper on my massage chair holding a brew.

"What's up, broham? This must be your wraith friend I've heard so much about." The tattooed Norwegian took a swig and let out a casual burp.

I sighed. "Comfortable, Kasper?"

"You know it. And don't worry," he said, addressing the

Spaniard, "your secret's safe with me. I'm practically family."

The cat was out of the bag and I didn't care. Secrecy was the wraith's hang-up, not mine. Ever since the Obsidian March blew up Kasper's tattoo parlor and home, he'd been crashing at my place. I had the space and countless amenities to accommodate him, including *my* massage chair.

A couple of people had gotten glimpses of the Spaniard, including Milena, but it was only me he generally revealed himself to. True family. And while Fran was, technically, his true family as well, Evan and Emily had a thing about exposing their daughter to a centuries-old undead necromancer. I did too.

Kasper set his empty bottle on the side table and approached the wraith with an appraising eye. "Did anyone ever tell you you'd make a kick-ass tattoo?"

The Spaniard ignored the comment and focused his glowing eyes on me. "If the black sisters are scheming in our world, you should be able to uncover their plans from up here."

I shook my head. "Too many dead ends and too much collateral damage. I need to go to the source."

"You are abandoning your city."

"I'm having trouble protecting it when I don't know what's going on."

Kasper retrieved fancy paper from the bar. "You talking about this?" he asked, waving the silvan invitation.

Of course my roommate had gone through my mail.

"Yes," I said, turning to the Spaniard. "You know, I

could use some backup down there."

The conquistador straightened. "I will not enter the Nether, brujo."

"So you're just gonna leave me high and dry again?"

He smoldered. The accusation was unfair because he had actually gone for help against the Igbo. But he didn't get into that. After a tense moment, he simply said, "That realm will be the death of me."

I blinked uncertainly, stalled by his prophetic words.

"I can go," chimed in my biker friend. "I've never been." He shrugged. "It's not like I'm doing anything up here."

I grunted. "Yeah, like keeping up your shifts at the coffee shop."

"Exactly!"

The sarcasm was lost on him.

But I considered his offer. Kasper was covered in powerful tattoos. They basically made him as tough as a tank. He'd be able to brush off whatever teeth and claws came his way. "You'll seriously be my plus one?"

"Come on, broham." He chuckled. "You're asking if I want to go to a place with topless half-horse women? I'm in. It'll probably only be the third craziest wedding I've crashed."

The life of a crazy Norwegian biker. I loved it. "Fine, you're enlisted. I'll get you caught up in the morning."

The Spaniard hissed and disappeared. I hadn't known him to have a hissy like this before, but he really disliked silvans.

One day I would need to ask him why.

Chapter 13

My head shot up from my pillow, ears pounding.

No. The pounding was at the door. There it was again.

I reached for my phone to check the time but it was missing. Right. A quick scavenge for jeans and a tank top later and I was hurrying to the visitor.

"What is it?" I grouched, carelessly throwing open the door.

Evan Cross released a tense breath. "Christ, you're okay." He stormed past me on his way in. "Why's there a key on the floor?"

I glanced down. Just inside my entry where it had been shoved under the door was the key to my Firebird. I snatched it and closed the door.

"I didn't know what to think," continued Evan, voice still frantic but obviously relieved. "I found out about the sting after it was too late. The feds had a perimeter up and were scouring the area. Agent Bell denied having anyone in custody but you went off the grid. Your phone's disconnected. I was half sure you were locked down in a secret government black site or something."

"You've been listening to Fran too much." I grimaced and rubbed my face, picking out an eye boogie. "Sorry about that. I had to destroy my phone. I didn't know how they were tracking me."

He shook his head. "Those burners should be legit, but better safe than sorry." He paused, hands on hips, shaking his head as he studied me. "Shit man, I'm fucking sorry."

"No worries. The trap was well sprung. The FBI tricked both of us."

"Still, it was stupid of me to walk right into it like that."

I wandered over to the bar. It was way too early to drink but the tall chair was a convenient perch.

"How did you get out of there?" asked Evan.

I dipped my head, considering how much to tell him, but he was my best friend. We were past keeping secrets. "A couple of Clan Beaumont spooks pulled me out through their tunnels."

His face darkened and he waited a beat. "You brought them in on this?"

"No, they were following me."

"That's even worse!"

I scowled. "I know that. I'm planning to speak with Beaumont about it."

"You should cut ties."

I chortled. The suggestion was ridiculous.

"I'm serious, Cisco. Think about who you're throwing in with."

"They weren't the ones who screwed up last night," I snapped.

We both fumed, more angry at ourselves than each other. The whole situation was concerning, desperate, and rotten to the core. It had only been sheer grit that had kept things alive. We weren't gonna be this lucky forever.

"Look, bro," I said, consolation in my voice, "we're threading the needle here. I know that. We can't last like this for long. With the Obsidian March on one side and the FBI on the other, we're bound to slip up somewhere. And then I'm gonna get picked apart."

He clenched his rugged jaw and paced to the other side of the bar so he could lean forward. His lack of answer was an answer in itself. I had spoken the truth.

But I knew exactly what he was thinking. Aligning myself with Clan Beaumont was a stopgap, and a risky one at that. It didn't stall the FBI's search for the Shadow Man. It didn't prevent whatever insidious plots the Obsidian March were cooking up. But it did, at the very least, keep us safe on the home front. Dealing with Leverett was political squirming at its finest, buying time to kick the can further down the road till we could figure out how to vaporize it.

"How's Operation Black Out coming?" I asked.

Instead of a full change of subject, it was more like a sidetrack. Evan was the sole commander of the DROP team, which stood for District Risk Overview and Prevention. The city of Miami was divided into five districts, each with their own commissioner, and the DROP team had jurisdiction in all of them. Basically, they did long-term threat assessment on a macro level and spearheaded campaigns to improve outcomes.

The team used to be answerable to all five city commissioners, but after some dirty business they got reassigned to the mayor. That's four fewer bosses for anyone keeping count, and the one they did have was a hell of a lot busier with bigger and more important things, like golf. This meant, as long as Evan got results and kept embarrassment away from the big office, he had full autonomy over his team.

It should be noted that this was the only law enforcement outfit that knew about the supernatural. Due to my actions they'd had brushes with revenants, immortal wolf cults, and a fire-wielding jinn.

Operation Black Out was a public face for a secret threat: the Obsidian March. Evan's task force was handling the case on the books by getting hooks into the human trafficking operation running through the city. In time this would uncover shell companies, safe houses, trucking lines, and more. All the while the DROP officers could keep the true depths of the upir menace under wraps. By keeping the operation slow and steady, and close to the vest, they avoided drawing the wrath of the fiendish syndicate.

Evan firmly shook his head. "Operation Black Out is proceeding slowly. We're months away from any sweeping actions. We're fighting the FBI over access to the family you found at the Cielo, but there's no way we can reveal our hand to the Obsidian March anytime soon."

I nodded. It was what I figured. I didn't envy Evan his

status as a police lieutenant. It came with a lot of power and respect, but it was hard to get anything unorthodox done. My investigative style was more instinctual and brash. Sure, it often backfired spectacularly, but no one could deny it also got results.

"Oh, is this your underground wedding invitation?" He unfolded the makeshift envelope on the bar.

"Does everyone know about this?"

"Like you said, you're all we talk about when you're not around." He skimmed the card. "This is in two days."

"It is, and I've made a decision. I'm gonna go."

He continued reading the card and absently nodded.

I blinked. "You're... not gonna try to talk me out of it?"

"Why would I? I think it's a great idea. I was the one that told you to take a vacation while Agent Bell's in town."

"That's what I'm talking about!" It was nice to finally get some support around here.

"Plus," he added, "it would mean fewer hotel explosions for a bit."

I glared at him.

"Wish I could let the DROP team escort you, but we have official duties that prevent us from disappearing into Wonderland."

"I'm taking Kasper. But listen, I hate leaving you guys."

He snorted. "You're the one that had babysitters, Cisco. We're fine without you."

I nodded. "Just do me a favor and stay in Beaumont's territory. He'll keep the vampire clans off your back."

"No one's making moves with the FBI in town. Trust

me."

"You're probably right. Still, if you get spooked in the slightest, come stay at my place. You have a key and the place to yourself, with a complement of full wards to protect the whole family."

He grinned. "That mean I can use your fancy electronic toilet?"

I sighed. "You do know that all toilet business goes down more or less the same, right?"

"That's not what Emily says. According to her, it's like springtime in your pants."

"Fine. Use the toilet. Just watch the hot setting. There's a problem with the temperature control."

His face contorted in imagined pain. "Duly noted." He set the silvan invitation down and pulled away from the bar. "And since we've reached the low point in this conversation, I think it's time to head out." He pressed his lips together for a serious moment. "I'm glad you're okay, brother. And call Milena. She's worried about you too."

I spastically gripped my forehead and fired my gaze at the wall clock. "Crap, I'm missing our date."

He arched an eyebrow. "You mean last night? I thought you called her. She has to understand—"

"No, I canceled last night. But we were supposed to meet up this morning. They have a yacht for the day." I paced the living room looking for a phone.

"You gonna pop the question on the water?" he asked.

"It'll be romantic." The drawer where I kept a burner was empty. Damn, I needed to restock. Then I remembered the emergency spare I kept in the car.

He chuckled as he let himself out. "Good luck, Cisco."

I was too panicked to respond. I raced to the bedroom to make sure the ring was safe. I opened the nightstand drawer and rummaged through the contents. A man's sock drawer was his secret stash. It wasn't the most savvy of hiding places, perhaps—a remnant of his formative teenage years— but it was close at hand and personal. If a man had a secret that could fit in his hand, it was tucked away under his socks. No doubt about it.

The ring was there. I hastily changed into swim trunks and *chancletas*. This was gonna be a day in the sun and the surf, away from the vampires and the feds. It was an easy way to get off the grid in Miami. Maybe we'd even head down to the Keys, spend the night in a sweaty beach paradise. We could sip margaritas in Margaritaville and gaze longingly at the sunset. That or watch the crazy dude on the dock jumping his cats through flaming hoops. The romantic possibilities were endless.

I stuffed the ring in the zippered pocket with a roll of cash and my ID, hooked my key back on my key chain, and threw open the front door. But I stopped there...

Something was nagging at me.

I strolled back inside and grabbed my belt pouch. Romantic getaway or no, as a black magic outlaw, one could never be too careful.

Chapter 14

I skipped my usual routine of checking in at the coffee shop. Outlaw Coffee & Colada operated fine without me, and I was late enough as it was. I did wonder if Kasper was downstairs or still passed out in his room in the penthouse, but he was a grown man. At least on the outside.

Exiting the elevator into the parking garage, I was relieved to see my silver Trans Am. I circled the car looking for scratches or dents. After my seal of approval I settled in the driver's seat and scowled. The car mileage was more inflated than it should've been. Whatever bastard had driven this home had detoured for a joyride.

I checked the ash tray and grumbled. My spare quarters were missing too. What did a vampire need quarters for? One out of ten, would not use again. This car service was worse than valet.

At least the spare phone was still in the glove box. I opened the clamshell packaging with ease. The trick is to pry the seams apart with a bit of shadow magic. If you don't know spellcraft you're screwed.

I moved the cash and ID to my belt pouch and dug around for a spare sim card. It only took a minute to put the phone together and plug it into the charger. I turned it on and added a few key contacts from memory. The routine grew easier every time I repeated it, and that was a lot.

"Sorry," I texted to Milena. "Just got back on the grid."

"I HADN'T HEARD FROM YOU!!!" she replied. A quick follow-up text said, "You better have a good excuse."

"Vampires?" I hurried. "Where are you?"

Things took a minute. She was likely updating her contact listing with my new number. My friends were used to this dance too.

"We started without you," she said. "But you're lucky we're close by. Pick you up?"

"I can drive."

"I mean in the yacht."

Oh. That complicated things. But there were any number of docks along the coastline. Most of them were private but could manage a quick pickup.

"Brickell Point?" I texted.

When she confirmed with a closer ETA than I realized, I forgot about making the walk. The park had a few parking spots and it was a weekday, so I was hoping to get lucky. I started the Firebird and turned onto Brickell Avenue.

One block in, a black Ford Explorer pulled out behind me. It was nondescript and I'd only been driving a minute, but I couldn't ignore that it was the same type of SUV that had participated in the federal sting. Luckily I only had a few blocks to drive. I pulled into the parking circle and snagged the last open spot, jumped out of the car and walked briskly across the grass. A casual glance showed the SUV had turned into the parking circle behind me.

"Suck it, FBI," I muttered. "There's a pay lot a block down."

Meanwhile, my ride was pulling up to a small dock fairly close to where I'd crawled out of the ocean the night before. Despite living in Miami, I didn't know anything about boats. It was a good size, maybe forty feet, and looked sleek and new. I smiled when I spotted Milena on deck. The yacht was closing cautiously because of the limestone shallows.

I covertly glanced behind me. Two agents in suits had exited the double-parked Explorer and were fanning into the yard. Okay, definitely following me then. Good to know I wasn't paranoid.

Pretending I was unaware of them and their containment effort, I waved at Milena and hurried toward the boat. The agents spread out, attempting to back me up against the water. I couldn't help but notice, the closer I got to the sidewalk, the farther away the boat seemed. By now I could make out someone else on board behind the angled windshield. A man stood behind the wheel wearing a captain's hat.

"We'll need to find another port," he called out. "This one's too shallow."

I saw his point as I stepped onto the dock. The tiny wooden outcropping was more for show, not even suitable to fish off of. Milena frowned, still eight feet out.

I glanced behind. The FBI was hurrying over now, abandoning all commitment to subtlety.

"Wait there," I said to the captain. "Don't move."

"Is he serious?" he asked Milena as I backed along the dock.

I launched into a full sprint and kicked off at the water's edge. It was a sunny day, but docks had shadow under them and I tickled a bit to help my launch.

Unfortunately, salt water had a habit of dispersing the Intrinsics and my *chancs* weren't Nike trainers. I didn't get the full thrust I'd been hoping for and tumbled through the air a little wildly. I landed on the deck and skidded on my haunches, which was all the better because it was a soft landing on an expensive boat.

"Let's go!" I shouted.

The man at the wheel chuckled and steered away from the shallows, completely oblivious to the converging federal agents. The throttled triple engines drowned out any late objections the FBI could muster.

Milena smothered me in kisses. "Who were those suits?"

"I don't know what you're talking about," I said with a shrug and a smile.

She helped me up and around into the boat's cockpit.

"That was awesome!" said the guy at the wheel. He flashed his biceps. "Strong guy!"

"Uh, yeah." He was talking about me since he was fairly scrawny himself. I wasn't really into the bromance dudes always trying to touch your muscles, but I gave him a polite chuckle seeing as how he did kinda rescue me from a federal inquisition. "Thanks for the pickup."

"Cisco," presented Milena, "this is Ahmed. He's the son of a diplomat."

"I am a diplomat," he corrected as we shook hands. "We're a diplomatic family. We're all diplomats."

I blinked, impressed. "That's gotta be a sweet gig. So, is your dad the actual diplomat then?"

"That's where you're wrong," he laughed. He kind of petered out without finishing the point.

Milena leaned close and whispered, "It's his mom."

This was obviously a sore point for Ahmed. As the boat cut through the water, I made a show of admiring it. "Well, this is an amazing yacht you got here." I didn't bring up whether the boat actually belonged to him or the family. That bought me a heartfelt thanks from the captain.

"So," he said, "you're a friend of the girls?"

Milena hugged me. "He's my boyfriend. But Cisco hasn't met Jem yet."

"Well," he told me with a wink, "it looks like we're two very lucky men."

"Guilty as charged," I said. "Where is the lead singer of the Holograms anyway?"

Ahmed scrunched his eyes at the missed reference but Milena slapped my shoulder. "Cut it out, Cisco. She gets that crap every day at the club. Think you can be a little more original than that?"

I snickered. "Is that a challenge?"

Ahmed nodded like he knew what we were talking about. "Jem's taking a shower below deck. She said she wanted to be fresh for me." His eyebrows waggled up and down suggestively like a cartoon character, and I was beginning to think he wasn't wearing the captain's hat ironically.

I managed a curt chuckle but my heart wasn't in it.

"Oh!" Milena's eyes lit up. "A little birdy told me you were going to pop the question!"

Full panic overtook my face. "What!?!"

"How could you not tell me?"

"What do you mean?" I blinked frenetically. Who spilled the beans? "I was gonna, obviously—"

"You get a fancy handmade wedding invitation from a mystery customer and you don't tell me about it." She slapped my shoulder again. "What were you thinking?"

I gasped for air and saliva caught in my throat. I broke into a fit of coughing, face red at the close call. "Of course —" I loudly cleared my throat and took calming breaths. "Of course I was gonna tell you about it. I just... Can we talk about it later?"

"Uh oh!" chimed Ahmed a little too enthusiastically. "Someone's busted."

"No, no," I stammered, "it's not like that. I just..." I withered under Milena's glare and pointed back to the foredeck. "Can we step away and talk about this?"

"Yes," laughed Ahmed. "I smell trouble. Take all the time you need."

I wasn't asking him but I let it slide. Was that some kind of rule about boats, that you had to ask the owner if you could move around? I didn't think so, but this guy probably overestimated his role as captain just like he did his position as "diplomat."

Milena and I rounded to the front deck. Ahmed could clearly see us, of course, but we were separated by ten feet, a pane of safety glass, and buffeting winds. We could talk in private.

"Why are you making a big deal about this?" I asked. "I was gonna show you the invitation. I thought you'd get a kick out of this."

She laughed. "I know, I just like giving you shit in front of Ahmed. He gets a kick out of it, and I get a kick out of *that*."

I groaned. "This guy."

"I know. I don't know what Jem sees in him."

"Really? Diplomatic connections, a party boat... You don't see it?"

She smirked. "Maybe our friendship isn't built on the foundation of deep mutual respect I thought it was."

We laughed.

Milena had a party girl inside her, no doubt, and she did work at a strip club. A girl had to make friends, right?

But she also had a head on her shoulders. As unlikely as it was, she was pure sex and smarts wrapped up in fun. One in a million, and she knew it.

At the same time, Milena was humble and the least judgmental person I knew. She lived in the moment and hung out with whoever, always aware of the line between meaningful friendships and simple pleasures.

And she crossed that line all the time.

"So a wedding in silvan land, huh?" she prompted.

"It's not called that. It's the Nether, and it's a very dangerous place."

Her excitement waned. "This isn't gonna be one of those things where you tell me how risky it would be for a normal person like me to go with you, right?"

I winced and my voice accidentally rose an octave. "Well..."

"Oh no," she warned, going serious. "Don't try to tell me I can't go."

"Look, you met Leverett Beaumont, you know how dangerous he is, and he doesn't even want *me* to go. It's for your—"

"Don't say protection, Cisco. Don't say it." She crossed her arms defiantly. "Don't you think you flaked on me enough lately?"

Ahmed laughed and pointed from the other side of the glass. I was in real trouble this time. I sighed. "Milena, my love, what kind of man would I be if I put someone so special to me in that position?"

She scoffed and laughed at the same time. "You're buttering me up!"

"No, no, I would never do that unless it was a warm day and we covered the bed with plastic. I'm just speaking sense here."

"Mmm hmm," she said in the most disagreeable way possible. "Or maybe you just have trust issues."

"Trust? Baby, I trust you implicitly."

"Yeah, you trust everybody. You just want to do everything by yourself."

I deflated. "That's different."

"It's not. You either trust me to handle myself or you don't. After everything that's happened, even you have to admit it's good to rely on friends every now and then." She leaned close. "We all do."

I frowned at the unfair argument. This was miles away from trust and friendship. The boat slowed in the water and we looked around. The Florida coast was still visible in the distance, but it was mostly Miami Beach and the other keys. The barrier islands were spaced away from Downtown, creating Biscayne Bay.

Ahmed said something and went below deck. We couldn't hear him. The moment of quiet and privacy was welcome. I rubbed Milena's hand and leaned in for a long, heartfelt kiss. Some people were magnetic together, and it was that way with us. Every physical touch just felt right and had the power to fritter away any anxieties and tensions. When I pulled back she smiled.

"Look," I said gently, "I had high hopes for having a relaxing day together. The wedding's not for another couple days and we can't do anything about it now. It's also not a great time to talk details, for obvious reasons. Can we table the discussion till we get back to my place?"

She pressed her lips out and chuckled. "You're right. I'm really not giving you a hard time, I just want to be included. We'll talk about it later. Pinkie swear?"

I dropped my head to her offered finger. "Wait a minute. I wasn't prepared for this kind of commitment."

"You better be, buddy."

"Then how am I gonna weasel out of this?"

She uncaringly shook her head. "You can't. It's impossible to renege on a pinkie swear. Everybody knows that."

I huffed loudly and locked my little finger with hers. "You got me."

"Game, set, and match."

Chapter 15

We chuckled and sat on the cushioned seats, enjoying the expansive view.

"This is beautiful," I said in awe. "I should get a boat." A gust of wind ruffled the wrap she wore, and I picked at it with my finger. "Please tell me you have a bikini under that."

She pulled it down to reveal the skimpy black top. I didn't know how she did it, but she had a new one every time. "I suppose this is as good a place as any to suntan, but I need you to help me with the lotion."

I cracked my knuckles. "A man's gotta do what a man's gotta do."

A minute into it, Ahmed came back upstairs calling Milena. We walked around to the cockpit.

"Everything sorted, huh?" He held up a hand to high five and I obliged him. "Player!" After his hand contacted mine, his face contorted and he wiped the extra lotion on his shirt. I shrugged.

"What's going on?" asked Milena.

"Jem was asking for you. Says she needs a little help with some"—he placed a hand on the side of his mouth like he was telling a secret—"*lady business.*"

The cabin door was open now and I glanced down the steps at movement. Jem backed away into the room. I saw her body from her toes to her breasts, completely naked. I jerked my head away and stepped back as Jem likewise retreated.

Whoa. That was one of those peeks where you felt guilty and extremely lucky at the same time. Jem was a top-heavy white girl with a Brazilian wax. Milena had told me I would like her, but I hadn't gotten the chance to see for myself since she preferred I not visit her at the club. I avoided eye contact as Milena hurried down the stairs.

"Yes," said Ahmed with a chuckle, "Jem's not particularly shy."

"Uh," I said, a little embarrassed he'd caught that exchange, "you were right. You're a lucky man."

"Maybe later we'll go skinny dipping." He winked. "You know what I mean, man?"

"There's literally only one thing that means."

"I know." He nodded suggestively.

I sighed. Ahmed was kind of a douche. And apparently I had some alone time to kill with him. "You have a beer?"

"Of course." He motioned to the built-in cooler next to the sink and grill.

The whole cabinet setup was sleek and unassuming, in easy reach of a central dining booth. I grabbed a beach pilsner and sat facing the rear of the boat so I could enjoy the view. Unlike the cockpit behind me, the table had no overhead roof. The sun warmed my skin. I twisted the cap off and pulled from the bottle.

This was nice. I wondered if I should take the plunge and get a boat. I could live like in one of those tropical thriller novels, operating a home base out of a bungalow and saving damsels in distress from heinous drug runners.

"So, my man..." Ahmed mimed a bodybuilder pose again and sat in the booth across from me. "You work out, huh?"

What was the proper etiquette here? On the one hand, I didn't wanna get chummy with the guy. On the other, we were on his boat and couldn't get more than twenty feet from each other at any given time.

"Not really," I answered. "But I guess you could say I do a lot of contact sports."

"Yeah? Boxing? MMA?"

I hiked a shoulder. "I dabble a bit. Street fighting."

"No way, that's amateur stuff. You should go pro. Can you flex for me?"

I leaned back in the seat, desperate to change the subject. I craned my neck behind but the girls were probably gonna be a minute. Who knows what kinds of things they get up to together? Instead I took in the horizon. Distant clouds of pure white boldly stacked to the heavens, but it was clear skies directly overhead. "What about you? How're you liking Miami?"

"Oh," he chortled, "this is the best city in the world."

"You got that right."

"So many beautiful women here. I take a different one out every weekend."

"I bet they love to hear that."

He shook his head. "This is the life, man. And to think I almost got married once."

Now that was the first surprising thing he'd said. "Really?"

"Back in my country. The wedding was delayed when I got this position. Diplomacy waits for no man."

Or woman, as was actually the case. I took a swig and nodded.

"Then it was party, party, party."

I held the beer in my lap. "I think you skipped the part about your fiancée."

"What do you mean?"

"What happened to her? She couldn't come with you?"

"Oh. She did, sure, but she didn't last."

"Can't imagine why."

"It requires very little imagination." He leaned in conspiratorially to give stern advice. "Never get married. Guys like you and me, we're lions. You know what I'm talking about."

I really didn't. I grumbled inwardly as I checked off the subjects to avoid with this guy: muscles, girls, and now, for some reason, lions. He was like a douchebag minefield.

"I don't usually go for Spanish girls, no offense, but your shorty is hot."

Urge to kill: rising. "Her name's Milena."

His face suddenly brightened. "Hey, I have an idea. Have

you seen that show, *Wife Swap*?"

Luckily, the decision whether to deck him with my fist or the bottle stayed my hand long enough for us to be interrupted.

"Cisco!" called Milena as she excitedly bounced up the steps. "Jem has a hookup in the Keys tonight!"

I spun in the seat to greet them and was floored by Milena. She'd put her hair up and taken off the wrap. A spaghetti strap clung tightly around her neck. I swore, I saw her body every day and still couldn't get past what a babe she was.

"Hello, lovely," said Jem, leaning over the side of the table and locking lips with Ahmed.

From that angle, I saw a wash of wavy brown hair on a *very* curvy girl. She wore red sequined short shorts but my eyes were on her hanging breasts. Instead of a proper top, Jem wore some kind of fishnet blouse. Her body type was similar to Milena's except her skin was pale and her nipples were pink. Inches from me, bent over as she was, and really thrusting into and out of an extended kiss, I suddenly felt like I was participating in a dirty movie.

Milena rolled her eyes. "They're just breasts, Cisco."

It was an easy attitude given that hers were bought and paid for. None of this was taboo in her world. Hell, in her line of work, it might've even been a little boring. "Hey," I said defensively, "I'm just a humble, simple man."

"I would say predictable and basic."

Jem finally broke away from the lip lock and faced Milena, turning her breasts out of sight. "Of course, darling.

That's what makes them so easy to control." They laughed.

"Guilty," I added, fighting a losing battle with staring at the bottom of Jem's ass hanging out of the shorts. Were my eyes even under my control anymore?

Ahmed leaned forward with a smile. Instead of a not-so-quippy remark, his eyes half closed in contentment. Wow, she could shut him up, too. Jem wrapped her arm around Milena's waist and seductively spun around her. It was hot but I hated the thought of Ahmed getting any ideas.

Jem shook the hair from her face as she hugged Milena from behind. "I've heard so much about you, Cisco." She rested her chin on Milena's shoulder and they both beamed at me.

You know that sudden pang you get when your ex-girlfriend meets your current one? I got that. *Hard.* Which was weird since I'd never met Jem before. But her face was familiar. Even more so were her forward behavior and—

I sprung from the booth, knuckles white. Jem jerked the two of them to the back of the yacht. Milena's face tensed at the rough treatment, but when she tried to turn Jem's grip tightened and held her in place.

Ahmed slowly leaned forward, drooling from an open mouth until his tongue hit the table. He was in a daze or half asleep or something.

And then it all came crashing back to me. This wasn't *Jem and the Holograms*, it was Gemma and the Glamours. My girlfriend was now held hostage by a mermaid with a score to settle.

Chapter 16

"Don't do it," I said, going for a growl but allowing too much panic into my voice.

"Do what?" snarled Gemma. "Snap her pretty neck?"

My vision went red. "It'll be the last thing you ever do."

We stood a few paces from each other, unmoving, as if this whole thing could be safely paused. But our muscles were taut. We were poised to strike.

My eyes darted to Milena's. She clutched the arm around her neck, afraid to move. I wanted to say something but it wouldn't come out. It would've felt like a lie. I settled for a stern gaze, something to convey the gravity of the situation, the gravity of what she meant to me and what I would do to protect her.

"Good," said Gemma with a slight nod. "I finally have your attention."

Her bucolic charm transformed to a sneer, enlarged smile full of sharpened teeth and fingers ending in claws. While still possessing human legs, she was showing more of her true mermaid features. Trust me, they were anything but the charming vixens from storybooks.

"You're the silvan assassin that's been asking for me," I spat.

Her words came out like venom. "You didn't think I'd forgotten about the wizard who killed my sister."

I fumed at her accusation. Her sister, Jade, was another mermaid of course—and another assassin. I'd merely defended myself against an attempt on my life, paid for by a now-defunct drug cartel. But reason wouldn't sway the rage that led Gemma here. She didn't care about right and wrong. She was an assassin and I'd hurt her. All she wanted now was revenge.

"I knew you'd come eventually," I muttered.

My mind continued spinning, things falling into place. I hadn't believed the silvans hired an assassin to go after me. It didn't compute. But Gemma operated independently. And she had all the reason in the world.

She grinned hungrily. "I bet you thought I'd come for you, though. Like I tried before. But even on the water, wizards are tough contracts."

I blinked at her incredulously. "So this isn't personal?"

"Oh, it's personal all right. I just figured out a better way to hurt you. You took away someone that I loved, so I figured I'd return the favor."

"Don't hurt her," I warned.

This was a hairy standoff. I was wearing swimming trunks and flip-flops. No belt, so my bag of tricks was sitting on the front deck where I'd shared a relaxing moment with

Milena. Not like it mattered. Gemma's teeth were inches from her bare neck, a split second from turning my world upside down. Any action on my part had to be faster than a twitch.

Which I could definitely manage. I just had to worry about protecting Milena first.

"Jem," pleaded my girlfriend, "this is me..."

"Shut up, bitch." Gemma jerked Milena's head sideways to further expose her throat.

I almost made a move but held off when Gemma did as well. Despite the hair-trigger dance we were locked in, my body trembled with rage.

"Let's just think this through," I said as reasonably as possible. "There's no endgame here."

"Just because you don't see it doesn't mean it's not there."

I shook my head, unsure who I was convincing. "No. We have a choice right here. One of two options, and we're both in control."

She smiled. "I'll humor you. Lay it out for me."

"One is we back down. You walk away from this, you have my word I won't retaliate. We go our separate ways forever."

"And the other option?"

"You hurt a hair on her head and I will utterly destroy you. Every waking breath; every ally I have topside and in the Nether; every animist, ghost, fiend, and silvan I can convince or contort will hunt you down for the rest of your rapidly dwindling life."

Her patronizing smile never faltered. "You drive a hard bargain, Cisco. Care to entertain a counter offer?"

"There is no counter offer."

"Such confidence. Such swagger." The mermaid's voice went flat. "I can see why Jade wanted you all to herself." Gemma traced a claw over Milena's throat, dragging the skin but not breaking it. "I can see why she likes you."

Milena shook her subdued head. "No, Cisco," she said softly. "I love you. I love you."

Damn it, why was she saying that now? It only gave the assassin more leverage. It only... Aw, hell.

My eyes watered and my voice broke. "I love you too, Milena, with everything I have and am."

Gemma rolled her eyes. "Okay, now you two are gonna break my heart."

My mind raced through contingencies. We were far removed from civilization. The land was a blur on the horizon, miles of salt water surrounded us and limited the flow of the Intrinsics.

But the boat wasn't drenched. Sure, it was wet with the occasional splash and the humid breeze, and the sun was high in the sky, but there was still some shadow to work with on the deck. The mass of it was behind me, under the canopy. Gemma had smartly maneuvered to the aft of the vessel where there was less I could nab her with.

And then there was the guesswork as to Gemma's part in this. She could've killed Milena by now but hadn't. Was that because she had other plans, or was it just to prolong my suffering?

"What do you want?" I finally asked.

Gemma blinked, taken aback by the question. Maybe she expected a fight. Maybe it was because I couldn't possibly give her her sister back. But her reaction was good. It meant she would keep talking.

"Heartstrings," she muttered. "You see that? Threats don't change us. Money helps, but what's really in control of everything is the heart."

That's what I was afraid of. If this was as simple as a contract, I could outbid her employer. But this wasn't that. And while talking was a sure way of delaying the inevitable, it wasn't a solution.

I took a soft step forward. Gemma hopped to the stern of the boat, inches from the water. I froze. I raised my hands slowly and swallowed.

"You're more hesitant than I remember you," she taunted. "You should've shot first and asked questions later. Now you're in a bind."

"Just tell me what you want."

The mermaid's lips curled over her teeth. "I wanna watch you squirm."

Milena suddenly jutted her fists up, striking Gemma in the chin. At the same time, she slackened her body and dropped low. The maneuver took the mermaid by surprise but couldn't overcome the headlock. Gemma held tight and leaned toward the water.

Lines of shadow shot past me from behind and latched onto Milena's legs. Another two grabbed Gemma's arm bar. While those yanked, I launched forward.

But the mermaid stepped off the boat's stern. Her weight came down hard. Although my shadow tendrils ripped the headlock loose, Gemma's other arm wrapped around Milena's waist, dragging her over the edge. The sudden fall shifted their positions. Gemma slipped around Milena's defending arms. Sharp teeth closed on her neck.

My spellcraft-bolstered fist slammed into Gemma's mouth. Fangs tore my knuckles open, but I followed through and knocked the danger away.

Two more fingers of shadow locked onto Milena. Despite Gemma's best efforts, I wasn't letting her take my girlfriend off the boat. The mermaid kicked up, and another length of shadow caught her foot.

Claws tore into Milena's side. I batted the arm away with my bloody hand, but Gemma moved in to bite again. I stretched past Milena and locked my grip around the mermaid's throat.

We were suspended there, toes barely on the boat, dangling over the water on tethers of black magic as Gemma attempted to rip Milena free and escape into the ocean.

"I warned you!" I growled. The blood on my hand bubbled around the silvan's throat and I squeezed.

Gemma screamed.

Milena, though hurt, still had a clear enough head to keep fighting. Her elbow rammed into the stomach behind her. I wrapped my arm around Milena's waist while using the other to squeeze the life out of the assassin, and I put all the power of the shadow into it.

But the flow of Intrinsics was spotty. Gemma had picked her strike location well. Somehow, her leg came free of my weakened magic. She flailed and grew heavier, throwing our delicate balance off.

A serpentine tail of sparkling scarlet kicked up, salt water splashing everywhere. Fingers of magic were doused. Milena's legs were released. It only took a second for my spellcraft to blink out and all three of us tumbled.

Warm water smacked my face and enveloped us. My shadows were gone, but I still had one arm around my girlfriend and one hand choking Gemma. I was upside-down and disoriented, but as long as I held tight I had a chance.

Gemma's thick tail slid between us. Twice the length of her legs and prehensile, it wrapped around Milena twice. At the same time, the water washed away the blood on my hands, stopping the burning and making everything slick. Now in her element, the mermaid rotated viciously like an alligator clamped onto a kill. We spun several rotations as if in a vortex, my weight pulling me away from them. I lost my grip on Gemma first, then spun in a dizzying blur before Milena slipped from my hand too.

Head over heels, awash in bubbles, I kicked toward the light. I broke the surface and turned in panic. If Gemma stole Milena down a rabbit hole, I might never be able to find it. But as I took a large breath and readied to submerge, the girls surfaced twenty feet from me, having moved impossibly fast.

"You want her?" called the mermaid. "Come get her."

I broke into a swim before Gemma made a move, but I had no hope of catching her anymore. A sharp finger tore into Milena's neck at the shoulder. She cried in agony as her blood spilled into the water.

I paddled furiously, but the seconds felt like forever. All I had were glimpses between frantic breaths.

Gemma laughed and held a vial into the air for me to see. "You wanted blood, Cisco. Here's some silvan blood." She unstoppered the bottle. "But it's not for you." She upended it. Black fluid drained into Milena's wound with a sizzle. The screams were agonizing.

My arm came around and locked onto Milena. As I pulled her to me, I readied a fist.

But Gemma was gone.

"It stings," cried Milena, convulsing as she attempted to wash the wound.

Some of the black blood had slicked away, but the majority of the water was red. I spun around, readying for Gemma and seeing the boat twenty feet away. "Come on."

Milena was instinctively treading water, but she couldn't get it together enough to swim. I pulled but she was fighting me.

"Come on!"

My breaths were starting to come too fast. The struggle hadn't been especially taxing—I was just worried at her desperate screaming. Milena was losing control and even more blood. I cursed, held my wounded hand above the water, and squeezed the fist to force as much blood as possible into it.

"I'm sorry," I said, and then clamped onto Milena's wound.

Her wail only lasted a few seconds before she passed out.

Chapter 17

I plopped Milena on the deck, both of us drenched in water. I didn't know why, but Gemma was gone. She'd had the upper hand in the ocean. She could've taken a shot at me, but she didn't. All I could figure was the damage was already done.

"Milena," I prodded, patting her cheek. She turned her head slightly, partially awake. Her chest rose and fell with shallow breaths.

I went straight to the wound, right where her neck met her shoulder. The tear of flesh was gaping but it wasn't fatal. The leaking blood wasn't an arterial spray. I snagged two nearby seat cushions to elevate her head and shoulder. The bleeding didn't visibly slow.

"Ahmed, can you get us back to land?"

The side of her stomach was clawed open as well. These lacerations were more jagged, the result of multiple claws, but they weren't as deep and had hit a less vital area.

"Ahmed?"

Damn, the guy was still facedown on the table. I didn't have time to worry about whether he was poisoned or charmed. I marched to the other side of the boat to get my implements of spellcraft and returned to Milena. The first thing I did was twist open a red ketchup bottle and squeeze toxic goop onto her neck. I could tell it was working when she violently jerked her head away.

I held her in place. "Easy, easy..."

The zombie toxin stung like a bitch—I knew from personal experience—but it had the best chance of cleansing the wound. Gemma was a fan of poisons, apparently. The more I thought about it, coming prepared with that vial, it was her plan all along. Funny way for an assassin to work; poisons were supposed to be covert.

As I finished sanitizing the second wound, Milena opened her eyes. "Cisco?"

I laughed madly for a minute, overjoyed to see her conscious. "I got you," I assured. "You're gonna be okay."

She groaned slowly. "I don't feel so good."

"There's something in your blood. Don't worry." I turned my head and yelled, "Ahmed!"

Milena's eyes lolled back into her head.

"Hey! Hey! Come back here."

She began convulsing in an epileptic fit.

"No."

I held her down and studied the wound. It was an ugly mess of black blood and gray gel. At least the bleeding had stopped. But Milena was pale and nearly delirious. She didn't have long.

I stood and pulled Ahmed's shoulder up. His pupils were rolled upward too. He was different, though. Peaceful. Dude was in a state of bliss. I tried to pull some shadow into my eyes but it was too bright out here.

"Shit."

I rushed to the helm and started the engines, easing the throttle to half and steering toward land. Once our bearing was set, I threw it to full speed.

Next I hurried back to Milena. She was still again, heartbeat faint. If I didn't use spellcraft within the next couple of minutes, Milena would be dead.

The problem was, much of my spellcraft was predicated for working *on* the dead.

I wasn't a healer. It wasn't my thing. But that didn't mean I couldn't attempt a new trick or two.

The first thing I did was lift Milena by the shoulders and drag her to the lower deck. Once out of the sun, I hugged her close and pulled her into the shadow. We stayed like that for half a minute. Part of me hoped I could isolate her body and leave the poison behind in the physical world, ridding it from her bloodstream, but that was wishful thinking. It wasn't usually how this sort of thing worked. Any toxins, like the zombie salve, would just come along for the ride.

I threw her onto the bed next, propping her up with pillows and wiping us both down with a blanket. The Intrinsics would work better without the salt water. Then I opened my shadow sight and examined her.

I didn't see much. The wound had a slight glow that

could've been the result of my salve. They say humans draw spellcraft in through spirit patrons but silvans are born with magic in their blood. If Milena had in fact been infected with silvan blood, it stood to reason that I could see it. But whatever it was wasn't strong enough to come through her skin.

Without a sure way to detect it, I had to go scorched earth.

I peeked upstairs to make sure the boat was still on course and to retrieve my bag. We were approaching Miami at a good clip but still had several minutes. I went back down and withdrew a lighter, flinching at the sight of the Spaniard standing over the bed.

"What are you looking at?" I snapped. "Do something!"

The skull seemed to wince. "You see what I have done to myself. It's not a curse I would wish upon her."

"You've gotta know something about blood and poisons."

He shook his head. "You are familiar with my magic, brujo. I can only help her body once the soul has fled it. Your skills are thus limited as well."

"I refuse to believe that. I can purify her."

Voodoo spellcraft was rife with poisons. I wasn't a houngan, or even a bokor that specialized in pestilence like Chevalier, but that didn't mean I was flying blind. I climbed over Milena's still form and worked my fist open and closed, forcing blood into my palm. I chanted some words and clicked the lighter on, bringing it to my bloody skin.

The Spaniard watched drily. "Have you attempted this

before?"

"First time for everything."

The blood in my palm swirled and the flame leaned into it. I gritted my teeth as my skin blackened.

And then the Intrinsics kicked in. The flame turned a shade of green and grew in size to encompass my hand. I began shaking involuntarily at the immense pain. My entire body was feeding it.

"Brujo..." warned the Spaniard.

"Help or shut up."

The spellcraft was working up something fierce and I wasn't sure I could take it, but then the Spaniard lifted rotted fingers and I suddenly felt nothing. The smell of burning flesh still filled my nose, so I was thinking he'd stifled the pain. Just a trick. He had power over human minds like that.

Finally, when I was satisfied with the product, I upturned the blood into Milena, just as Gemma had done. I stuck a finger directly into the wound, seeking out foreign Intrinsics or impurities.

Amazingly, I sensed them. The Spaniard's eyes flared as I pushed in deeper, in touch with Milena's pulsing blood and beating heart. She shrieked and opened her eyes but I continued on, burning out every last piece of venomous blood I could find.

When I was done, Milena was sweaty and exhausted, but awake. I panted heavily and cradled my hand, blackened and curled. I ignored the pain and leaned my forehead onto Milena's, relief washing over me.

"You're okay," I whispered. "You're okay."

She grunted, still a little out of it.

"Hey!" called Ahmed from outside. "What the hell?"

Crap. I jumped off the bed to deal with Ahmed but my legs noodled under my weight. I collapsed. I caught myself with my blackened hand and spikes of pain fired up my arm.

"Brujo, you are weak."

Whatever spellcraft I'd just slapped together wiped me out. I bit down, pushed to my feet, and went halfway up the steps. Ahmed stood by his captain's seat, though his hat was now missing.

"What happened to you?" he demanded, slightly confused.

I shook my head innocently, pulling off my tank top and wrapping it around my wounded hand to not draw attention to it.

"You're not down there with both girls are you?" His eyes narrowed. "Did you roofie me? Because I know what they feel like and this is pretty similar."

I chuckled. This guy. "It was Jem, bro. She split."

He whined in annoyance. "Man, not again."

"Can you take us back in? Milena's not feeling so—"

My eyes widened as I took another step up and glanced at our surroundings. The yacht was bearing straight toward Brickell Point at full speed. We were so close I could see the panicked eyes of people on the river walk. I'd been so casual because I'd seen him at the wheel. I didn't realize he was still drugged.

"Ahmed!"

I hurried to the helm and shut off the throttle. Steering was another problem entirely. I turned the wheel but forty-foot yachts didn't turn on a dime.

"How do you stop this thing?"

Ahmed snapped to it and reversed the throttle lever. Triple engines kicked on but we were coming in too fast. All I could do was try to make land on the smoothest incline possible. The front of the boat scraped limestone and kicked into the air, sending me and Ahmed to the deck. A few bounces and scrapes later and the collision was over.

All things considered, much better than it could've been.

Milena moaned. I hurried over and found her sweating profusely, hot to the touch. She was still infected.

Damn Gemma. I was gonna find her and pay her back for this, but not before she told me how to fix it. Until then I considered other alternatives. The Bone Saints. Beaumont was nearby—they might know something of this. And Kasper. The Vietnam medic had patched me up before. I just wasn't sure his fancy markers could deal with blood toxins.

I grabbed my bag in my teeth and carried Milena across the deck, shirt still wrapped around my hand. Ahmed lay on the floor whimpering, "Not again." I felt a little bad for the guy but didn't have time for it. We hopped off the boat onto dry land.

"Ugh..." groaned Milena.

She looked sickly. It was obvious she was still in trouble and whatever I'd done had only staved off the inevitable. Maybe I needed to do something right now. But we were in public. The Spaniard wouldn't help me here. I wasn't strong enough...

My eyes shot to the Miami Circle, the site of countless ancient rituals. It was a location of power, either because of anomalous terrain or due to repeated spellcraft from Tequesta shamans. The reasons weren't important. What mattered was the Intrinsics likely flowed more freely within the Circle, and that was good enough for me.

I hurried across the lawn and set Milena down. The same federal agents from before sprinted toward me. Damn it. Not now. I unzipped my belt pouch to grab a lighter but the agents reached for their guns. They converged and drew down on me.

"LET ME SEE YOUR HANDS! LET ME SEE YOUR HANDS!"

I put my hands in the air slowly, but the shirt still covered my right hand. That kept the agents yelling another minute. My eyes darted behind them as Special Agent Rita Bell took over.

"Keep it cool, boys. Is there a weapon?"

"He went for a bag."

I rolled my eyes. "It's Milena. She's hurt. I'm just trying —" I paused, realizing how screwed this situation had become.

Rita shooed the guns down with a hand motion. "Cisco, it's about time we talked."

Milena coughed and I put my hand on her cheek. She was way too hot. One of the agents came to pull me away. When I resisted, he forced my arm behind my back. I spun and punched him in the jaw. That got the guns trained on me again. The other agent shoved me to the ground and they both piled on.

"Agents," eased Rita, "no one's under arrest at the moment." She frowned at Milena. "What's wrong with her?"

I swallowed. I didn't have time for this song and dance. "She was swimming and something bit her." Agent Bell leaned in but I nodded toward the crashed yacht to keep her from looking too closely. "Ahmed took a tumble on the boat. He's hurt."

Rita sent one of the agents over and studied us as they allowed me to sit up. As she did, a Fire Rescue truck pulled to the curb. Of course. If the FBI was sitting on my car, they would've called this in the second the boat jumped the river walk. Paramedics unloaded and hurried over with a stretcher.

"Anybody been drinking out there?" asked Rita.

"Agent Bell," I said calmly but clearly annoyed, "we're in a panic over my girlfriend. She's not doing well."

Milena writhed on the grass. I wished it was an act but it wasn't. The paramedics attended to her and I spun the same lie. They didn't need to know what was going on to help. In fact, maybe this would work out after all. They could treat the wounds and the fever, give Milena conventional help while buying me time to do my thing. But it didn't hurt to give them a little.

"One other thing," I added as they moved her to the stretcher. "I think she was poisoned."

The paramedic arched an eyebrow. "Poison? I thought this was a shark attack?"

"I don't know what it was. I didn't see it. But she complained of pain all over her body."

He nodded. "She's running a high fever and showing signs of nausea. We've seen it before with scorpionfish, but they don't usually bite." They loaded her onto a stretcher.

On the sidewalk, Ahmed had his hands on his head and was explaining what happened to the fed. The good news was he didn't know anything. I just hoped he left Jem out of the story. Otherwise the police would be looking for a missing person too.

We walked with the paramedics to the truck. As they climbed in, I went to follow. The agent tailing me grabbed my shoulder.

"Where do you think you're going?"

I turned to him with the stare of death. "I'm getting on this truck with my girlfriend."

"Not a chance. You assaulted a federal agent. You're under arrest."

He reached for my arm and I shrugged him away before Rita jumped between us.

"Carter!" she snapped. "Stand down."

"But he decked me."

"We'll deal with that later." She looked me in the eye. "You're free to go, Cisco. But we're gonna talk later. Got that?"

I nodded in thanks and stepped into the truck.

Chapter 18

The rest of the day gave me a *lot* of time to think.

Sometimes thinking is the enemy. Instead of making a choice, instead of reacting or taking a shot, you get bogged down in trivial details. They call it analysis paralysis, and I hear it's a bitch.

Lately that particular problem hadn't plagued me. I was a man of action, reactive and proactive. I was motion. I was force. I was fucking nuclear fusion when I needed to be.

But moments like this, when the enemy struck too close to home, when they got my daughter or my girlfriend or my friends, that's when inaction threatened. Insecurity. Maybe I shouldn't be doing this. Maybe I had no business keeping friends and family. I stared at the silver wedding ring for an hour straight. Maybe I had no business asking someone to be a permanent part of my life.

But self pity can only take you so far. I'd come back to this world on a mission of revenge. It had driven me through voodoo gangs, haunted spirits, unimaginable monsters, and most of a drug cartel. Revenge was a powerful motivator. It drove me when nothing else could. But it wasn't all I had.

Pride. Pride in this city. Pride in my life. For better or worse, I'd mowed down my enemies and staked a claim to Miami. Cisco Suarez was here to stay. It was everybody else who could get the fuck out.

Because this was finally about more than revenge. We were building something, my friends and I. Maybe we weren't so important that we could make a better world, but no one could convince me we weren't damn well trying. So if witches from deep in the Nether were sending serial killers and vampires into MY world, if they had designs on MY people, well, my friends and I weren't going to let them in.

It's called taking a stand, and by definition it means not backing down.

So I used my time to think, to plan, and talk. After ensuring Milena was stable, I paid a visit to Beaumont. I told him I was charging into the Nether whether he liked it or not. I updated Evan on the situation. Gave my daughter a hug and urged them to stay safe.

I also let Kasper work on my hand. It was blackened and raw. It hurt to wiggle my fingers. The damage, however, wasn't permanent. I might be shooting lefty for a while but I'd be right as rain.

That night I stayed with Milena in the hospital.

"I'm sorry," I told her.

She winked. "You need to stop apologizing. It's not

sexy."

"I'll remember that next time I take you out for pizza."

I felt her forehead. Her fever was under control. She'd gotten some color back in her skin. The staff had administered a blood transfusion since she had lost so much. They'd also expertly patched her up.

All progress aside, Milena was weak. There was something in her, acting on her, and I was afraid what it could be. I was up half the night, holding her while she slept, considering how lucky I was just to have those tortured moments.

The nurse roused us in the morning and chided me for crowding Milena on the bed. I stepped out to let him do his thing and bought a Mountain Dew and a water from the vending machine. I returned just as the nurse left.

"So," I said, handing her the water bottle, "are they letting you check out?"

"They want me to stay another day." She ignored the water and grabbed the Mountain Dew. "What?" she asked, rebuffing my look of surprise. "You're rubbing off on me."

Emily knocked lightly at the open door. I stood as she came to the side of the bed and placed a bouquet of flowers down. "The family sends their love."

"Thanks, girl," said Milena.

The women kissed and hugged. "Are you all right?"

"I feel like an ash tray, but I'll live."

Emily sat at the bedside. "Cisco, will you get the door?"

I drew it closed to give us privacy. Emily pulled a few stones from a silk pouch and placed them in a line from

Milena's neck to her groin.

"Ooh, can you do me next?" I asked.

The white witch rolled her eyes and leaned forward in study. I decided to go a few seconds without being an ass. I wasn't sure what she was doing. Light magic couldn't heal as far as I knew, but it was pretty darn good at exposing truths. Unfortunately, Emily's expression wasn't promising.

"You're... tainted somehow."

"Probably my fault," I joked.

"Yeah right," said Milena. "If anything, I tainted you."

"Do you guys always talk about sex?" asked Emily.

"Only when we're together," I said.

Emily shook her head like a disappointed older sibling. "Anyway, I can't get a handle on the enchantment, which is strange. This is utterly foreign to me."

The nurse poked his head in and froze at the sight of Emily reading stones on top of Milena.

"Uh... homeopathy." I hiked a shoulder.

The nurse glared and retreated.

My face dampened with dread as I thought about the serial killer. "Is she cursed?"

"Hard to say, but I don't think so." Emily looked at me. "This isn't like Manifesto."

That relieved me slightly.

"Still, it might as well be a curse. There's something in her blood that doesn't want to come out. You're saying it was silvan blood? The mermaid's?"

"That's what I don't know. Silvan blood is poisonous to humans. It's black and putrid, but it generally dissolves in this steppe. If Gemma wanted to infect her, she could've used her own blood. Instead this came from a vial."

"To preserve it, possibly." She pressed her lips together. "So it could've been poison, or some other blood, or a concoction of things."

"That's where we are."

We all frowned.

"All I know," said Milena, "is I'm getting out of here. Help me up."

It may not have been advised, but at this point Milena's problem was supernatural. It was best to keep her close at hand and under supervision. Emily helped us sign out and saw us to my car.

"Remember," I told her. "Stay in Brickell. There's a silvan assassin trying to hurt my friends."

"Don't worry. Evan told me about your offer and we're packing up for your place. I can't wait to get him on that computerized toilet."

"At least your priorities are well placed."

I hugged her goodbye and drove behind her until we returned to Beaumont's territory. Then I split off to my condo. Kasper was upstairs and immediately went to work marking up Milena's stitches with his gold paint pen.

"These are no problem," said the scribe. "With any luck she won't even have battle scars to show for it."

"I owe you another one, buddy."

"Nah, the wedding is a good enough perk."

Milena gave me the side eye. "Oh, so *he* gets to go now?"

I sighed. "You don't want me going alone, do you?"

"And what about me? I can shake this off. I—"

As she moved to stand, Milena doubled over and puked on the carpet. Liquid ejected from her mouth, foul and rotten.

"She's still sick." I pulled my knife and slashed my hand.

"Hey!" complained Kasper. "I just patched that up!"

I crisscrossed Milena's wound with blood and rested my hand on top, feeling out the situation.

"That didn't work last time," chided the wraith as he blinked beside us.

"It helped."

"Will you cut her open too?"

I worked my jaw, weighing the value proposition. There had to be better methods than reopening her stitches. "I could go to the cookhouse. You could help me."

"With our combined knowledge of the poisons of the wild folk?" posited the wraith.

I frowned. I was in over my head and everyone knew it. "Jean-Louis. He's a poison expert. Kasper, help me to the car."

The three of us hauled ass to Little Haiti. Given the Spaniard's history with the gang, he stayed out of it this time. Past the rapid development of Wynwood, Little Haiti was still impoverished and run-down. As I slowed in front of the peach-colored apartment block where the Bone Saints headquartered, low level bangers hurried to open the gate. Without questioning the hospitality, I pulled in.

Kasper and I unloaded Milena and turned to the nearest guard.

"This way," he said before I could prompt him.

The feeling that we were not only welcome but perhaps even expected sunk in. We were led into a ground-floor apartment where Chevalier, without his ornamental face paint, waited.

"Suarez," he announced. "I take it you are not here to buy product?"

"Cut the shit. Milena's been infected with silvan blood. A mermaid assassin."

We set her down on the dirty carpet and he cocked his head at her. "This happened yesterday?"

"Yes, do you know about it?"

The bokor didn't answer as he leaned over Milena and pulled her blouse off her shoulder. His finger traced over the stitches and her neck. Then he produced a white powder that he sprinkled over her nose. Milena immediately gasped and sat up partway. We both grabbed and eased her back down.

"Calm down, baby," I whispered. "We're getting you looked at."

Her eyes blinked at me like she wanted to say something but was too tired. To me, it was a plus she wasn't convulsing or throwing up.

Chevalier barked some orders and two men hurried away to retrieve supplies. I squeezed Milena's hand tight. Jean-Louis turned and examined the old white biker standing in the middle of his ghetto block and arched an eyebrow. "You are the scribe?" He nodded toward my tattoos and the healing glyphs on Milena.

Kasper crossed his arms. "I'm expensive," he said.

Chevalier nodded sharply. "So am I."

"Lookie here," said the biker. "You just fix up the little lady and I'll return the favor. Got that?"

The leader of the Bone Saints frowned at his lethargic patient. "Suarez has made me enough money," he returned. But before my hopes shot up, he added, "And I am not sure how much I can do here."

His men returned with a wooden box, some sacks and jars filled with homemade salves, and a bundle of candles in a metal bowl. Chevalier lit a match and held it close to study Milena's eyes. Then he lit a fat candle with a charm tied around it and set it on an end table. He took a spoon carved from bone and mixed two powders in the bowl, adding a few ounces of a nearby sports drink. I considered the lemon-lime flavor an optional bonus. Then the bokor served a few spoonfuls to Milena. Kasper's face puckered at the noxious scent.

Milena sat up again and choked it down. Chevalier nodded in satisfaction.

He opened another jar of a glycerin-like substance that he rubbed on the stitches. "For the pain," he explained.

"Ugh," grumbled Milena. "I'm on painkillers. It doesn't hurt that much."

"It will."

The bokor picked up the lit candle and poured the wax onto her wound. I'd seen it coming in time to hold her down. She yipped but didn't scream so the gel was doing its job.

"How do you feel?" he asked.

Milena turned an icy stare his way. "Peachy."

Her sass didn't last. About ten seconds later, she was half asleep on her back again. Chevalier waited several moments until the time was right. Then he opened the large wooden box. Very gently, he lifted a large copperhead out and placed it on his patient's chest.

We all watched as the reptile tested the new environment with a tongue. It lazily slithered toward her face, seeming to examine her mouth until noticing the wound. The snake then curled around it as if for warmth.

"You know that thing's poisonous, right?" I asked nervously.

Chevalier merely held up a hand for silence. That didn't reassure me. The moccasin's venom could cause quite a bit of pain and swelling. In Milena's state, death wasn't out of the question. As we waited with tense breaths, Jean-Louis slipped a silver gauntlet over his right hand.

Suddenly, the copperhead reared its head. The bokor and the snake both struck at once. In a split second, bared fangs hovered over Milena's neck. Chevalier's silver hand held its open mouth, just behind the teeth. He quickly grabbed another jar, this one empty with a paper cap, and pushed the snake's fangs through, releasing the venom inside. When he was done, he took a knife and sliced the moccasin's belly open. It silently writhed as he cut out its heart and tossed the body back into the box.

The heart went in the jar of venom, as did a few other powders. He took it to the kitchen and put a pot of water on the stove. Kasper and I glanced at each other. He was good and freaked out by the show, but this was old hat to me. You run in voodoo circles long enough and you see everything. I held Milena a little while longer until she closed her eyes to rest. With her out of immediate danger, I paced to the kitchen to relax.

"That wasn't so bad," I said.

He watched the water on the fire without emotion. "She'll be dead in two days."

"What?"

He blinked calmly and met my eyes. "I cannot purge her blood. She hasn't been poisoned, she's been tainted."

That was the same word Emily had used. "What's the difference?"

"Our people say the ancestors of the silvans lusted with Baron Samedi, toying with his emotions and shaming his wife Maman Brigitte. This incurred her wrath, and so she banished them to the underworld." He frowned stoutly. "You incurred somebody's wrath, Suarez. This isn't regular poison."

"It has to be," I said, voice getting heated. "Why would the mermaid tell me it was silvan blood? I saw it. It was black. She was infected."

"How much?"

I stifled further assertions and held up two fingers to show the size of the small vial.

Chevalier shook his head. "I have known that to be poisonous, yes, but not fatal."

I hooked my hands on my hips in wilting denial. How

could he say so matter-of-factly that she would die? "There has to be something." I motioned to the tributes and charms. To the jar of snake venom. "What's all this song and dance for?"

"I am fighting it off as Maman Brigitte would, with snakes and fire. I am giving her time, to set her affairs in order."

I shook my head. "No. No."

"I'm sorry, Suarez. This is something more than mere pestilence. Your girl is going to die."

I kept shaking my head while I glanced at Milena but froze as I saw her sitting up, staring at us, mouth open in horror. She'd heard everything.

"No," I said, stomping over. "That's not gonna happen. You hear me? If he's giving you time, we'll go to the Nether and find a solution together." She blinked distantly. "You hear me, baby? You said you wanted to go to the wedding, right? Right?" I turned her face to me and she slowly nodded. I kissed her and smiled. "We're going to a wedding."

Chevalier poured the raw heart and venom in the pot of simmering water. Then he filtered it into a cup with a cheesecloth. He brought the cup over and handed it to Milena.

"Drink it, poor girl." She took it down like a shot. Chevalier unrolled the cheesecloth and handed her the snake heart. "This too."

The news totally removed any hesitation from the equation. Milena chomped the heart down. The bokor blew out the candle and unwrapped the charm tied around it on a string. He placed the necklace over Milena's head. The medallion was a flattened piece of clay stamped with a snake symbol. She closed her shirt over it. Chevalier took her hand and helped her stand. Amazingly, Milena's strength had returned with her wakefulness.

"This will buy you time. It is all I can offer."

"It's all we need," I told him, locking my hand with his. "We're gonna find a cure. The wedding's tomorrow, but we're going to the Nether right now."

Chapter 19

Yesterday was time to think, today was time to *do*.

We had over a day until the nighttime silvan wedding, but only a day after that until Milena's health took a sharp turn for the worse. She was up and walking now, which made the thought of her death in such a short span so unbelievable. But I couldn't deny the roller coaster she was on; sheer drops could come without warning, and often when riding highest. Reaching the silvans early and getting her healed was the best play. They would know how to counteract their own blood.

Beaumont had been set against my plan, but he curtailed his objections after learning the stakes. It was a strange sight to see a vampire so taken with a human life, or at least sympathetic for the ones I cared about. Every time I thought I had the crime boss boxed in, he surprised me.

He sent a limo outside my coffee shop. Darcy waved goodbye as Milena, Kasper, and I met Lago outside the car. Sure, I only had a plus one but I couldn't take away Kasper's moment. He actually liked the idea of being a wedding crasher, and I still needed the backup. The truth was, Milena was going to be more of a liability than usual in the Nether.

"What's in the bag?" asked Lago as the trunk popped open.

I tossed it to him like he was my valet. "I think you might appreciate it."

The vampire set it in the trunk and zipped it open. He flashed a grin of admiration at the firearms. He even loaded some of his own gear into the bag before closing it back up and shutting the trunk.

We slid in and Lago came in last. We sat on one side of the cabin while Trinh, Lago, and Beaumont himself sat opposite. Kasper watched our company very closely.

"They brought guns," Lago reported.

Leverett nodded as he studied Milena. "You're looking quite healthy, if I may say so."

She cleared her throat, nervous at the attention. "I feel good."

He nodded as the car pulled away. I wasn't sure where we were going specifically, but it would be a rabbit hole convenient to our destination.

"Just the one bag?" asked the crime boss.

I shrugged. "We travel light."

The debonair vampire clicked his tongue. "You're going to a wedding, Cisco. With silvans." His companions soured at their mention. "They're very big on ceremony."

"Useless," muttered Trinh.

"On the contrary, ceremony is quite revealing. Power isn't just bashing heads and pulling triggers."

I traded glances with Trinh and Lago. The advice was lost on them. To be honest, most of the people in the car were of the bashing-heads variety, myself included.

"Hear me if you hear one thing, Cisco. A projection of your power is just as important as recognizing a projection of someone else's. You'll be traveling into unfamiliar territory with a desperate request. You're behind the eight ball before you even set foot below. There'll be a line of people ready to take advantage of you."

"Sounds like silvans," muttered Trinh.

I bit my tongue. The last thing I wanted was to play games with the wild folk, but taking his advice at face value seemed the wisest course of action. I would, given the circumstances, need to sway the minds and hearts of any power brokers in the Nether I could.

"I'll keep that in mind," I finally said.

Soon enough it became clear we were headed into the Everglades. I thought over all the rabbit holes I'd been through, and they were pretty much always in sections of wild land, whether ocean or forest or swamp. I wondered if the act of creating a city, of razing land and paving roads, wreaked havoc on the network of rabbit holes. Maybe that was why the wilderness was so scary at night.

Then again, night was my scene. And though it was the middle of the day now, as soon as we entered the Nether Steppe, the shadows would take over and I would be energized.

"What are you looking at?" asked Beaumont sharply. I turned to see him challenging Kasper with inquisitive eyes.

"Not much," said the biker gruffly.

"You have nothing to fear here."

"Oh, I know that. I kicked plenty of vamp ass after they wrecked my shop."

"We're not the March," said Lago.

"Same difference from where I'm sitting."

"Kasper..." I warned.

"It's all right," announced Beaumont, showing his teeth. "We've arrived at our destination."

The limo pulled over and I scooted out before Kasper could start a fight. Lago got out to unload our bag.

"Cisco?" called Beaumont.

Trinh slipped by me as I leaned into the open door. "What is it?"

"I have a gift. If you're going to a silvan wedding, you'll need to look the part."

I sighed. "I appreciate the gesture, Beaumont, but I'm not too concerned with—"

"Milena may only have hours left with you. She might enjoy seeing you in a tailored suit. And for her, I've packed the finest Parisian dress. She'll love it."

Again, I was at a loss for words. I hadn't dwelled much on romance the last twenty-four hours. Dressing up and enjoying what time we had together... well, wasn't that exactly what I wanted to do with my life?

I gave him an earnest nod. "Thank you, Leverett."

"My pleasure."

I turned just in time to catch the bag that Lago tossed back at me. Beaumont's gift bag was being held by Kasper. Lago only held his M27. Trinh shut the limo door. "Let's go." She marched toward a line of trees.

"Wait a minute," protested Kasper. "Why do I get the feeling you're coming with us?"

Lago turned to follow. "Because we are."

We headed into the dry woods for a short hike. I stayed at Milena's side but didn't baby her. She really did have her strength back. Whatever Chevalier had done, it was a blessing. After some time, we detoured through scraggly brush and found a dip in the ground. The rabbit hole. Trinh and Lago jumped in without a word.

I eyed my companions. "You guys ready?"

I put my arms around them both. Even having never done it before, Kasper could probably manage on his own. Milena was a different story. Without spellcraft, she wouldn't get any further than the dirt.

Kasper grunted. "I don't like this, broham."

"What's not to like?"

I pulled them into the ditch and we fell into the ground.

Chapter 20

"A bit gloomy down here," murmured Kasper.

"It has its charm," I said, "but it's not sunny Miami. I'll give you that."

We trudged down Yet Another Dirt Passage, which is most of what I'd seen of the Nether. The wide tunnels appeared ancient, as if carved out by the pilgrimage of giant sand worms eons ago. A network of roots hung loose overhead. Bugs crawled through clumps of earth. Ambient light permeated the depths here and there, starting and ending nowhere in particular while leaving plenty of room for shadow. It was my kind of place.

"I think it's cool," said Milena, eyes wide as if she were Alice finding Wonderland for the first time.

For the record, that's as far as the metaphor went. Milena wasn't blonde, she definitely wasn't a kid, and she was strapped with a Micro Uzi in a drop-leg holster.

Now that we were no longer topside, we'd unpacked our bag of goodies and loaded up. The Nether had no laws banning open carry.

In like fashion, I wore an MP7 on a strap around my shoulder. There was nothing like a submachine gun with armor-piercing rounds for fending off cretinous beasts. Past that, I cracked my trusty sawed off open and loaded it with a custom fire cartridge, with two more in the side saddle. The discharge was similar to dragon's breath except it used a voodoo powder to ignite. The preternatural fire gave baddies an owie.

I dropped my shotgun back into the shadow and stretched my fingers. The skin on my right hand was black and blistered. I had a full range of motion, it just hurt a ton to actually move. I forced through the pain to keep it limber.

"Is it healing?" asked Milena tenderly.

I dropped the hand to my side. "Don't worry about me. I'll be good in no time." I winced, wondering if my callous mention of healing in time was insensitive to her predicament. She didn't seem to notice.

"I thought you couldn't get hurt like that?"

I sighed. "Yeah, a bunch of zombie toxins and charms were pumped into my system. My skin is pretty tough."

Trinh cast a sidelong glance at me, and I realized I was giving her a rundown of my defenses. I supposed it didn't hurt to reveal what I had. It was Beaumont's theory of projecting power.

"Anyway, I did this to myself."

She pouted. "The spell you cast to purify my blood."

"It seemed to feed on my life force or something. But

seriously, don't worry about it. It was a small price to pay."

She pondered that silently for a while.

We reached a four-way intersection. Trinh pulled a pistol and cleared left while Lago faced his automatic rifle opposite.

"You expecting company?" I asked.

They dropped their weapons and continued straight. "In the Nether," said Lago, "you should always expect company."

Kasper snorted. "I thought you guys were like kings down here?"

He shook his head. "The Nether Margins aren't under any dominions."

"Better for you," said Trinh, breaking her long silence. "You wouldn't like visiting the upir homeland."

"Is it as stifling as this place?" Kasper pulled a cigar from a travel box and lit up.

"I'm sure that's gonna help," mocked Lago.

Kasper blew out smoke toward the vampire. "Sorry if I don't take advice from you. You're about as unimaginative as that tribal tat on your shoulder."

"It's traditional for my people."

"Your people? You're a vampire."

"As you keep reminding us. Better than being a redneck."

"I'm not a redneck. I'm Norwegian."

"Cool it, guys." I moved between them so they couldn't glare at each other so easily. "How do ethnicities work with upirs, anyway? They call Beaumont the Frenchman.

Magnus was German, emphasis on *was*."

Trinh snickered at that, proving she just might have a sense of humor stashed somewhere.

I pointed to her. "*Chinita?*"

"Vietnamese," she said, strangely forthcoming.

"And you're Samoan?" I asked Lago.

"Italian Samoan," he said.

"That just raises more questions."

He smiled. "Human guises pass through our lineage, just like you. Some of us are even born and live with humans. We're not all that different."

"Except for the subsisting-on-blood part," noted Kasper gruffly.

Trinh walked and talked without looking. "The humans would fear and hunt you just as they would us."

I recalled the militia video Fran had found. A direct result of Manifesto's warnings.

Kasper wasn't so introspective. "The difference is, I *understand* what you are."

Trinh abruptly turned and marched up to us. She met the biker's eyes and then nodded toward Milena. "Silvan blood is potent. What if she was afflicted and turned into a monster? Would you still take the moral high ground?"

"Hey..." I warned.

I didn't like using my girlfriend's life as a morality case, especially right in front of her. Kasper, for his part, knew better than to continue with the conversation. He took a drag from his stogie and pressed ahead. I stared Trinh down a second until she moved on. Then I hugged Milena tight.

She was trembling.

Trinh and Lago suddenly snapped their guns ready, facing forward. Something skittered away.

Kasper hefted his double-bladed ax. "What was that?"

A long whine echoed from the passage, starting low and throaty but ending with a high note. Several other yips resounded in response, coming from ahead and behind. I spun and scanned the reaches with enchanted eyes.

Milena's breathing sped up as the high-pitched howls kept coming. "Are they... laughing?"

"Gnolls," grumbled Lago. "They have us surrounded."

"How did we get surrounded in these passages?" I asked.

"Not by accident."

The group pulled closer together, covering both directions.

"There's a lot of them," said Trinh. "This is a hunting party."

"Will they listen to reason?"

"Not unless you speak hyena. Let's move."

Our formation pressed forward. Given the intersection behind us seemed to be the source for the majority of the howls, it was sensible to relocate. I gripped my SMG in my wounded hand to reserve my left arm for defense. I'd never seen gnolls before and didn't know what we were up against. That didn't shatter my confidence, however. We had enough firepower between us to take out a terrorist cave network.

"This is gonna echo down here," said Lago, digging through his pocket and producing ear plugs. They weren't for him so it was a curious thing to carry. Kasper and I turned them down, possessing our own supernatural defenses, but I thanked the vampire and passed them to Milena. Beaumont had really thought of everything.

Piercing barks followed in our wake as we raced forward. With any luck, the resistance ahead of us would be less than what was coming from behind.

"There must be side tunnels," said Lago. "No other way for them to get around us."

"We need to break out before they set a perimeter," I said.

Trinh hissed. "If they don't already have one."

Beastly shadows danced against the dirt walls behind us. The pack was closing fast.

"Keep going!" I yelled, pushing Milena forward.

I stopped, dug into my belt pouch with my off hand, and sprinkled a line of red powder across the ground. I lit a match and sparked up a wall of incendiary fire. As I backed away from the heat, the yips and growls grew more intense. The fire wouldn't block pursuit entirely, but it might slow it down.

I turned and hurried away. The group was covering good ground as it took me a few minutes to catch up. When I did it was only because they slowed as the vampires took corners and cleared another intersection. Kasper wasn't so furtive. He stepped right into the middle of both tunnels and brandished his ax.

"Which way?" I asked as I stopped beside them.

Lago pointed straight. "That was the plan, but plans

change."

I nodded. He was thinking what I was thinking. The gnolls couldn't possibly cover all passages. If they had somehow predicted our destination, they would've put heavier resistance along our path. Taking a detour might enable us to slip through their net.

But that also meant a delay in reaching the silvans. Milena only had so much time.

"How do you feel?" I asked her.

She retracted the bolt of her automatic pistol and released the cover to spring forward. "Locked and loaded. Is that right? Is that how you say that?"

I chuckled. She was fine.

With her health holding up, and trusting Jean-Louis Chevalier's word that it would do so until well after the wedding tomorrow, it was best to focus on the more immediate threat to her health: say... dozens of raving Nether fiends.

As we stood idle, the passage behind us that had somewhat silenced began to fill with the laughing howls of our pursuers. The gnolls made their presence known ahead as well.

"They're everywhere," muttered Kasper.

"No," said Trinh. Though Lago maintained his rifle coverage of the right tunnel, Trinh stepped out into the left and lowered her pistol. "Listen."

I faced each passage in turn. It was hard to delineate echo from original source, but there were definitely cackling gnolls coming through the front, back, and right tunnels.

The left seemed clear.

Lago dipped his head. "What are we waiting for then?"

We all bounded left. I briefly hoped the converging gnolls would be stymied by wondering which direction we took. That thought fled fast. Besides their various hunting parties covering the other three tunnels, it was a good bet they were tracking us by scent.

Back in a single corridor, we had the sum of the enemy behind us. Progress. The group sprinted for several minutes. Kasper began to slow. I would've made an old man joke, but to be honest I was breathing hard myself. Ironically, Milena was in great shape due to her workouts. Maybe I should've taken her instructor up on the gym lessons. And as for the vampires... well, they didn't fatigue as easily as the rest of us.

"Are they running us down?" I panted, growls still at our back. "Getting us exhausted before they move in? There's no way we're faster than them."

"They're cautious," spat Lago.

"No," said Trinh. "They're cowards. They smell upir."

Kasper snorted. "I bet they smell Norwegian badass."

We bowled forward into a large space, weapons fanning out to cover a multitude of passages.

"What the..."

I spun at the dizzying sight. The chamber we found ourselves in was large and circular, with over a dozen passages outward, most on the ground but a few short climbs overhead.

"Anyone have any idea which way to go?" asked Milena.

"Not that way," said Kasper, pointing to the tunnel we'd come from.

Trinh balked before so many choices. I caught movement in a raised passage. Large, round ears on a dog-like face. I spun my MP7 at the gnoll but it ducked down and laughed. Milena's Uzi went off. Sprays of dirt pattered the walls of a dark tunnel.

"Did you see that?" she asked frantically.

We tiptoed to the center of the room, backs together.

"There!" shouted Lago. He charged five steps forward as his rifle fired a barrage. When he released the trigger, there was no body.

Yipping cries came from a tunnel on the opposite side. A snort to my left, a hiss on the right. Our gazes snapped from passage to passage as, one by one, every single one filled with ravenous howls.

Damn it. We hadn't slipped the net, we'd stepped right into the middle of it.

Chapter 21

"They herded us here," I grumbled, the edge in my voice revealing the only thing left to do.

Trinh nodded grimly. "This is a bad place to make a stand."

"They can come at us from anywhere," Kasper said.

Milena stepped forward. "Let's pick a tunnel."

As if on cue, a gnoll emerged from the passage she headed toward. The furry beast had matted hair, a wide jaw brimming with uneven teeth, and pads of leather armoring its body. It stood upright, frame more slight than bulky, standing shorter than us but more than making up for that with primal hunger. Despite paw-like hands, it comfortably wielded a sword and wooden shield.

Milena's Uzi went off as the animal charged on hind legs. The spray started wide but quickly corrected. Rounds popped into the shield and the gnoll's legs. It tripped to the ground and received another barrage in its back.

Trinh pushed Milena's gun down and the firing stopped.

The beast lay on the floor, whimpering, trying to lift its sword. The vampire pointed the pistol and planted a single bullet in its head, ending the pain.

"Conserve your ammo," she instructed. "You'll need it."

All at once, the passages filled with angry howls. Gnolls leaped and bounded at us with swords and axes. We defended our respective angles.

A hyena ducked his head behind his shield and blind charged me with a dagger. I pointed the MP7 and fired. The alloy-plated round punched through wood and skull, dropping him in one shot. I swiveled to the next threat.

Two came at me next. I fired at one and it sidestepped. I tracked it as the second closed on my side, blade coming down. I met her with my tattooed left forearm. The arm bar blazed a flash of turquoise and the sword flew from her hand. I stuffed the SMG into her neck. The burst of fire nearly decapitated her. As the other converged, I kicked her body into him and gunned him down.

A throwing ax came at my head. I puffed into shadow but realized, too late, that I had allies at my back. Luckily there was a slight upward trajectory to the throw and the weapon flew above Lago's head. He turned to me with a scowl.

"My bad," I called.

I sprayed forward to suppress the incoming gnolls as I chose a new target. A shield splintered under my barrage. Another savvy fighter saw the shield was useless and pitched it my way like a Frisbee.

The Helm of Awe tattoo on my left palm flared to life and my own shield of light-blue energy covered my face.

The wooden shield ricocheted to the ground and I mowed the following gnoll down.

But my mag ran empty and I needed to disperse the shield to reload. As I did that, I triggered a wide wall of shadow to protect me and Milena at my side.

Lago's rifle went off like a drum beat. Short, controlled bursts that took care of nearly half the room by himself. Trinh worked slowly but precisely, taking stock of the battlefield and placing strategic headshots where they most helped, but she didn't have the ammo to keep that up. She tucked the pistol in her back and drew the two knives on her hips.

"About time you got dirty," said Kasper, the runes on his body glowing red through the spattering of black blood. The biker had refused a firearm and was going to town with his ax.

"I'm dry," cried Milena, digging at the empty ammo belt on her leg.

"Here," I said, looping my gun strap over my neck and handing her the MP7. "Hold it with both hands. Shoot slowly."

As she accepted the intimidating weapon, I snapped my blackened hand free. Tentacles lashed out everywhere, spearing gnolls through torsos and limbs. In this chaos, it was near impossible to be accurate with this many manifestations. On the plus side, there were so many of them I could strike blindly and stand a good chance of hitting something. With the shadow wall protecting us from direct charges, the tentacles disrupted whatever unified front was left.

Kasper was being a bit careless, I noticed. Out of all of us, he strayed the farthest from the circle. He collided with oncoming gnolls dead on, batting weapons away and splitting heads. The blades that hit him met similar resistance to my arm tattoo. The difference was Kasper didn't need to aim his defenses. His body flashed red and blue on his back, his legs, even his head, which didn't have visible tattoos. The primitive weapons simply couldn't penetrate his protected skin.

Two gnolls teamed up and got lucky by disarming him of his heavy ax. That just made Kasper angry. His entire arm energized with a surge of golden light and he punched one in the chest, collapsing its rib cage and sending it flying. The other gnoll widened its eyes and loped away.

Trinh was like a ninja, and that wasn't a racist Asian thing. She performed literal cartwheels through lines of enemies. They took a few steps before falling, realizing too late that they were dead. She switched between several wide stances and flashed her relatively small karambit knives with great effect. Small, ergonomic handles made up half the length of the weapons, with the blades being short and curved to resemble the claws of a big cat. The gnolls had larger swords and daggers, but she was faster and ripped them to shreds.

"Last mag," called Lago.

I tossed Milena my last two. Two bags sat in the center of our defensive circle, holding whatever ammo we couldn't carry on our persons.

I growled and recalled my set of tentacles. I merged them into the shadow wall and balled it into a dense black mass. Then I played a little roulette.

"Kasper," I warned, "fall in."

The biker saw the giant wrecking ball and converged in the center with Trinh as I sent it spinning. It bowled through gnolls living, dead, and dying, knocking them up and about like rag dolls. The shadow swept over the walls of the round room, around and around, forcing those in the tunnels to retreat or have their heads bashed in.

The Intrinsics pumped through me quickly now, which was a great way to burn yourself out, but we had too many enemies coming from too many sides. As our last two guns reloaded, Trinh pointed down a narrow tunnel. "This way!"

Lago headed in first, clearing a path with automatic fire. I pushed Milena close to Kasper and grabbed the two bags in my left hand. As the giant ball of shadow came around to us, I waved my blackened hand around. The shadow dispersed into a giant wall. Everyone backed into the tunnel as I pulled the shadow close.

"That's a hell of a lot of spellcraft you're pumping, Cisco," said Kasper. "How long can you keep that up?"

"Shorter than forever, but maybe for the rest of our lives," I quipped.

"We're clear," shouted Lago, dropping his spent M27 to his side.

Milena advanced to him and aimed my machine pistol forward, in case there were any stragglers. I cursed as I noticed her Micro Uzi on the floor in the circular chamber.

Hyenas were scampering from their tunnels and advancing. One picked up the weapon and studied it. Nothing happened when it pulled the trigger.

"We can defend this position," said Trinh, hooking her knives back onto her hips.

"It would be easier with ammo," said her partner.

I tossed the bags at his feet, and he dug into it and passed mags around. Meanwhile, I concentrated on the shadow wall as the gnolls began to pound it with weapons.

"Just another second," said Lago, strapping ammo to his belt.

Milena stared down the passage. "Anybody know where this leads?"

The vampires didn't answer, which was answer enough.

"I should be in there," growled Kasper, watching the gnolls pile up on my wall.

"No reason to risk it," said Trinh. "Better to use the choke point and defend the narrow tunnel."

"She's right," I said. "I could even drop the shadow for seconds at a time and let them trickle in." My confidence was high but the strain was getting to me. Eight or nine weapons were poking and stabbing my wall.

"Fine," said Kasper. "Let them at me."

Lago and Milena covered the escape route as Trinh smiled, pulled out her blades, and converged on the biker. "You're more fun than I thought, old man."

"You're probably as old as I am," he muttered.

"But I have more beautiful genes."

Before I could lower the wall, a guttural sound filled the

chamber. The growl was deep and long and resonating. Dirt rustled onto our heads as the walls shook. The gnolls snapped their heads to each other and released sharp cries, quickly dispersing. Like a pack of panicking rats, they skittered into darkness and emptied the chamber in seconds.

And then a single large beast launched from a high tunnel and landed lightly in the center of the chamber.

Trinh's jaw dropped. "It's the man-eater."

Chapter 22

The beast in the chamber was huge. Twice the size of the largest lion you could imagine. Her pelt was bright red and her mane was dark brown, but the hair was longer, like a human's. Exacerbating this likeness was the very human female face with its aquiline nose and sunken eyes. Fangs peeked from behind plump lips set into a smirk.

Heavy paws patted forward. "I smell wizards and vampires," she said, voice deep and resonant, yet playful. "What treats shall I devour first, and who shall I save for later?"

"Later," volunteered Milena, raising a sheepish hand. "Actually, since I'm not a wizard *or* a vampire, maybe you consider not devouring me at all?"

"Thanks a lot," I whispered to her.

The human head studying us was unnerving on the animal body. As the lion paced sideways, a long tail snapped around. A flurry of barbs protruded from the tip like a spiked mace.

"You're a manticore," I said. "I didn't know you actually existed."

"Most of your monstrous legends stem from the bowels of the Nether, one way or the other. You'd be surprised what you can find if you live long enough to look." The beast fluttered her eyelashes at my shadow wall. "Is this paltry magic yours?"

"Trust me," I warned, "you don't want any part of my paltry magic."

She snorted. The light burst of air came out like a growl, and the ground rumbled. "Claw or tail?" she asked.

I narrowed my eyes, ready for her strike. "What?"

Her tail whipped around and a single quill fired my way. It came at me like an arrow, effortlessly piercing my wall, which was made for more massive objects. My spellcraft just barely deflected the projectile so it hit me in the hip. It embedded there and threw me to the ground.

My wall faltered but held. The manticore lunged and smacked into the shadow, forcing through with scraping claws and pouncing atop Kasper. Red and blue runes flared as she raked his chest. He punched upward but missed. The manticore clamped onto his arm with her teeth and, despite the defensive magic sending sparks in the air, she bit down.

I pulled the barb from my hip and yelled, "Shoot her."

Milena blinked unsteadily. "But Kasper..."

"Don't worry about me," the biker snapped. "Just shoot!"

Lago was the first to act. He stepped forward with his newly reloaded M27 and let the manticore have it. Bullets pummeled her massive hide. It wasn't immediately obvious if they were penetrating their target because she recoiled. She flipped and landed sideways on the wall, running along it and leaping to Lago.

Trinh ran and slid under the beast, swiping upward with twin blades and slashing the exposed underbelly. The shallow knives didn't dig deep enough to register. The man-eater knocked Lago's firing rifle to the side and tackled him.

The vampire was tough. Not only did he punch away the second swiping arm, but he'd held onto the M27. The beast didn't relent, however. Her jaws crunched down on the weapon, snapping the steel in half.

Lago still held the portion of the weapon with the action. He shoved the shorn barrel into the manticore's mouth and fired. She howled and batted it aside. Her jaw was bloody this time, but just as strong. Teeth clamped down on the weapon once again and crushed it beyond usability.

Before the manticore could switch from chomping metal to flesh, a much tighter grouping of shadow struck her side. She hissed and sidestepped to face me. Milena's weapon barked next, though she had trouble holding steady against the recoil. Armor-piercing rounds pounded dirt, but some struck the beast in the chest. She roared and her tail snapped. Several quills rocketed out.

My energy shield exploded as I jumped to cover Milena. A quill missed my position as I caught another with my shield and another bounced off Kasper. The last quill struck Milena's weapon and disarmed her. The SMG bounced to the ground, stuck through with a hardened spine.

The man-eater pounced. I grabbed Milena and spun her out of the way, but Kasper was her target. His back slammed into the wall as daggerlike claws scratched out. Trinh's pistol rang out in the tunnel but the manticore ignored the small arms fire. Over and over, muscled paws pummeled the biker as the manticore's human head bit down on his shoulder.

Trinh and I closed. Though the beast's back was to us, preternatural senses warned her of the threat. Still goring Kasper, the shifty tail swept into us.

I melted into darkness and the spikes whizzed through me with barely a scratch. Even though the beast was magic, its quills were not powerful enough to break through my spellcraft.

Trinh didn't have such defenses. Through a combination of not being quick enough and being unused to my fighting style and having the tail unexpectedly pass through me, the barbs gashed her leg as she was flipping over it. Her right pant leg tore open. Unfortunately, so did her right leg. A dark gash cut through a dragon tattoo. Trinh upended and slammed into the wall.

An angry roar flew past me. A twisted figure in a blackened carapace slammed into the manticore. It was Lago in his true form, body pitch black and covered in hardened plates, white eyes and teeth and blood-red tongue the only visible splashes of color. His fingers, now a foot long and ending in razor points, gouged the manticore's side.

Several barbs fired blindly as I ducked away, back in

physical form. Shadow leaked from my hand and I folded it over, strengthening it. Meanwhile, the spiked tail rammed into Lago. He was shoved away but lunged again. The manticore met him head on, claw against claw. Kasper, released from being pinned against the wall, collapsed to the ground, body sparkling blue and red.

Lago was formidable but the manticore was four times his size. She exerted her weight advantage and bowled him over, slamming the center of his chest with her spiked tail.

The vampire cried out.

"Yes," taunted the she-beast, "I know how to pierce your magical core." Both of Lago's hands held the spikes at bay. Multiple stab wounds pierced his hands and chest, and it was all he could do to keep them from sinking into his heart. "It's where you keep all your delicious blood." The manticore licked her lips as she pressed down.

The amethyst sword snapped into form, protruding from my hand. "Then maybe it's time to dock that tail of yours."

I slashed horizontally over Lago's chest. The man-eater hopped into the air, heavy paws deftly avoiding my strike. The vampire, however, had different plans. Both hands tightened over the bundle of barbs, squeezing as the manticore tried to pull her tail away.

Spines tore from Lago's bloodless hands and others fell away as she desperately shed them, but she couldn't withdraw quickly enough. My shadow sword sliced clean through the thin lion tail, severing off the menacing weapon at the tip.

The manticore shrieked and landed at the head of the

tunnel, squaring defensively towards me.

"Do I have your full attention now?" I asked coarsely.

She growled viciously. "You'll pay for that, wizard."

I raised the sword toward her. "Come and get me."

Still sneering, her eyes turned and focused on my sword. It blinked out.

I opened and closed my hand, trying to catch the Intrinsics as they slipped away like sand. Using only trivial effort, she'd completely dispelled my sword.

"You were saying?" she snarled.

In my moment of confusion, she pounced on me. Claws opened my chest and my head bounced on the ground. The manticore roared. Kasper and Lago struggled to their feet. Milena scrambled for a working firearm. Trinh's knives flew into and bounced off the beast's jumbled mane.

But her eyes were fire, and she was unstoppable.

Neatly pinned, there was no way I could escape into the shadow. Her teeth came at me. I shoved my armored forearm into her mouth. Blue magic exploded outward, but I wasn't covered in tattoos like Kasper. Her jaw was too large and her bottom teeth caught the unprotected backside of my arm. Blood welled, her bite only stymied by the explosive spellcraft pushing her away. Her unbelievable strength and weight were crushing me.

And then the entire passage darkened. A screeching, slithering sound filled my mind, painful just to hear. I shook violently as my friends covered their ears and screamed. Even the manticore shuddered.

When a grating voice penetrated the cacophony, it was

all I could do to hold my sanity together.

"DO. NOT. KILL. HIM."

The manticore cowered, shriveling away backward into the circular chamber. She growled in supreme anger, standing her ground for a moment of ill-conceived defiance.

"The explosive," said Lago, reverted back to his human form. He pointed at the ammo bag.

Milena rushed to it and grabbed the bundled block of C-4. She handed it to Trinh so the vampire could set the charge.

The manticore growled, but her intelligence won out. Her anger was no longer directed at the ghostly voice. She fixed her eyes over each of us, no doubt wondering which would be her next snack. The deafening scratching at our ears ceased.

"Fire in the hole!" Trinh hopped forward on one healthy leg and tossed the plastic explosive at the mouth of the tunnel.

I rolled away and projected the shadow wall to cover us. Kasper hugged Milena behind him just in case. The man-eater's eyes lit up. She spat a curse and leapt into the upper reaches of the chamber, disappearing into the maze of the Nether just as the tunnel exploded.

The shadow wall couldn't stop the full concussive blast, but between it and the wide open chamber on the other side, most of the force expended that way. Dirt filled the tunnels. It was a minute before we could easily breathe again. The mouth of the passage had collapsed, barring further pursuit from the manticore.

I rolled to my knees, cradling my gashed chest with my mauled arm. Trinh attended Lago, bearing similar wounds. Milena was crumpled on the ground, sobbing. Kasper struggled to sit up beside her. We'd all been knocked around like bowling pins. While the biker had suffered the worst of it, he amazingly didn't have a scratch on him.

We exchanged a grim stare before I crawled to Milena's side. I pulled her head into my shoulder and let her cry. There was something comforting about the sound, something inherently human and safe.

I closed my eyes and released a long breath, quite shaken myself.

Chapter 23

We basked in the silence for several minutes, interrupted by pained grunts and worried sniffles. Recovery was vital, though at some point it worked against us. We were deep in the Margins, and they were proving more dangerous than I remembered.

"This was a planned attack," grumbled Lago, the last to rise to his feet. "Someone doesn't want you to reach that wedding."

I ground my teeth at the implication that this had to do with my business. It was hard to deny.

"Who was that woman who scared off the manticore?" asked Trinh.

I shook my head but she remained suspicious. Do not kill him. That's what the vaguely female voice had said. But I had a feeling it wasn't for my protection. Only, if the manticore wasn't here to kill, what was its objective?

I recovered my MP7 and pulled the quill from it. The center gun muzzle was punched clean through, jamming the barrel with bent metal and effectively destroying the gun. Lago likewise grumbled and kicked his retired weapon. "Junk."

Milena glanced at the dirt wall blocking the chamber. Some of the soil shifted, opening up holes of light to the other side. The wall wouldn't be permanent. "I think the Uzi's back there."

"The gnolls are hearty scavengers," explained Trinh. "No use going back for something that's not there."

"Probably shouldn't leave them the ammo then." I pulled the meager supplies we could still use and stuffed them into the bag with Beaumont's clothes. Then I grouped the junked weapons and magazines into the ammo bag and prepped it to burn. I pocketed a couple manticore spines but added the tail stump to the pile.

"We should get going," prodded Lago, nodding to the temporary wall. Curious bug creatures that resembled lobsters emerged from the soil and snapped at the air.

"Scourgelings. I assume we're headed deeper down this passage?"

"It's the only place we know the gnolls aren't."

I nodded. As one lobster creature tumbled to the ground and ventured our way, I dropped a match on the gun bag and stepped back. Flames roiled across the way, sending the scourgeling scampering away in a hurry. "Let's move."

Kasper reached for the clothes bag, but I shooed him off, hooked it over my shoulder, and started our trek.

We were a sorry lot. Trinh was limping. I didn't think Lago could grip any weapons even if he had one. Kasper was slow and Milena was scared.

The vampires had turned down my zombie toxin. It mostly staunched the flow of blood and kept infections at bay. Upirs didn't need to worry about either. Their bodies were bone dry and their healing top-notch. By my estimation, Lago would be doing curls tomorrow.

As we hiked, I treated the scrape on my chest and the puncture in my hip with the toxic gel. I only stopped a moment to let Kasper mark me up with his gold pen.

"Not a great start to our silvan party," he muttered. The biker was moving around a little tenderly, looking more his age than usual. Although his skin was never broken, he was probably a little banged up on the inside. "Sorry I wasn't much help back there."

I snorted. "Are you kidding, bro? I can't believe you're walking right now. That thing came at you hard."

He frowned, finding little solace in my point of view. Kasper was a proud man and rarely found himself on his back unless it was after a drinking binge. "That should do ya," he said when he finished. He took the moment to check my blackened right hand. "This is healing nicely. I can touch it up."

"Later."

I pulled away and kept walking, careful to hide my left arm from him. Given his skill set, he doted like a grandfather sometimes. I didn't want to slow everyone down with it, especially when all this was very possibly my fault. Getting Milena to safety was my priority, even if it meant healing a little slower.

We turned down a couple of passages and passed a rabbit hole. All eyes fixed on the mystery doorway, wondering if we were better off taking a chance with it or not. But we had a mission, and everyone here was determined to see it through.

Five minutes later, footsteps shuffled down the corridor, and that chance to peek topside was looking like a missed opportunity.

Trinh drew her pistol on her last mag and we pressed into an alcove on the wall and waited.

The pattering sounds coming down the tunnel filled out. We traded glances. This wasn't a wanderer, it was another hunting party.

Muttering gave voice to our fears. "Dun de dun doh."

I furrowed my brow. Instead of laughing howls, wall-shaking growls, or demonic voices ripping through our brain cases, this was... lackadaisical singing?

We paused in confusion as the trampling neared, neither the silent footfalls of hunters nor the jeering calls meant to sow fear. One thing I did know: there were a lot of them.

Figures finally came into view. Short humanoids, three feet tall with enlarged heads and grimy gray skin covered in warts. The creatures were clothed in leaves and sticks that covered mismatched sections of hair and bare skin.

Trinh pointed her gun at the nearest bulbous head.

"Wait," I said.

The bumbling spriggan leapt in surprise at my voice. A few others advanced with raised clubs. The fiends weren't especially bright, but they were brave.

Trinh didn't fire but Lago moved.

"Wait."

He stepped into the center of the corridor, shifted to his true form, and brandished menacing claws. "Who sent you?" he demanded.

Being a denizen of the Nether, he knew spriggans often served higher fae. While there was a chance this group was acting autonomously, it was unlikely given the day we'd had so far.

"Upirs!" called an unseen voice down the tunnel.

Barely perceptible *thwips* snapped. Lago darted aside as two arrows zoomed past him and lodged into the wall.

With an exhausted hiss, I jumped between the spriggans and vampires and thrust my arms to either side, blasting both battle lines with waves of shadow and knocking the eager combatants on their asses.

"I said wait!"

Yellow spriggan eyes and the solid whites of the vampires fixed on me in anger. I looked past the servants to the approaching figures. They were only a head taller than the spriggans, but large curved ram horns extended their heights an extra foot.

"I should've known," I muttered loudly. "Fauns."

"Not just any," rang a nasally voice.

The elite guard of three stepped to the side, short bows still drawn on us. Coming up the rear, behind his spriggan party and faun bodyguards, was Orpheus.

He stood in a hunch, as if his large horns weighed him down. Unlike the others, his seemed inscribed with natural runework signifying his nobility. A shaggy mane extended over his shoulder and into a pointed beard, and his torso was bare except for similar shag on his forearms and legs, which ended in cloven hooves. His only dress was a leather skirt and belt, albeit nice ones. His only weapon was a cross between a boomerang and a hatchet, made from a bone like his horns. It was a property that made it dangerous to me, even in shadow form.

"The baron of the Circle of Bone," I announced.

"Not a baron anymore," declared Orpheus. "I'm a duke now."

I chewed my lip and pondered the difference between dukes and barons, but came up short. Orpheus snorted at my obvious ignorance.

Unlike most silvans, fauns sported monstrous faces. Humanistic, sure, but more animal than even the manticore. A flattened, goat-like nose, wide-set eyes, and small-yet-protruding fangs. Orpheus flicked long pointed ears as his orange eyes studied my companions.

"You have business with upirs now?" he asked with disdain.

"Our business is done," said Trinh. "We were to escort the wizard through the Margins. We have no wish to enter your territory."

He snorted at our obvious wounds. "Lot of good it appears your escort is doing. I heard of your ill-advised passage and ventured out to save you. It wouldn't do for royal guests of the principesse to die before the wedding."

Lago shifted back to his human form. I didn't know if

the glamour settled silvans the way it did us. I took it for a sign of peace, but his words didn't follow suit. "Interesting that your *help* came after we needed it."

"Maybe you don't want me around at all?" scowled Orpheus. He turned to me. "What say you, human? Shall I leave you to plot with our enemies?"

Trinh mocked him with an easy chuckle and tapped me on the shoulder. "This is what you wanted, wizard." She pressed her lips together. After a moment of thought, she handed her pistol to Milena. "Most of a mag. Don't shoot unless you need to."

Milena nodded. "Thanks. You're kinda cool for a vampire."

Trinh smirked. "Shall we, dear?" She started down the way we'd come.

Lago glowered, disappointed there wouldn't be a fight. "You're lucky I'm with her." He turned to go, giving me a businesslike nod.

They disappeared behind us, likely headed to that nearby rabbit hole for a much-needed vacation. I didn't exactly trust the vampires, but I preferred their company over the present. At least Trinh and Lago had risked their lives for me. Twice.

Orpheus was allied with the Table of Oak now, which included the bride's family. In the past, the idea of a union between Ceela and Throok was an affront to many silvans, Orpheus being the prime objector. Our previous meetings had involved a Nether curse and the loss of two of his loved ones.

And then it was all erased by an opportunistic alliance.

Silvan politics. Now I remembered why I hated the Nether so much.

Chapter 24

We marched as a group, not particularly concerned with stealth or caution. Orpheus was a savvy fighter. His elite bodyguards didn't look to be slouches either. One woman, two men, bows across their shoulders and swords at their waists.

The duke's eyes flicked from my bloody chest to my blackened hand. "What beset you in the Margins?"

"What didn't?" groused Kasper.

Orpheus stared at me, waiting for more information.

"A gnoll hunting party and a manticore."

The duke's gaze shot to his bodyguards in concern. He quickly regained his composure and shook his head. "Vile she-devils. It is said their fur is stained with the blood of a thousand humans."

I pointed my eyebrows his way, and not just because of his startled reaction. "I never said it was a she."

"All manticores are female, wizard."

I bit down. "Fine, but I never said she was red."

His lips pressed tight. "Did you not? It's a common color and a fair assumption. Anyway, it's an old human saying. Silvan blood is black."

I frowned in silence, feeling like I was being lied to. The bodyguards kept their eyes ahead, not revealing any clues. The rest of his traveling party didn't know anything.

The spriggans were just dumb muscle, making up in numbers and ferocity what they lacked in size and skill. Besides fodder, they seemed to act mostly as an early-warning system. With a pack of spriggans taking the lead and the tail, no one could sneak up on us. And a horde of trampling feet warned any curious scourgelings into hiding long before we saw them. It was an elegant, if blunt, solution.

"Where are we going?" I asked, making sure to keep myself between Milena and Orpheus.

"Where do you think we're going?" The faun snickered. "You don't trust me, do you?"

"Is there a reason I should?"

"A lot's changed since last we met." His gaze strayed to Milena, curious.

Made nervous by his stare, she dove into pleasant conversation. "You're a duke? Does that mean you're royalty?"

"It means I'm the head of my circle," he said.

I took an extra step to block his study of my girlfriend. "About that. You're still allied with the Table of Oak?"

"Of course. It's the strongest silvan alliance in centuries. It would be stupid to endanger that."

Lust for power, I believed. Unfortunately, I didn't put it past Orpheus to lust for power too much. Last I remembered, he was the youngest of three brothers, last in line for the dukedom, which was why he'd desired a wedding with the principesse so badly. It was the only way for him to significantly raise his station.

"Speaking of stupidity," he said sourly, "you shouldn't deal with those fiends." He was still ruffled by the vampires.

"No dealings," I said a bit trivially. "Just mutual benefit. Is it so different from utilizing spriggan fiends?"

"Vastly," he said with a scoff. "I command these spriggans. Let's see you manage that with an upir."

The duke turned his attention to Kasper, quietly trudging nearby. The old man was playing it cool, staying out of the conversation, hoping he was forgotten. Which was as far from reality as possible. If a fight broke out, he would be the first to swing.

"I was under the impression you were bringing a single guest," said Orpheus.

"Kasper?" I laughed. "Don't worry. He's the entertainment."

The biker twisted his ax over his shoulder and grunted.

We walked for a long time. I wondered why the silvans hadn't given me better directions to their dominion. They had, after all, sent me an invitation. But maybe that's how they operated. Enigmatic yet practical. Being difficult to reach was a defense. I considered asking our host but, honestly, the less we chatted, the better. There was no love lost between us.

Patches of grass and moss began dotting the packed soil on the walls and ceiling. Conversely, the well-trodden ground remained barren of plant life. Still, the landscape of the Nether was beginning to transform and brighten. As we encountered luminescent mushrooms shining red light, things were about as colorful as I'd ever seen in this steppe.

"We're approaching silvan territory," said Orpheus. "You arrived a day early, but it's past feastime. There'll be no reunions tonight."

I was amazed that it was night already. In the Nether, it was impossible to tell. My friends and I *were* exhausted, though. I was gonna need to start listening to my internal clock.

The thought of the passing time darkened my thoughts. Milena was still trudging along fine, but a nagging cough had set in. It could be nothing or it could be everything. I put my arm around her protectively.

"We need to see healers," I said.

The faun frowned as he considered us. I, at least, had visible wounds. "Of course. I should have suggested as much."

A low rumbling filled the passage as we walked, gentle and steady. It soon became apparent the white noise was running water. Greenery began to overtake the dirt. The ground softened with plant life. Slowly, the cavern began to widen. The ceiling angled upward. We found ourselves in a large open space that might've been the countryside except for a wall of green above. A bubbling brook washed by, alive with fish and other things.

"It's beautiful," said Milena, eyes wide.

She wasn't kidding. I didn't know the Nether could open up like this. I'd only ever seen the Margins, the fringes and the borders of the true realm, where it connected with ours. This... this was something else.

The pack of spriggans scattered in different directions, walking in lines like troops of dwarves from a Disney movie. Some crossed the stream and others rounded along the rocky wall. They were returning home, perhaps, their job done.

Milena twirled at the sight. "It must be so peaceful to live here."

Orpheus flashed a rare smile. "This is just the border of our dominion. The real treasures are deeper yet."

Kasper huffed. "I don't get it. All this wildlife... What's keeping all the other monsters from marching in here and having their way? And don't tell me those guys." The biker waved at the dispersing spriggans.

The duke flicked his eyes upward. Kasper turned and stretched his head high. "I don't see—"

The entire mountainous wall rumbled, kicking down a stream of dust as we collectively stepped away.

"Is that...?"

"A giant," I finished, stupefied. "I've never actually seen one before. I'd assumed they all died out long ago." I remembered the manticore's mention of human legends. What were we in for down here?

Kasper moved ahead, cowed by the being that could probably get through his protective tattoos. "You were saying about the treasures being this way?"

Orpheus chuckled and led us to the stream. We hopped across several large rocks, but the fauns just stepped right in. We passed lush trees and a field of purple flowers. The cavern narrowed and widened again, as if the territory was a network of separate rooms. But each successive space was larger than the last. I'd always imagined the Nether tunnels to be just underneath the earth, several yards or so, but now the ceiling stretched twenty stories overhead. I even caught sight of a few birds.

"This way."

Orpheus finally broke away from the open terrain and headed into a doorway in the wall. Like the rest of the silvan territory, it was solid rock instead of packed dirt. Directly inside was a guard post. We marched past an armored minotaur with a three-headed dog. Down the hallway, the fauns split up.

"Hera will take you up," said Orpheus. "I'll fetch your healers." The duke turned and left us with his female bodyguard. We eyed each other warily.

Chapter 25

With all the reverence of someone taking out the garbage, Hera led us up a flight of stairs and down an extended hall. Finally she stopped before an open door. "Your guest room."

"Do I get one?" asked Kasper.

"Just the one that was prepared." She watched us a moment, in case we had any requests, and then, like Orpheus, hurried away without looking back.

"Guess they're not very big on customer service down here," muttered Kasper.

The suite was large, with an open sitting area with several day beds and furs. Good for entertaining company. I peeked in the master bedroom and it was likewise grand, with a sturdy wood bed and plush sheets.

"This is good," said the biker. "I'll crash on the couch."

He started adjusting a blanket but Milena sat on it, fingers over her eyes.

"You feeling okay?" I asked. I stood by her and kneaded

her shoulders. I'd never seen Kasper hit the sack so early so he must've needed it. Still, he didn't complain about the intrusion. He wandered to the bathroom.

"I'm just tired all over," breathed Milena. "On the inside too."

"Travel was pretty rough." As I massaged her neck, I brushed the necklace Chevalier had given her to the side. A spot on the charm caught my eye and I took it in my hands. A portion of the clay had blackened, maybe a quarter of the medallion. It was like some kind of enchanted hourglass, only I didn't want to find out what happened when time ran out.

Milena grabbed my hand and pulled me around so I could sit with her. She smiled, but I could tell she was doing that for my benefit. I clenched my jaw and broke eye contact.

"Where are we, Cisco?" She squeezed my hand. "If you tell me we need to be here, that we can fix this, then I'm with you all the way. But if we're wasting our time..."

"Hey," I said, putting my finger over her lips. "We're going to a wedding. We're gonna dress up and have fun. You'll see things you've never seen in your life. And besides, it's the fancy dinner I've been promising you."

She snorted in laughter and leaned her head into me, carefree for the briefest of moments. Except she brushed the tear on my chest and I flinched ever so slightly. She stiffened, realizing what she'd done. "I'm so sorry."

"It's nothing," I said. "Really." I pulled her back into me. She rested her head on my shoulder, but it wasn't quite the same. The innocent moment had passed.

She sniffed and pulled away. "Did you mean what you said? When Jem had me in the water?"

I rubbed her neck tenderly, growing conscious of the ring in my belt pouch. "Yes, Milena. I love you. And not just 'cause I was afraid of losing you. I've loved you for a while."

The blackening charm around her neck snapped into my mind and I threw caution to the wind. I furtively unzipped the belt pouch and dug for the ring.

She kissed me. "*También te quiero.*"

We stared in each other's eyes as I fingered the ring. Was I really gonna do this now? Part of me felt she deserved a better moment, but we had to work with what we had. A fear had been gnawing at me—ever since I heard that awful voice with the manticore over me—a fear that we would never live long enough to be married.

And then I wondered. Did the marriage matter? Wasn't it just the sentiment? The expression of love and the commitment to each other? If Milena only had a day or two left, maybe the best thing was to tell her what I wanted as early as possible. To give her that confidence of my love, of what she meant to me.

The moment held as I deliberated until she broke out laughing. "I can't believe it took a mermaid assassin for us to tell each other!"

I flashed a smile, annoyed I had taken so long but trying to keep the moment light. "A *stripper* mermaid assassin, you mean." I shook my head. "Man, that has to be a cliche."

She laughed. It was infectious, but I wanted to move us

back to serious. I kissed her. She was surprised but went with it. When we broke away, her smile lingered, but I stared at her with deep affection.

"Milena..."

She squinted, concern on her face. "Cisco?"

Kasper strode out from the bathroom with a wash of steam in his wake. "Can you believe it? This place has no indoor plumbing. I had to crap in a bucket."

I gritted my teeth. "Kasper..."

"I'm not kidding. The bathroom has covered tubs and sinks with warming stones in them. You ever accidentally rested your balls on warming stones, broham? Activated my protection enchantments."

Milena's jaw dropped in sheer joy at the bit of gossip. "Your balls have tattoos on them?"

The biker grunted. "Of course. Otherwise it'd be like Achilles not protecting his heel."

"What about your... you know?"

"Same deal. And here's a bonus tip. Those strengthening tats are useful for more than just protection."

Milena burst into hearty laughter. I sighed and leaned back into the cushion, stuffing the ring safely back in the pouch and zipping it shut. The moment was officially ruined.

"And what's this?" he griped, stumbling to some cabinets. "There's no kitchen? Ah, here's the good stuff." He beamed at the open ice chest and pulled out a bottle stoppered with a cork. "I don't know what this is but we're finishing the bottle. Tell me you're in this with me, Cisco."

I sighed again. "I could actually use a glass right now."

We turned to Milena, who smiled apologetically. "I don't think it would be a good idea. After a good sleep I'll have some at the wedding."

They didn't have glasses, per se, but Kasper dug out a pair of metal goblets. He filled them and passed mine over, joining us on the opposite couch.

"So do we trust these people?" he asked. "Those fauns didn't seem too friendly with you."

"It's a long story," I admitted.

He shrugged. "We got time."

"Sure," cut in Milena, "but before you tell it, I think he has a good question. We passed through the gauntlet of monsters in the Margins, but now that we're in silvan territory, is it a sure thing we're safe?"

A light knock on the door made us all jump. It opened before I could answer, and I jumped to my feet as shadow filled my hand.

Three naked ladies stepped inside. They were lithe, pale, and with the same shade of red hair. They had to be triplets. And while naked was technically an overstatement, their ensembles consisted only of three strategically placed leaves. Use your imagination.

"Sorry," I said. "We didn't order any—"

I nearly doubled over from the pillow Kasper hit me with. "Yes!" he called out. "We're here! Come in, come in." He cleared his throat and winked at me. "Now, I assume all three of you have authentic masseuse licenses, right?"

The women giggled. "We're the healers."

Another grinned. "We don't get to see humans often."

"That's okay," I said, releasing the building Intrinsics from my fist. "We don't get to see silvans all that much."

"How're the leaves staying on?" blurted Kasper.

They laughed and approached, splitting off with us one on one. A girl took my hand and pulled me to the third couch, sitting me down.

"Are you ladies nymphs?"

"Dryads," she answered, sitting confidently on my lap. "And experts in the soothing ways."

"Watch it, lady," warned Milena. "I know what that means."

"It's nothing, really," explained the girl sitting with her.

"Just make sure you check on her," I said. "She was infected with silvan blood."

"Curious."

"Seriously," asked Kasper. "The leaves. Do you use some kind of feminine glue or what?"

The girl on me kissed my chest wound. Instead of pain, the contact sent tickles through my rib cage. She checked the manticore bite on my arm before frowning at my blackened right hand.

"It's okay," I said, lightheaded. "It's already healing." She weaved some kind of magic into it and I was hit with a wave of euphoria. "Hey, this is kind of cool..."

I jerked as her weight shifted onto the puncture wound on my hip. She backed away apologetically. Then her eyes flashed mischievously. "You naughty boy. You didn't tell me about this one."

It took her announcing my wounds to realize how banged up I was. The dryads were quick workers. When Kasper spoke next, he was slurring so heavily I couldn't make out the words. Or maybe my senses were muddied.

By the time I recognized the charm working over me, I didn't even want to fight it. I closed my eyes and smiled.

Chapter 26

I sat up on the couch and paused, waiting for the voice to return. Everything was still. Milena and Kasper were sleeping on their sofas. I craned my neck, searching the room. The dryads were absent. A bottle of bubbly was tipped over on the floor, half its contents spilled. My goblet rested overturned at my feet.

I stretched and felt... amazing. I wiggled the toes on my bare feet. I wasn't sure where my boots and shirt were but my jeans were on.

"Wake up."

I nudged them and checked out my hand. The skin was no longer black, but ripe and pinkish. My fingers danced freely without the slightest hint of pain. The manticore bite was likewise healed, as was the hip puncture, though the gash on my chest still had some ways to go. It was a hardened scab across my heart. Pressing against it prodded no pain.

"Incredible," crowed Kasper, jumping to his feet. "I feel

like a million bucks. I can't remember the last time I woke up without a hangover."

"My bra's missing," said Milena.

We both looked at her boobs, but they were well covered by her shirt.

Come to think of it, I did need to adjust down there. I pulled the waist of my jeans. "My underwear's on backwards."

Milena pointedly narrowed her eyes. "What kind of 'healing' did you get?"

"The nymph kind. I don't know, I swear. What about you, Kasper?"

He shrugged. "I always go commando."

Milena grinned. "I feel like I'm learning so much about you."

"Does anybody remember anything?" I asked.

Milena came over and checked the scab on my chest.

Kasper put his hands up in celebration. "That was the best sex I don't remember!"

"No one had sex," I countered.

"You tell it your way, I'll tell it mine." He picked up the half empty bottle of suds and sniffed it.

"Isn't it a little early for that?" chided Milena.

"Hard to tell. There's no sun down here."

"Fair."

"Forget about Kasper," I cut in. "You're not coughing. How do you feel?"

She pulled her chin back as if just remembering her predicament. "Come to think of it, I feel rejuvenated, like

I've just been at the spa for a week."

"That's a hint if I ever heard one," chuckled Kasper, retiring to the bathroom. He peeked his head out. "Hey, someone changed my shit bucket!"

We chuckled at his excitement, though I wasn't sure I liked the thought of being undressed and having the room serviced while we were passed out. I supposed, if we were truly in danger, we could've been killed where we slept.

But it wasn't all sunshine and rainbows. I grabbed the charm around Milena's neck and worked my jaw. The withering black had begun to grow over the snake symbol, now covering half the medallion. Milena was still on the clock.

"Don't worry," she pressed. "I feel better. And we have the whole day to figure it out."

"A whole evening anyway," called out a boy's voice.

We spun to the open door where a child had entered. He might've been ten, but it was hard to tell with silvans, especially when their human torso sat atop the body of a horse.

"*Ay que cute!*" chimed Milena.

The little centaur boy was adorable. Short and lean, wearing only a leather belt slung around his neck and a bag on his back. His top half passed for completely human except for the little horn nubs and pointed ears poking through his short tan hair. His tiny horse half was a smooth coat of ruddy brown.

"I'm sorry to startle you," he said in a crisply polite voice. "I wouldn't want you to travel all this way and miss the wedding."

"I thought it wasn't until tonight," I said.

"That's what I'm trying to tell you, sir. It *is* tonight. The folkmoot begins thirty minutes hence."

Damn it. The intense healing had come with a cost. Milena had very little time left and we'd just snoozed the whole day away. I could only hope the healing had done her good.

"Hey, a little pony dude!" Kasper chuckled as he strolled up to the boy. "Give me five, broham."

The boy smiled, eager to partake in the human custom. He missed. They tried again but the boy's timing was off.

"Don't worry. It takes practice." Kasper held the boy's hand and guided it into his. "What's your name?"

"I'm Kory, sir. Pleased to meet you: Kasper, Milena, and Cisco."

"We slept the whole day," explained Milena. "It's nighttime."

"You see?" said Kasper, picking up the bottle of beer again. "It's not too early to start." He took a swig and offered us one. We passed.

"Where are the healers?" I asked.

"Healers?"

"The dryads. They were in here last night."

Kory's front two hooves rapped the floor as he mulled it over. "Hmm, they must have left before I was assigned to look after you."

"Can we get them back? I have some questions for them."

"I can request a visit, but I'm not sure who you saw. You have no need to worry, however. Our healers are quite proficient." He klopped toward the unused bedroom. "I hope you don't mind, but I took the liberty of laying out your clothes. My commendations. They are quite fashionable."

I sighed as we followed for a look. "Kory, I still need to check in with them. There—"

"*Que preciosa!*" Milena hurried to the ruffled bundle of cloth on the bed and set it against her body. The gold dress looked expensive.

I pulled the centaur aside and lowered my voice. "Listen, I understand if you don't have the full details of what's going on. Orpheus was the one who sent us the healers. Maybe you can lead us to him?"

"As is customary for all folkmoots of this magnitude, the duke sits at the Table of Oak until he is announced."

"Sure, but if we could just chat with him before that..."

"It's impossible, sir. The wedding is imminent."

I gritted my teeth, but Milena backed me off. "Cisco, baby, by the time we shower and change and get down there, everything will be starting. There's no point going against the grain to save an hour." She led me by the hand to the bed. "Now *you* are gonna be wearing the fuck out of this suit in half an hour or I'm gonna be extremely irritable."

I smirked. "How irritable?"

"*Extremely.*" She turned to the centaur. "Kid, you mind waiting outside for us?"

"Of course, madam." He bowed slightly in deference

before shutting the bedroom door.

Milena slipped out of her shirt, and she still hadn't found her bra. "Now, I just know *these ladies* do more for you than all the scrawny dryads in the Nether combined."

I grinned. "I don't know... I'm pretty into leaves."

Her hands shot to her hips. "Turns out, they don't provide the support a woman like me needs."

"Amen to that."

I pulled her in and kissed her, our bare chests squeezed tight. I was suddenly thrilled at the chance for a date night with Milena. Her mood had been understandably dark lately. If she was determined to have a good time, then I was too.

"You're gonna need help getting in that dress."

She winked. "But first I'll need help in the tub."

The master bedroom thankfully had a separate bathroom without Kasper's poo bucket. In the center of the room, a round wood cover was set into the floor's stonework. It swiveled aside on wheels and a wash of steam hit our bodies. We stepped into the sunken tub lightly, hot water shocking our skin, and then we embraced. Our hot tub sex wasn't too quick or too slow. Time didn't seem to matter. We stared into each other's eyes, full of passion, and the stresses of the world receded far away.

That was always the way with us. We both cared about a whole lot, but we still found moments when nothing else mattered besides us. Kasper, the centaur boy, and the whole wedding entourage could wait; my girl and I were getting dirty.

Kasper was right about those warming stones, though. After we were done and relaxing, I accidentally sat on one of those hot shits. Suddenly I sympathized with the methhead at the Cielo who was stuffing his pants with ice cubes.

We fit into our new wardrobe next. I took Beaumont's word that Milena's dress was Parisian in fashion—I would've described it as Victorian. The main fabric was made up of bold stripes of honey and gold, with an extravagant trained skirt, puffy in the back but practical on the bottom where it thinned out for easy walking. Gold sashes and frills hung at the waist. The back was tied, leaving her shoulders and neck bare, and the upper arms ended in modest puffs. Red trim highlighted the edges, putting that last touch of panache on an already larger-than-life outfit. Milena looked like she walked straight out of a fairy tale.

My suit, on the other hand, was the definition of modern debonair. Silky black with a metallic sheen, perfectly cinched at the waist and cuffs. Beaumont must've had a good eye because even the seat of my pants was expertly fitted. At least if Milena's groping was any indication. The lapels of the jacket puffed out stylishly, opening to a cream-colored shirt and a light-red tie. Milena slicked my hair back to complete the look, and it was a good one. She may have been a walking fairy tale, but I was a secret agent.

Cisco Suarez cleaned up well.

As Milena was at the mirror putting the final touches on her hair and makeup, I fitted the belt pouch under the jacket. It sort of spoiled the look but was a necessity. I also stuffed Trinh's pistol in there.

"What do you think?" asked Milena.

Straight hair hung over her shoulders, curling at the bottoms to frame her bust. She had tightened the snake charm around her neck like a choker. And she'd splashed green color over her eyes in a nod to the silvans. I hardly noticed the large scab on her shoulder, still slightly blackened.

"You're beautiful."

I walked over to kiss her, but a finger over my lips cut me off. "My lip gloss is still drying."

I rolled my eyes.

She slapped my shoulder playfully. "Don't make fun. This is a big day for us."

She went back to the mirror and I turned away, fingering the silver ring as I pulled it from the bag. This *was* a big day for us, and I was gonna make sure it was successful on all fronts.

Neither of us could predict what was gonna happen tomorrow. Today was much more certain. I was determined to show the love of my life a good time, no matter what. And then, to cap off a magical night, I was going to ask her to marry me.

I dropped the ring into my jacket pocket, promise on my lips.

Chapter 27

We strolled down the hall and I couldn't stop chuckling.

"What?" grouched Kasper, my mirth getting to him.

I shrugged like it was nothing but had to ask, so I kept my question casual. "Where'd you get the duds?"

He pressed ahead with a scowl.

Kory, our little centaur companion, answered. "It wouldn't do to have a guest attend a royal union in casual attire. With Sir Kasper lacking a packed outfit, I took it upon myself to fetch him one from the silvan stores."

I snorted. "I'll say."

The old man didn't look that bad, truth be told, but a few of the flairs were comical. He didn't have a jacket but wore a dark-gray pinstripe vest with matching pants. So far, so good. The shirt, however, was the stuff of legends. For one, the pale rose color didn't match Kasper's grumpy demeanor. And hey, I'd be the first to say a guy in a suit can rock a pink shirt, but when it had large dangling buttons and puffy arms to rival those of the most extravagant pirates, it was funny. Luckily Kasper's full beard hid the button situation.

There was also the fact that the old man stood at a normal height and his pants were more... silvan sized. The short legs gave us full view of his tan checkered socks. Which wasn't the only fit problem. Kasper was a mostly scrawny dude, but he sported one hell of a beer belly, and his poor vest wanted to burst at the bottom. On second thought, maybe the super-sized buttons were a good idea.

Topping the whole ensemble off was the pièce de résistance, the pointy-toed shoes that ended in upraised curls.

"I think you look great," said Milena. "Can you do me a favor, though? This year when you're helping Santa pack the presents, can you just send me a Porsche?"

The biker adjusted his red-tinted glasses. "I know when I'm being baited, and it's not going to work. Ole Kasper is taking the high road."

"Who is Santa?" asked Kory. "And what is a Porsche?"

"An overpriced status symbol," I answered. "When you want a real ride, you go with American muscle."

The centaur chewed his lip, probably thinking about horses instead of cars. Instead of using the side tunnel back to the guardhouse from the night before, he led us the opposite way, entering a majestic hall with a ceiling two stories high. Candeled chandeliers lit our path.

"This reminds me of Game of Thrones," murmured Milena.

"Let's just hope with less dying," I said.

"I can deal with the nudity though," mentioned Kasper, no doubt happy for the change of subject.

A few members of the help staff darted this way and that in hurried last-minute preparations. Many of them resembled humans, but we did pass several others. Another minotaur guard, dutifully stomping by. A young satyr, who resembled a faun but was prettier, with horse features instead of goat. Satyr's tails were lush and their faces more humanlike. Kory briefly exchanged pleasantries with a centaur girl about his age.

We were in another world, no doubt about it, and all banter deferred to wonder. I squeezed Milena's waist, excited by this once-in-a-lifetime opportunity. The hall ended with grand double doors of glass which opened onto a stonework veranda. Tables and lounge chairs were aflutter with guests, but the real show was on the lawn below.

And we were not prepared.

This cavern was huge, with a ceiling so high and filled with yellow light you could mistake it for a sun-filled sky. Besides the endless greenery, on the only distant wall visible from our vantage, a waterfall tumbled from above. These were the royal grounds.

Even more stupefying were the guests. There must've been a thousand silvans in attendance. They crowded the yard, lined up at tables, huddled over games, wandered the grounds, and cheered, sang, and laughed uproariously. This was more Lollapalooza than wedding.

"Holy hell," said Kasper. "Now *this* is a party."

Kory beamed proudly. "It is much more than that, sir.

It's a folkmoot. A gathering of all the major circles and their allies. Hunters, brewers, and traders hawk their wares. Friendships are crafted, marriages arranged. Events like these will last days, and the high king has spared no expense."

We nodded along and took it all in. The boy had reason to be proud. It reminded me how important the wedding of Ceela and Throok was. The satyr girl was a princess. Two great houses were merging.

"Where're the bride and groom?" I asked.

"They'll be announced when it's time. Until then, please enjoy our amenities to the fullest. And don't forget to mingle." He leaned close. "I don't know of any other humans in attendance, so you'll be a big hit."

Kory bowed and cantered back indoors, leaving us with a bit of vertigo.

"Wow," said Milena. "Well, what do you think we should tackle first?"

Kasper and I looked to the table of refreshments, then at each other. "Definitely the food," we said in unison.

We'd been sleeping for a whole day. I was starving.

The three of us started slowly down the steps. The plush lawn was full and soft under our feet. Milena's slippers were provided by Beaumont. They were raised but had wide heels, making it easy to walk on the grass. The vampire boss had kindly supplied me with a pair of comfortable loafers, but I'd shirked them in favor of my cowboy boots. The red alligator leather kinda matched my tie.

I chuckled, realizing I should've given my loafers to

Kasper. But then no one would appreciate the elf shoes.

We made our way into the crowd, weaving past characters of all shapes and sizes, in all combinations of scales, fur, and skin. Satyrs and fauns, sirens and nymphs, and more. Harpies with the wings and legs of birds. Kitsune women with several foxtails each. A crew of hairy wild men. We'd gone through the wardrobe and were now in Narnia, except these creatures weren't full of sparkles and whimsy. There was an element of danger inherent in each of these beings.

Silvans were said to have been human once. Stories abound of shape-shifting Greek gods, curses inflicted, and relegation to the underworld. There was probably a kernel of truth in it all somewhere, but it was hardly relevant to modern times. What I did know was that, just as the upirs hated the silvans for domination of the best parts of the Nether, many silvans despised humans for inhabiting the Earthly Steppe.

A big hit indeed.

However, this was a party and a place of friendship. In contrast to the single-minded staff going about their duties, the guests on the lawn idled with luxurious treats and showy outfits. They were here for pleasure. And a surprising number of them wore masks straight out of a masquerade ball.

Most silvans were shape-shifters. They couldn't take any form they wanted, but they had human guises, and the mechanics of constant transformations made clothes troublesome, especially when so many of them wore so little by default. So most silvan clothes were illusions, part of their glamours. Which was why Kasper drew the short straw when it came to actually finding real clothes for him to wear. Even in a kingdom of riches, those were a rarity.

We arrived at a long table with a bustling line. Metal and clay dishes were arrayed with crumpets, exotic fruits, poached eggs, and various cheeses.

Kasper sighed. "You think they're hiding a smoked brisket around here?"

But the line moved quickly, and there were loaves of bread, vegetable husks, wild rices, hearty mixed stews, roasted fowls.

"I don't know what this is," said Milena, "but I'm scarfing it down."

My belly rumbled at the sight of a flank of pork being thinly sliced, but when I noticed the cook had a pig-like face, I cowered. "Uh, sorry for your loss," I blurted out. Thankfully, I had said it under my breath. I hoped.

"Looks great!" exclaimed Kasper, shoving his plate forward. "Gimme four of those."

I opted for spitted chunks of meat that resembled beef and hoped I didn't see any minotaurs for a bit.

One particular that caught me pleasantly by surprise were the different buffet rules in the Nether. Instead of loading up plates and taking them away to sit like civilized folk, the silvans meandered in endless lines, hopping and looping from table to table, eating and chatting as they walked. The immediate style suited me because I was about as hungry as I'd ever been. As we munched, a passing man on the other side of the table leaned across.

"Forsooth! Are you not witches and wizards?"

The sudden interaction startled me, but it was harmless small talk. The man was blond and exceedingly handsome and wore a tunic that ended in a skirt. Really, besides the outfit I would've pegged him for human, but I didn't want to admit that. Lack of knowledge was a weakness. I remembered Beaumont's advice: project power and recognize power.

"We are." I smiled wide.

No one needed to know Milena wasn't an animist. The stronger they thought she was, the less likely she would be messed with.

The man's eyes sparkled. "I knew it! We silvans adore our dresses down here, but we wouldn't be caught dead in those constrictive formalclothes." His smile faltered. "I'm sorry, I don't mean offense. Of course, for you, the outfit must be a natural fit."

Milena laughed it off. "Don't worry. Cisco usually doesn't know the definition of formal." Her comment made what could've been an awkward moment a fun joke instead. She was better at making friends than me and Kasper.

The man looked ahead as the line began to move. "Might I ask, if you don't mind, how you know Principesse Ceelandra and Champion Throok?"

It was strange hearing their formal names and titles. Maybe Throok had been promoted since I last saw him.

"Just a chance meeting in the Margins a year or so ago," I said.

"I hear wizards never do anything by chance."

A plump woman behind him wearing a mask butted forward. "The human happened upon Ceela and Throok while they were on the run. His highness thought they were eloping."

"How deliciously juicy!" insisted the man.

The line bumped again. Since the opposite sides of the table were headed in opposite directions, the handsome man waved us off. The plump woman turned around and told her consort who we were.

The ancient man had bushy eyebrows that covered the top half of his face. "What's that?" he grumbled.

She raised her voice. "THESE ARE THE WIZARDS WHO FACILITATED THE ELOPING OF THE PRINCIPESSE."

I flinched at the attention the comment garnered. The old man squinted. "Who are?" he asked, oblivious.

The woman huffed and pointed. "They are. Across the table."

He leaned toward a roasted turkey and said, "Nice to make your acquaintance."

I nodded politely as we walked on, but the whispers were in full swing.

"I heard he was cursed by Orpheus himself."

"Nonsense. No one survives a Nether mark of that degree."

"If that were true, why would they be here now?"

"A shadow charmer? I've never heard such a thing!"

"Humans bring only trouble with them."

I focused on ladling fondue onto my plate and adorning it with toasted breadsticks. A woman with white hair to her hips waddled ahead of me in line. It was only when she turned around that I noticed she had duck feet peeking out from under her dress.

"Now, now," piped the prim woman. "Orpheus was a jealous pursuer, and we all know you can't trust fauns." She shared a conspiratorial look. "Does anyone else think it coincidence that, as soon as his ambitious marriage plans faltered, his father and elder brothers were mysteriously killed?"

"Tut," said a man sporting a scorpion tail. "The Margins are a dangerous place."

"And I would agree," said the duck-footed lamia, "if the attack was the single incident. But Duke Prospero was soon-after poisoned."

"You think the son poisoned the father?"

"Of course. It's well known Orpheus and Prospero never got along."

Another man snubbed the idea. "He took his own life, in grief at the loss of his favorite sons."

The lamia knowingly shook her head. "Just because the Table tells you a thing does not make it truth." She turned to us now. "I know these things. A baron doesn't rise to duke so suddenly. Orpheus orchestrated his rise in station by his usual trickster means. I'd die on that oath. Oh!"

She jumped as an armored faun marched by. It was one of the duke's bodyguards, I thought, though I couldn't be sure. He eyed us suspiciously.

"A disgrace!" shouted the lamia. "Humans at a folkmoot!" She turned from the table and stomped away.

And she'd seemed like such a generous woman a second ago. The whole scene brought even more focused attention to us, including from the faun guard.

"Excuse me," I cut in politely, trying to make the best of it. "Is there any way we can talk to—"

The goat-man looked away and passed without the slightest acknowledgment of my request. I stared after him, angry and daring him to look back.

Kasper moved close. "Did he just snub you, broham?"

"I think so."

"Then how are we ever going to find those nymphos again?"

"Nymphs," corrected Milena. "They're nymphs."

"I've heard it both ways."

I stretched my neck to ease my scowl. "I'm not sure, but I'm getting a little sick of high society."

I dropped my plate on the edge of the table and abandoned the line. Then I stopped, went back, and angrily dipped a breadstick in delicious cheese sauce. "No sense wasting good food." I crunched down and stormed away with the plate.

Chapter 28

The party-goers congregated in bunches so having a moment alone required searching for a clear patch. We loitered beside a bird bath with glittering water that looked good enough to drink. No birds though. I assumed my foul mood projected an unwelcoming air. I didn't trust the silvans down here, and even the birds were probably filled with venom.

"The human wizard!" announced a man, hurrying over.

"Great," I muttered.

He was a satyr, and a royally dressed one at that. His top half wasn't very furry at all. He did have a healthy mane of black hair that matched his horse legs and tail. His clothes were made up of a series of ornate sashes: a wide one at the waist like a cummerbund, and arm and leg bands, with a matching yellow headband over his large drooping ears.

"Francisco Suarez, I presume!"

"Cisco," I said.

"I would be honored to use the epithet. We are friends,

you and I."

He included his wife in the statement, hugging her close. I didn't recognize either of them. She was a stocky satyr of mixed brown and white fur and held a bright-red mask over her eyes.

"Friends?"

"Of course. Did Ceela not mention me?" He looked to his wife. "My cousin, ever aloof." They laughed.

"Family!" chimed Milena, smoothing over my rough edges as usual. "I'm so honored to witness such a momentous occasion." She held out her hand and the man kissed it with practiced poise. "I'm Milena and this is our friend, Kasper."

The biker suddenly straightened, surprised at being pulled into the conversation, and quickly shoved a fatty pork flank into his mouth, slurped his greasy fingers, and held his hand out in greeting.

The man pursed his lips at the waiting hand and settled on a polite nod. "I love the shoes."

Kasper grumbled and went back to his food.

"Nice to meet you and your friends, Cisco. My name is Baron Ludwig of the Juniper Circle. This is my esteemed wife, the Lady Fenn."

Her only clothes were a shawl over her shoulders and chest and numerous bracelets on her arms. I shook their hands as cordially as I could. I wasn't really looking to make friends, but it wouldn't be the worst thing to have allies around here.

Milena mirrored the woman and stood at my side.

"What's the Juniper Circle?"

"Oh, dear," said Ludwig as graciously as possible, "it is our silvan circle."

"The major factions are organized into them," I explained. "Fauns are bone, satyrs are juniper."

"Yes," he agreed, "but the Juniper is no ordinary circle. It's the High Circle, ruled by the high king himself."

I blinked back surprise. "You mean Ceela is the princess of the entire silvan kingdom?"

"Look at that, he's modest too." The baron kept his chuckle light and airy. "Do you mean to say you helped my cousin without knowing who she was?"

I shrugged. "Seemed the right thing to do at the time."

He smiled approvingly while Lady Fenn interjected. "Bravo to that. I've always been proud of the faith we satyrs place in humans. You've proven to be a shining example of our sentiments."

The baron nodded. "Without a doubt, my dear." He noticed my empty plate and waved at a centaur boy, who came and retrieved them from us. Kasper tugged his away like a dragon hoarding treasure. Ludwig nodded and the waiter left. "I trust you're finding your accommodations suitable? If there's anything you need..."

"You guys have any flushable toilets?" asked Kasper.

I waved him off and the baron and lady laughed. "Actually, we were looking for the healers Orpheus sent up last night. I had some follow-up questions."

Ludwig jutted his lips out for a moment. "That's strange. Did he send the castle healers?"

"He means the dryads," said Fenn. "Don't you?"

"That's them," answered Milena.

Lady Fenn nodded. "Yes, those triplets make up the duke's personal troupe, but they aren't classical healers. Were they up to mischief again?"

"Now, dear..." prodded Ludwig. "We shouldn't concern our guests with trickster antics." He locked his eyes with me and sighed. "I do regret that the fauns have a reputation as practical jokers. Trust me when I say they're harmless."

"I've heard worse things about their reputation," said Kasper gruffly.

The baron nodded. "History has its share of villains all around, wouldn't you say? Orpheus and the Circle of Bone are strong supporters of the Oak Table. The duke is a more important man than he's been his entire life. He's not about to lose that over a petty vendetta." Ludwig placed a comforting hand on my shoulder. "I understand if you have reservations, Cisco, given your past with our mutual friend. Especially because he's not the type to apologize for past behavior. But have no worries. The alliance is as solid as oak."

"Fenn!" called a woman. The voice was deep, almost sensual, and the woman sauntering over fit it to a tee. Large hips, dark olive skin, and eyes like the abyss. "Don't leave me alone like that. I have no one else to talk to!"

The women kissed and Fenn chuckled, holding her mask at her side. "You must watch yourself, my girl. Everyone's laughing on the outside, but you're in a pit of vipers."

"Vipers I can handle." The woman's eyes electrified as

she took us in and leaned close. "Be careful with silvans, darlings. Everything is a negotiation, which means everything comes at a price." They chortled.

The newcomer appeared perfectly human, wearing a tight red ball gown, which was more modern than other silvan outfits. No mask or animals parts. I didn't want to show ignorance by asking, but Kasper wasn't thinking that far ahead.

"Aren't you a silvan too?"

"Of course, but I'm upfront with my transactions."

The group chuckled again, including Milena. Like a breath of fresh air, this woman radiated charm. There was something intensely personal about having her in your presence. Perhaps it was her disarming smile. Kory was right about us drawing attention.

I glanced at our surroundings, making sure other wedding guests weren't waiting in line to pounce on us as well. We were okay for now.

Lady Fenn gave our names before pressing the mask to her face and taking a melodramatic breath. "I would like you all to meet my personal friend, Eden."

"The pleasure is mine," said the throaty woman. Thin and curvy at the same time, she gave a slight wiggle at the hips as she spoke. "The truth is we just met, but Fenn and I are fast friends."

The lady leaned on Ludwig and nodded. "We've taken her under our wing, haven't we?"

"Yes, dear," said the baron.

Eden looked us over. "We were just talking about the

famed shadow charmer."

Ludwig's face reddened. "You know women and their gossip."

Eden studied Kasper carefully before turning to Milena and grinning rapaciously. "And look at you, a beauty in your own right. I love the dress, darling. You would've been a hit at Le Chat Noir and the Parisian dance halls." She sighed. "Ah, but that was a lifetime ago."

"Can you believe?" asked Fenn. "She's not even projecting a glamour and she looks like that. I'm officially jealous."

Eden's eyes fluttered. "May I?" Milena nodded, and both women felt at her gaudy dress. Ludwig rolled his eyes in embarrassment but didn't speak up, as if we had to allow the women this concession. Eden's gaze ended on Milena's choker. "Now *that* is a curious piece of jewelry."

Lady Fenn huffed when she noticed it. "But why ornament yourself with a snake, my girl? They're such vile creatures."

"Not necessarily," countered Eden, stroking the charm and Milena's neck. "Snakes are like most animals in the Nether, both predator and prey. They're more honest than most silvans."

Milena pulled the blackening charm away. "It's just for good luck," she murmured, for the first time self-conscious.

But Milena wasn't easily unnerved by longing stares and sensual dispositions. She was a professional dancer, after all. It wasn't Eden's touch that had made her step back, but the subject of her limited mortality.

Eden seemed put off at making Milena uncomfortable. She backed away and smiled reassuringly. "Then I say wear it proudly. Too many of us are forced to hide our true natures. I find it freeing to let loose when I can."

Milena nodded, no stranger to wearing her freedom proudly. Eden's eyes flashed and she did another hip wiggle, and I got the feeling she was far more interested in Milena than she was in me. Something about her set my guard on edge.

I rubbed Milena's back encouragingly, placated the others with a smile, and scanned the crowd for signs of Orpheus or the dryads. Instead I caught sight of a man in layered sheaths of leather. He wore a small red cape with the cowl down and white fur over his shoulders.

And despite standing at ease by himself, he was staring right at me.

I glanced at the present company and found them discussing the merits of silvan wedding customs. Something about gifting or regifting. But my eyes kept flitting back to the mysterious guest, afraid he would vanish without a trace if I looked away for too long.

I couldn't waste the opportunity. I excused myself and cut through the crowd as the man waited.

He wasn't a silvan and he wasn't a stranger, but his presence here made me suspect trouble. Not that I had a concrete reason for that assessment. It was just a gut feeling.

The man's sculpted features didn't brighten at my approach. The expression on his face was flat, cheeks and lips made from marble, sky-blue eyes the only noticeable movement. I grabbed two glasses of beer from a passing waiter's tray and converged on him.

"I didn't know you were allowed to leave your house in the sky, Malik."

"The Aether's not my home any more than this place."

"And the Earthly Steppe?"

He turned his attention to the offered glass and took it. I'd seen him smoke and drink before, as our last meeting was a friendly one, but Malik didn't seem jovial now. Maybe there was something bothering him. Maybe it was all the people around. The nest of vipers. I wondered if they could even see him.

I set my jaw. "You're not following me, are you?"

"Do you think yourself so important?"

"Do you?"

Malik was cold now. Distant. He was an enigmatic figure and I wasn't sure about him. He'd given me helpful advice in the past. And he'd known about the Taíno shadow clinging to me, my Wings of Night. I just didn't know if I believed in *his* wings. In what he claimed to be.

But then, the ally who introduced us had told me plain enough. The thought of the volcanic elemental's ultimate sacrifice soured my tongue. I chugged half the glass to quash the taste. Then I dropped the tough-guy routine and turned to watch the crowd with him.

"Tyson was noble," I avowed, "on his way out."

"I know. But do not fret for him, Cisco. Rarely are the paths we choose the ones we want. Our friend lived and died by his own reckoning. That's exceedingly rare for his kind."

I hadn't forgotten Malik's lesson about the three chosen races. Jinns represented duty, so mere elementals were relegated to servants of duty. Humans were characterized by freedom, and Celestials by guidance.

I sighed. "Why do I get the feeling this lawn would be a lot less populated if only honest people were in attendance?"

"Because you're an awful politician, Cisco." Malik's bronze skin seemed to sparkle in the cavern's light. "Everybody here has hopes and desires. Everybody here puts on a face or wears a mask. Even you."

"Is that why you're alone out here?"

"Snakes don't cavort with eagles. But there are some who keep me apprised."

I glared at him. "Informants? Is that how you keep tabs on the steppes?"

"You know my style. I act from the fringes, when I am authorized to act at all."

I nodded toward Kasper and Milena speaking to our new benefactors. "About that. I'm down here because Milena's sick."

"You were ending up here anyway," he said flatly.

I frowned. "Yeah, maybe. But she's my priority. You need to help me cure her."

A thick eyebrow arched. "Need to?"

"Don't give me that. You're an angel, right? You can heal her if you want to."

"Want has nothing to do with it."

"So forget wanting. Just do it."

A simple shake of his head. "I understand your position,

but it's impossible for me to interfere."

"What's the purpose of watching then?"

"Poor choice of words in regards to me."

I killed the glass of beer and bit down. His damned Celestial bylaws were getting in the way of possible assistance from someone I thought was a friend. But the truth was I didn't really know who he was, or what he could do.

I scoffed sharply. "What are you doing here?"

His voice came confident and collected, in sharp contrast to mine. "I'm where I'm always needed."

"Yeah, that's what troubles me. Let me know when you grow a pair." I tossed the glass to the lawn and made my way back to the satyrs. Malik made no attempt to stop me.

Halfway across the yard, I slowed. Baron Ludwig and Lady Fenn had broken away from their conversation, and they were speaking to entirely different people. In a crowd of silvans, I should've spotted Kasper in a second. I didn't see him anywhere.

I hurried ahead until I caught sight of Milena, a short way from where I'd left her. She was still speaking with Eden, who was whispering in her ear. What was it with her?

I zeroed in on them. Unfortunately, I must've had tunnel vision because I was suddenly grabbed into a bear hug from behind. A guttural voice screamed so loud it hurt my ears.

"CISCO SUAREZ, HERE AT LAST!"

Chapter 29

Shadow enveloped my elbow as I readied a counterattack, but recognition flashed quickly enough for me to stop. The reason I was flailing in a vice grip a foot off the ground was because I'd been accosted by a fearsome minotaur.

"Throok? Is that you?"

He snorted and his voice returned to his normal, undisguised caliber. "I *hate* wizards. Too crafty. No fun at all."

Instead of being released as expected, something knocked me through the air like I'd been hit by a car. I spun with my pistol up... aimed squarely at Kasper and the gold magic glowing off his arm. I blinked and turned my head, tracking Throok from his previous position to where he was now, several yards away on the ground. If I'd been hit by a car, he'd gotten the bus treatment.

Several snarls shoved the crowd away, revealing a crew of minotaurs brandishing axes and clubs.

"No," I called. "Kasper, it was a joke!" I hurried over,

sheathing the pistol in the back of my pants this time.

But the minotaurs didn't look like they had senses of humor. They advanced on the biker with blood in their eyes.

"Bah ha ha ha!" laughed Throok, pushing to his hooves. "I haven't been sucker-punched like that since the schoolyard!"

He converged on us with a large gait, towering over everyone in the immediate area, including his own crew. He was an imposing figure: a bull snout, red eyes, horns and ears studded with earrings. While he had the classic nose hoop, he also sported a not-so-traditional red Mohawk and chin-beard. He was covered in short brown fur that thinned on his muscled chest and arms, and his leather vest and pants were a huge upgrade from his old clothes.

When he stopped at my side, I swore he'd grown several inches since I'd last seen him. Throok was now approaching seven and a half feet and might still have some in him yet. He was only eighteen.

The minotaur appraised Kasper. "That was impressive, old timer, but you're a wizard too. Am I wrong? Fortifying your blows with magic is cheating."

Kasper straightened his red glasses and lit up a stogie. "Last I checked, you were half man and half bull. There's nothing about you that *isn't* magic."

Throok grunted. "That's one way to look at it."

The minotaur seemed more jovial than his usual self, especially considering the sneak attack. But then, Throok had a lot to be happy about these days. He was an exgladiator from a lower circle who had no business marrying a princess. Now he was a champion on his wedding day.

I snickered. "Throok, this is Kasper. Kasper? You just decked the groom."

"Fuck me," he said, slightly ruffled. "I was just—"

"I understand, and you have nothing to fear. This man"—Throok put a heavy hand on my shoulder—"more than anyone has made today possible. I owe my life's dream to you, Cisco."

The other minotaurs were disappointed to put their weapons away. Disappointed, but clearly loyal and moved by their champion's words.

"Thanks, big guy," I said. "But that's kind of overstating things. In the end, Orpheus backed off on his own."

"Orpheus," he snorted, distaste evident on his lips. "The faun had some heavy encouragement. You bore a Nether mark for our union."

Milena squeezed into the group with a concerned look on her face. I hugged her, glad to have everyone together again.

"Again," I protested, "Orpheus removed the curse of his own will before I could be overwhelmed by hunters."

But not before the mermaid sisters tracked me down. My run-in with Jade was a direct result of the Nether mark. I killed her, Gemma hated me for it, and Milena's predicament was the fruit born of that tragedy.

Fucking Orpheus. Maybe he'd sent his personal healers out of guilt.

Throok snorted. He did that a lot. The gust of stinky air

ruffled his nose hoop. "I remember you being more cocky."

"Cisco's matured a lot since last year," teased Milena.

"I liked you better cocky," said Throok. But he turned and produced what I presumed was supposed to be a smile. "What is your name, little human?"

"Milena."

"She's my princess," I said.

Throok nodded solemnly. "Then you are forever welcome in these lands."

I pointed at Kasper with a smile. "I don't really know that dude."

Guffaws broke out in the ranks of the minotaur crew.

"Laugh it up," said the biker. "I ain't scared of you."

"Good," announced Throok, setting his arm around Kasper's shoulder. "Then you'll join us in the fighting pit. A human with a punch like that will draw a crowd."

He pulled the biker ahead and the rest of the minotaurs pressed us forward. I chuckled at the irony of being herded by cattle but figured the joke wouldn't play well. We crossed half the yard to a round patch of dirt in the lawn about twice the size of a sumo ring. Silvans, mostly minotaurs, lined up with padded gloves.

"You want me to get in there?" asked Kasper, stogie still in his mouth.

"We won't force you," said Throok, "but know that it is a great honor to—"

"I'm in." The biker stowed the cigar for later, slipped off his vest and glasses, and stepped toward the line, tattoos on his torso and arms glowing pale red.

Throok bellowed and looked over his crew. "Volunteers?" A couple hesitantly stepped forward. Throok nodded them to the front of the line just as the current fight finished. One minotaur had twisted another's arm up his back and held him pinned to the ground. They had minor flesh wounds from each other's horns.

I crossed my arms. "I assume people don't die in these things?"

"It's just a carnival game," Throok assured.

"We passed some groups playing dice and cards," said Milena. "You call this a carnival game?" She turned to the minotaur, her eyes level with his rock hard abs breathing in and out. "Never mind. I get it."

He beamed as Kasper was announced. "My proud people make up the Amethyst Circle."

Milena nodded along thoughtfully. "Are you their duke?"

"Minor circles have no duke. Even so, I'm far from a headman. I grew up with no formal title."

"Oh," said Milena. "Well, good for you. Amethyst is so cute."

Throok spat. "It is not cute."

"Sure it is! A light purple, almost pink at times. It's so pretty and sparkly."

The minotaur huffed a cloud of spittle. "Amethyst represents passion through temperance, solidarity, and protection from negative energy."

Milena shrugged. "Well, I think it's cute."

I chewed my lip as Kasper and his wrestling opponent

crashed into each other. The silvan circles were all based on aspects of nature. Juniper, bone, amethyst. Hell, even the fiends of the Obsidian March followed the naming convention. I would've thought a minotaur circle would go with something in a similar vein, like some kind of stout rock. Throok's insightful description was surprising; there was more to silvans than meets the eye. And now that I finally had an ally at my side that I trusted, I could dig for information.

"I just found out the satyrs run the High Circle. You're really marrying up."

"Tell me about it," agreed the minotaur.

"What does juniper represent?"

"Fertility." He smirked knowingly at me. "But health and life as well. Satyrs champion that which makes life worth living. Ceela embodies those qualities to their very essence."

We jumped out of the way as Kasper tossed the minotaur out of the ring. The biker hooked his hands on his hips. "Where's the other guy? I thought I was doing two at a time."

The crowd applauded. Plenty of snorts resounded, more volunteers eager to take him on now that he'd offered a two-on-one handicap. Throok nodded as a new pair of contestants entered the ring. A husband and wife team, it looked like, and the woman was beefier than the man.

"You're asking for it, Kasper," I called. He just smiled and cracked his knuckles to more applause. We watched the fight start before I continued. "What about the Circle of

Bone?"

Throook harrumphed. "You're inquiring about our mutual friend, Orpheus."

"He showed up in the Margins yesterday, somehow knowing where we were, and he was grumpy the whole way."

"He has no love for upirs, Cisco."

"Word travels fast. Anyway, those upirs fought off gnolls and a manticore with me."

"You fought a manticore and lived?"

I arched my brow. "Didn't hear about that part, huh?" I worked my jaw, deciding to voice my concern. "The point is that Orpheus was conveniently late to the party."

"That little surprises me," he said gruffly.

"And then we asked for healers when we got in, and he sent his personal dryads."

Throook's ears flicked. "You haven't seen the Amaranth Circle? That's unacceptable." He looked around as if he could right the indiscretion on the spot.

Kasper had been doing okay keeping the minotaur duo at bay, but the woman finally locked around his waist and tackled him to the ground. The crowd collectively "oofed."

Throook grunted approvingly. "The nymphs are experts at healing and protection. I'll ask the high king to personally assign the best in the kingdom." He snorted. "Fauns and their roundabout ways."

Kasper somehow rolled out of the pin. A blast of golden power fired the husband out of the pit, disqualifying him, but the blow had taken too much of his attention. The woman grabbed him in a sleeper hold.

"He's in for it now," boasted Throok. "Maura's an expert at chokes." He leaned into me. "Ask her husband."

"I wanna be a minotaur," said Milena dreamily.

"I like my neck, thanks," I said. "Plus, I don't think I can date a woman taller than me."

She turned to Throok. "They call that Cuban machismo."

I winked. "That's why you love me."

Blue energy bubbled around Maura's arms as she constricted Kasper's airways. The old man was in trouble, thrashing all four limbs. He sideswiped the minotaur with gold punches, but his tattoos weren't as versatile as my shadow magic. The scribe's spellcraft was ingrained in his skin, built for specific cases. He couldn't adjust his blows on the fly, and she had him at a dominant angle. Unable to force Maura off him, and with her strong enough to squeeze despite the defensive energies, the biker started to go limp. Kasper tapped out.

The crowd roared. Maura released Kasper and hopped up and down. Her husband ran into the pit to hug her, but she lifted him off his hooves and spun him around. I clapped along with Throok at the impressive show.

The old man stood on wobbly feet and Throok's crew converged into the ring, overwhelming him with congratulatory pats and shoves. Kasper was a hit with the minotaurs.

"That's the longest I've seen anyone in that headlock, and she's bested griffins!"

"Two at a time! What a bull of a man!"

The second one of them shoved a tankard of ale at him, I knew Kasper was in heaven. They asked about his tattoos, and a few minotaurs with ink traded stories.

"I like your friend," said Throok. "He'll fit in with us fine. Feel free to party with the Amethyst Circle and join the pit. It's about time I get going."

"I was gonna ask about that," commented Milena. "Don't you have a wedding to prep for?"

"They want me at the Table of Oak, even though I hold no rank. It's customary. But this is my wedding day, and I wasn't about to lose the chance to hang out with my boys. Cisco, I'll get you your king's healers. Until then, enjoy the folkmoot."

Throok congratulated Kasper and the other combatants before heading off. We joined the raucous fray and got our own tankards of ale, excited to finally be in some honest company.

Chapter 30

We enjoyed the next half hour with the minotaur crew. Silvans were the same as people. There was good and bad in all of them; your personal cocktail just depended on where you spent your time.

Minotaurs were a rough and boisterous lot, but they wore their hearts on their sleeves. There was no room for bootlicking or subterfuge. You always knew where you stood with a minotaur.

But trickery must've been in the air because I finally spotted Orpheus and his bodyguards emerging from the center of the yard. I made eye contact with Kasper and Milena and pointed to the contingent of fauns. Then I marched straight for them.

As I did, a troupe of horns sounded from a grand balcony above the veranda. An announcer called for attention. The ceremony was about to begin.

Man, Throok had really cut it close with his partying.

I ignored the announcements and forced through the

crowd as it bunched together, eventually closing on Orpheus.

"I thought you were supposed to be at the Oak Table," I said in greeting.

He clenched his teeth, displeased to see me. "Duty calls, even today."

I fell in line with the group of fauns as they marched the lawn. "About the healers you sent..."

"I trust they met your needs?"

My smile tightened. "They patched us up. I'm surprised to hear they weren't from the Amaranth Circle."

He gave me a peculiar eye. "It was after feastime. I thought it most efficient to send my personal people your way."

"I get that." Despite the smaller stature of the fauns, their goat legs had an impressive stride when they were so determined. I hurried to keep pace. "Was there any news on Milena's condition?"

He strode without his attention on me, like I was an inconvenience. "Condition?"

"The silvan blood. From Gemma's attack."

He sighed. "I warned you the mermaid would come. Did the dryads not check on her?"

"They did but I wanted to follow up. Did they mention anything unusual? Any expectations?"

"They reported nothing out of the ordinary. I'll have them talk to you. If you need further consultation, the Circle of Amaranth does good work."

"That's what everyone tells me."

I marched alongside him, wishing we'd just gone the official route in the first place. By this time we were on the outskirts of the crowd, with no signs of stopping. The fauns obviously had urgent business elsewhere.

"Is anything wrong?" I asked.

He scoffed. "Just the usual security concerns." Orpheus stopped and stood in my path. "There's no need to worry, Cisco. We're just staying on top of things. Enjoy the wedding." He spun on his hooves and hurried away.

I stood idly as Kasper and Milena caught up. "What was that about?" she asked.

I shook my head. "I think I just had my second faun brush-off of the day."

"Forget about that guy," grumbled Kasper. "The minotaurs will take care of us."

"That's a great idea," urged Milena. "You hear that?" The crowd cheered as the high king's court was announced. Milena straightened my tie and hooked her arm in mine. "Let's go to a wedding."

I contemplated the fauns disappearing in the distance and decided to rejoin the masses.

I hadn't noticed when exactly, but by the time we were thick in the crowd, the high king himself was giving a speech from the head of the veranda, going on about the time-honored traditions of the silvans, what a powerful people they were, how strong they were together, and how the heart of their dominion was the shining beacon of the Nether.

Ceela's father was a stately figure. Wide for a satyr, with

a short graying mane. His fur was dark gray more than black, mottled with bits of charcoal. His royal dress consisted of a flowing green-and-white robe that trailed into a cape. The golden crown resembled a branch of pine needles dotted with small cones, tightly fitted around his forehead.

High King Vesuvius introduced his court again, the dukes and their various circles: Clover, Cypress, Ivy, Thistle. Various silvans bedecked in ceremonial garb lined the stage, though I wasn't quick enough to tie all the races to their corresponding circles.

Notably absent was Orpheus himself, the Duke of Bone. His seat remained empty and the king glossed over his details. Which meant his security outing wasn't expected and was anything but routine.

"Today finds me with a heavy heart," announced King Vesuvius. "While I have complete faith in young Throok to guide and protect my daughter, it's never easy for a father to truly let go of their child. Not even one as exceptional as Ceela. She will rule the Table one day. Let me now introduce to you the man that will protect her with his life."

The crowd cheered as Throok strolled down the veranda steps. He wore the same high-quality leathers, but now had two green banners hanging over his shoulders and trailing behind him as he walked. He curved down the right staircase toward a little glade on the lawn under the veranda. The minotaur stopped in a circle beside one of two Stonehenge-looking pillars.

Horns blared four times in sequence, and then there was

silence. No music, no cheers, no speaking. The entire crowd knew this was the moment, and the anticipation was palpable.

"Blessed silvans of the circles and beyond," boomed Vesuvius, "I present to you the soul of the Juniper Circle, Principesse Ceelandra."

I clapped my hands in celebration but abruptly stopped upon realizing it was just me and Milena. A few silvans sent disapproving stares our way. Thankfully, the mock sun darkened like it was on a dimmer. Aside from our embarrassing faux pas, the only thing that broke the silence was a set of fluted instruments on the balcony above.

A solemn, almost sad, song played as Ceela rounded the veranda at the top of the left staircase. She was beautiful. Light-brown eyes, dainty horse ears with a large hoop on each. Her curly black hair was rolled into several buns on top and at the side on her head in the fanciest pony tail I'd ever seen. Her hair ended just above the start of her literal pony tail, likewise styled in a series of knots.

Ceela had powerful horse legs with a rich black coat that ended over white hooves. Her human half was much more dainty: a tiny waist and small chest, yet well toned. She wore a green sash across her upper arms and chest that left two trailing trains behind her. The deep green matched the colors of Throok and Vesuvius.

Once Ceela was on the grass, she blew kisses at the audience. The light exploded above us and the crowd finally cheered. I stubbornly crossed my arms after the last fiasco. The bride made her way beside her own pillar, opposite

Throok.

Satyrs generally stood a bit taller than fauns. Ceela was about five feet, which approached Milena's height. Still, she looked like a child beside the muscular minotaur. They faced each other and she put up her hands for him to hold. I thought it odd no one else was around them leading the ceremony, but of course the king himself stood on the veranda above.

"These two will be the pillars of the next generation," Vesuvius continued. "And like all pillars, they are stronger together."

Two centaurs trotted onto the stage hefting another length of stone. This one curved around, and I saw why as they set it atop both pillars, completing them into an arch.

"Let this symbol of their love forever stand on this lawn, so that everyone may be inspired by the everlasting courage and commitment they now share."

Several nymphs suddenly mobbed the stage, causing me to flinch in concern, but the crowd was delighted at their appearance. The naked ladies grabbed the trailing lengths of sashes and ran circles around the couple, forcing them together in a loose wrap.

"I'd like to get some of that treatment," murmured Kasper.

"You two are now bound," announced the king with great joy. "I bid you proceed with your new lives together."

Throok leaned down, lifted Ceela off her feet, and planted a big kiss on her. The nymphs giggled and crowded the couple with blessings.

While most eyes were on the stage, Orpheus discreetly snuck up the staircase. The high king backed away to share a concerned whisper. Then the duke retreated with the other heads of circle and took his chair.

"That's it?" asked Milena. "That's the whole ceremony?"

The crowd was moving up now, fighting for a word with the bride and groom. It did indeed appear they were now officially married.

"What are you complaining about?" asked Kasper. "This is the best kind of wedding. Light on the words, heavy on the party."

"They could've at least traded vows or something. What a gyp."

Kasper's eyes suddenly widened and I traced his gaze back to the head of the veranda. Instead of a king there was a woman, announced as Duchess Ariadne of the Amaranth Circle. The head of the nymphs, and she was appropriately beautiful. She appeared completely humanoid, as nymphs often are, though she wore some kind of sash or skirt around her waist and it was hard to make out with the veranda railing. But what Kasper and I and likely everybody else focused on were the most perfect breasts in the world.

The second thing I noticed was that she had aquamarine skin.

"It is time, my esteemed guests, for us to enjoy the fortune cake!" Ariadne waved and smiled like a Miss America model. "Remember, fate binds us all, but it's only the lucky few who grasp its design."

Nymphs flooded the lawn from behind us, where they

had obviously prepped. They passed out slices of cake to everyone with a pair of hands. I wasn't sure if Kasper even liked cake, but the old man wasn't about to refuse an offering from a naked lady. And despite their duchess, these nymphs didn't wear clothes of *any* sort, not even leaves.

I grabbed my dessert and took in the smell of spiced vanilla. The plate itself was a shaving of wood thin enough to bend but thick enough to provide support. A fluffy mini-cake sat atop a papery napkin. The frosting was white with orange glaze, and I suspected the recipe included alcohol.

"Don't judge me," said Milena, a white ring of sugar already coating her lips. "I'm eating with my hands."

No one had received forks or spoons or even sporks. It was just the way they did it in the Nether, and that was fine by me. We dug in.

"I got one!" shouted a woman. The crowd gleefully turned to a stairway as she revealed herself. A winged woman, like a harpy. "The coin of wealth!" She flapped up the steps holding the piece of gold high.

At the height of the veranda, the king and dukes and duchesses had receded to their chairs, all except for Ariadne. She accepted the harpy beside her, eyes glittering.

"The first brings good luck," she decreed. "An auspicious sign."

"Go... Go!" urged a group at the other steps. A hesitant young man, appearing human but with a lion head, was prodded up a few steps before he relented and waved his coin in the air. He trudged upwards and presented it to the duchess.

"The coin of death," she announced grimly. "It is not always undesirable, remember. It promises a fine end. Can any of us ask for more?"

"This is weird," said Kasper, munching on his cake, "but I'll go for a spin. Is there some kind of silvan slot machine around here?"

"Can't be," said Milena, taking a big bite of cake. "It's gotta—" She rushed her hand to her mouth and almost spit up the food. Instead she pulled out a single gold coin. It had been baked into the dessert. "What the...?"

We traded a heavy stare. Then the centaur woman beside me screamed, "Immortality!" She grabbed Milena's hand and pulled her through the crowd, parting before them. "She has the coin of immortality!"

The centaur pushed a frazzled Milena to the foot of the steps, where she boldly continued up on her own.

Chapter 31

We pushed forward, watching Milena step to the veranda.

"A human," whispered a voice behind me. "It's the only reason she was picked."

A juicy conversation followed. "You think the nymphs gave her the coin on purpose?"

"Of course. It's an obvious plant."

"A good one, though. She looks stunning in that dress."

"Yes, but those breasts are an obvious glamour."

I snickered. Silicone wasn't exactly magic, but it achieved the same ends.

"A human?" asked her companion. "Really?"

"Oh, honey, this is the biggest folkmoot of the year. Half of everything you see is a glamour of some sort."

Kasper frowned as he squished the remainder of his cake, turning up nothing but fingers full of frosting. "I never win anything," he griped.

I smirked. "Not even a wrestling match with a girl."

He stiffened. "For the record, she's a cow. And she's

twice my weight at least. And I was distracted by her husband."

"I'm hearing a lot of excuses, bro."

"And I didn't see you join the fighting."

I hiked a shoulder at his point. Maybe I would once I'd taken care of Milena. For now my concern was her being separated from us onstage.

Milena met the duchess, clasping both offered hands. The women peeked at each other's breasts and arched their backs like it was a competition. Honestly, Milena *stacked up* pretty well against what some might consider a sex goddess. Pun intended.

Duchess Ariadne held Milena's hand with the coin up high for all to see. "Now *this* is a surprise. Immortality for a *human*."

It was hard to make out, but I thought Orpheus narrowed his eyes at the announcement and watched Milena like a hawk, as if she had cheated. Then again, his animalistic features were tricky to read. It could've been nothing more than cold curiosity. Certainly the other dukes and duchesses and even the high king himself watched my girlfriend with rapt attention. The whole situation made me uncomfortable.

I absently finished my cake as we pushed ahead, cutting the distance to the veranda in case we needed to jump into action. The change of angle made it so we could only see the silvans standing at the veranda wall, cutting the royal court out of view. Ariadne introduced another coin winner. Fame. But I tuned it out when I spotted ink on my napkin.

I furrowed my brow. I wasn't sure what the napkin was made of, possibly a very fine cloth, but it was thin and disposable like something stuffed in a fast food bag. I flipped it over on the wood plate. Someone had written a message in fanciful script.

> *You are in danger. Meet me by the Wishing Tree at once. Come alone.*

I clenched my jaw and scanned the crowd. We'd changed our position since receiving the cakes. The nymph waitresses were all gone by now. I didn't even remember the face of the one who'd served me because, well, because I'm a red-blooded man. In case I need any more defense than that, many of the sprightly girls looked alike.

I studied the napkin. It bore no indication of who it was from. No signature or clue. I wasn't even sure what the Wishing Tree was. I turned backward, with hundreds of silvans facing me and the veranda, but not a single eye was on me. In the distance was a sparse grove of trees with only occasional passersby. It was opposite the wall with the waterfall.

I passed the note to Kasper. The group of winners stood beside the duchess. High King Vesuvius announced the recommencement of the folkmoot. Cheers rang out all around, and it was clear the ceremony was over.

Amid applause, Kasper handed the message back to me and leaned in. "What are we waiting for, then?"

I shook my head. "No. I'm not leaving Milena."

"Broham, that message sounds urgent."

The Duchess of Amaranth waved and said a blessing. There was a final round of applause and the winners scattered down the stairs.

I pulled Kasper toward her. "Listen, nobody's gonna protect Milena like we can. We need to stick together."

"Then let's grab her and go to the Wishing Tree."

"The note says to come alone."

His beard ruffled as he pouted. "Broham, you can't just ignore the warning. This place is full of silvan plots and trickery."

"Exactly, and for all I know this note is more of the same. What if it's a ploy to draw me away from her?" We strode toward the foot of the stairs, and I allowed a slight grin to pierce my gruff mask. "Besides, when are we *not* in danger?"

The biker chortled as a satyr child collected our plates. I made sure to keep my napkin, and that Kasper's was blank. I couldn't remember what had happened to Milena's plate.

While the ceremony was short, sweet, and anything but stuffy, it had drawn a crowd with devout attention. Now the lawn was quickly devolving into a party. A string quartet played fast-paced dance music. Silvans around us jumped, jigged, and scattered back to their games. The foot of the stairway was packed, but we shoved in.

I pulled Milena into a hug. She squeezed tight before sensing something was amiss. "What's wrong?"

Several nymphs with seashells on their lady bits crowded

around us. I eyed them and shook off the question. "Just happy to have you back."

Kasper peered at her closely. "Are you immortal now or what?"

One of the nymphs giggled. "No, silly. The fortune coins give glimpses into a winner's future."

"What does that mean?" I asked. "You're saying she can't die anytime soon?"

"So says the Duchess of Amaranth."

The crowd tugged us away. We chose to go with the flow for now.

"I won a spa treatment!" chimed Milena. "They're taking me right now. Youth and... what else? I just focused on the youth."

The young nymph smiled at her. "Amaranth enforces healing, protection, youth, and immortality."

"Yeah," nodded Milena. "Youth. Gimme some of that."

As we pulled away from the dense crowd, we approached the distant waterfall. The healing waters. And the hell was I letting Milena outta my sight.

"Hey cutie," started Kasper discreetly. "Someone told me I couldn't leave before seeing the Wishing Tree. You know where that is?"

"Of course," answered the nymph. "It's pretty but it's sooo boooring." She pointed at the grove I'd guessed at. Unfortunately, every step now took us farther away from it.

Which left me a choice.

I could leave my friends while I looked into the cryptic message. This was the obvious thing to do. The thing the note *wanted* me to do. I contemplated it but ultimately didn't trust my anonymous benefactor enough.

A safer option was to ignore the instructions, forget the coin of immortality, and skip the spa. We could stick together and investigate the tree, consequences be damned, even if it was likely to net us nothing.

Or I could pretend like the whole thing never happened. I never got the message or never saw it. We'd still be together, but instead of going on a possible wild goose chase, Milena would get the healing treatment she needed.

Because wasn't that precisely what we wanted? Why we were here? All day I'd been wondering why Orpheus hadn't sent the Amaranth Circle to heal Milena, and now we had that very opportunity. To be clear, I wasn't sure I liked the ominous-sounding coin of immortality and any possible baggage it brought, but if the greatest healers in the Nether were promising Milena she wouldn't die in the immediate future, I'd be stupid to brush that off.

The more I pondered it, the more I suspected Milena's slice of cake *had* been a plant. Maybe Throok had shoved my request through to get Milena her healers. The whole thing was a show to help out a friend in need. And if that was the case, the choice wasn't a choice at all.

I searched for familiar faces in the crowd. No minotaurs, but I spotted Orpheus in the vicinity. I slowed to intercept him. Instead, someone else intercepted us.

"Ho there, human friends."

We turned to the sight of High King Vesuvius himself, approaching with his throng. The nymphs escorting us dropped in unison, prostrating themselves in his presence. Kasper and I just stood tall, waiting, but Milena had the presence of mind to offer a bow.

"Formalities!" said the satyr monarch, lifting her hand and kissing it. He blinked at her strangely for a second, but his manners got the better of him. "You are the man that brought happiness to my daughter."

The high king looked even more impressive up close, in his later years but still carrying the build of a once-warrior. His mottled gray coat bore several war scars. The man's mere presence projected power. I straightened my jacket and took his firm grip in mine. He shook Kasper's hand after.

"It's nice to put faces to those causing such a stir at my party," he said. And to Kasper, "I hear you bested an opponent in the minotaur pit."

The old man puffed out his chest. "My count is two."

The king's eyes widened in admiration. "Admirable. It takes a rare satyr to attempt the same." Vesuvius turned to his short pant legs and curly shoe tips. "I see you have the best clothes in the kingdom."

I did my best not to snicker.

"Minotaurs are a proud people. I must confess I needed to get used to the idea of welcoming Throok into the family but, as always, Ceela knew best. Throok will do her right. I'm proud the groom was her choice instead of mine."

"Orpheus?" prodded Milena, who was probably a little hazy on the details.

Vesuvius sighed. "Yes, he had asked me for my blessing

and I granted it. The Circle of Bone is a historical giant. And think what the union could've been now that he is a duke! Alas, love hath a different heart."

Milena smiled. "It's nice that you came around."

"A good king listens to his people. It's not an easy job. Decisions are rarely as simple as right and wrong, but what is to the benefit of the kingdom." The satyr's tail whipped. "But let's not bore ourselves with politics. I needed to meet the wizard my daughter spoke so highly of."

"It really wasn't a big deal," I admitted. "Ceela's a strong girl. I have a feeling she would've gotten her way with or without me."

The high king erupted into bellowing laughter. His entourage and the prostrate nymphs laughed along. "How right you are, Cisco! But still, you did the Juniper Circle a great service, and no self-respecting satyr should find himself so indebted. Is there anything I can do for you?"

I put my arm around Milena and pushed her forward a step. "Now that you mention it, my girlfriend has been afflicted with silvan blood. Her prognosis isn't good."

His face went stoic. "This is the first I'm hearing of it. Come here, child."

The nymphs peeked up as the king laid a hand on her neck and frowned. "Yes, I thought I noticed something..."

"What is it?" asked Milena.

"Nothing immediately evident."

"The tainted blood is resistant to spellcraft," I explained. "She looks fine but might deteriorate fast."

He nodded. "Silvan blood isn't poison, but it is potent.

Human manipulation of the Intrinsics slicks off it. It's worse than salt water in that respect."

Wow. I'd known the black stuff was useless for blood magic, but I didn't see the extent of it. I wondered if Nether blood explained the magic resistance of some creatures down here. Though I'd dished plenty of hurt to plenty of them in the past.

"It's good you brought this to my attention," he said. "And lucky indeed the coin of immortality found her. Arise, my ladies." The nymphs all jumped to attention. "Apply your very best work to Lady Milena at once. I will not let such a beautiful flower wither in my dominion."

Chapter 32

High King Vesuvius and his entourage accompanied us to the healing waters. Instead of approaching the waterfall against the rock wall, we headed for a section of river downstream.

"By the way," I told the king, "I feel I need to come clean about a few things. We were attacked on the way here."

He nodded. "Orpheus reported as much to me. The Margins have been more volatile of late."

"Well, I don't know if it's related, but Milena was poisoned by a mermaid assassin." I frowned, deciding to stop short of mentioning the secret note. "I noticed Orpheus leading the security team around, and I just wanted to warn you in case something was compromised. He wasn't exactly straightforward with me."

Vesuvius grunted. "Tricksters are an unusual lot, always saying one thing and thinking another. But such suspicions should be cast aside. I'm sure you're aware many of our people say the same thing of wizards. Despite that, I broke with tradition and invited humans to this wedding. I wouldn't have it any other way."

I smiled drily, feeling I was given a political answer rather than a real explanation. The king must've picked up on my expression.

"Let me assure you, Cisco, that you couldn't be further from danger on these grounds." The hike ended as the nymphs settled into a gentle spring. "Ah, here we are. I'll check in with Orpheus, if it will ease your mind. Until then, I'm confident the Amaranth Circle will give Milena their finest work."

The nymphs all bowed again, some even dipping below the surface of the water, as the high king dismissed himself. Then the naiads grabbed Milena and started helping her out of her dress. She stopped them when they went for her corset and underwear.

"Watch it! A lady needs to leave something up to the imagination."

The nymphs seemed to have trouble with the concept, but they granted her concession. One woman giggled. "The full treatment for all of you."

Kasper's vest and shirt were already on the ground. "My kind of party."

"Free massage?" I wondered aloud, reviewing the numerous ladies on staff.

Milena butted her hand to my chest. "Sorry, player. Last night is all you're gonna get."

Kasper shrugged and cannonballed into the water. His elf shoes sat on the grass but he hadn't taken off his pants. It seemed out of character for him until I realized he didn't have underwear. He was being modest in front of Milena.

"You know," I said indignantly, hands on hips, "you really should be confident enough in our relationship to let a guy have a little fun."

A few very burly and very naked men showed up out of nowhere and pulled Milena into the stream.

"Wait a minute," I gasped. "You have male nymphs?!?"

"Yeah," moaned Milena. "That's the spot." She opened her eyes with a quizzical expression. "What? You're not telling me you don't have confidence in our relationship, are you?"

I worked my jaw as several nymphs held her in a back float as they massaged her from head to toe.

"Does anyone have a beer?" asked Kasper, who quickly had his request granted. He chilled in the stream while a single maiden gave him a back massage. It wasn't the full coin-of-immortality service, but it looked fun.

Kasper tossed a wet pile of pants to the grass.

"Are you naked down there?" I asked, incredulous.

"I don't make the rules, broham."

"You're getting a back rub!"

He shrugged. "It's how they do it down here."

I hissed, more than a little jealous that my companions were living it up. I didn't know when the magic started. It certainly didn't look like Milena was being examined by trained medical staff. I figured I'd just let this thing run its course while I stood guard. I briefly considered visiting the Wishing Tree, with Kasper and Milena safely tucked away, but decided it was too risky. For better or worse, we were sticking together.

"If it isn't my favorite wizard!"

I turned as the bride made her way to the edge of the stream with open arms. We hugged and kissed cheeks.

Several onlookers gathered to address the principesse, but Throok snorted and shooed them away. "Leave the principesse privacy with her special guests." Most scurried away immediately. The ones that lingered took the hint at the minotaur's glare.

Finally, a moment alone with the couple.

"It's good to see you," I told her. "You're beautiful, by the way."

"Gracious," she said excitedly. "So what do you think of the place?"

I shrugged. "It's all right, but I don't think the *Pan's Labyrinth* theme is wedding appropriate."

She slapped my shoulder just like Milena did. "The theme is the Harvest, silly!" The satyr princess smiled at my companions in the stream. "I'm surprised you're not getting the full treatment with them."

"Yeah, I'm... standing guard."

Ceela chuckled. "It's lucky she received the coin."

"It is, isn't it?" I winked.

Her brows furrowed. "What's that?"

"You know..." I exaggerated a gigantic wink. "Lucky to get the coin."

She frowned. "Is this some human custom?"

"Wait, that wasn't you guys?"

The princess adamantly shook her head. "I couldn't possibly interfere with Ariadne's moment. But it's not exactly luck, in the usual sense. Fortune is the result of fate, you know."

I nodded. Silvans.

"Oh," I remembered. "I was supposed to give you a gift. I left it—"

She threw her hand up. "Don't hurry into the gift exchange. Let it come naturally over the course of the night."

I blinked. "Is this not natural?"

"Just wait for it, Cisco. Otherwise I'll be afraid you'll skip out on me."

I grunted, not entirely catching her meaning.

"And I'm sorry for the late invitation," she said. "It took a while to convince my father to allow guests from outside the circles."

Interesting. Vesuvius had seemed to imply inviting me was his idea.

"Nobody cares about such nonsense," said Throok, swooping in and giving his bride a kiss. "Something tells me Cisco's the type of person to decide things at the last second anyway."

"Guilty as charged." I grinned, a stranger in a strange land but somehow surrounded by friends. I motioned the silvans away from the stream and lowered my voice. "Hey, did either of you write me a note with my cake? I got a warning that I was in danger."

They froze for a moment before laughing. "Really?"

asked Ceela. "It sounds like a practical joke. There unfortunately are a few among us who would delight in tormenting a human."

"Okay, but how safe are we? Gemma's the mermaid who attacked Milena. She's not gonna stop coming after me until I find her. Is there a mermaid contingent I can speak to?"

She pressed her lips together. "Mermaids run the Coral Circle. They don't sit at the Oak Table so they aren't in attendance."

I checked the stream, suddenly nervous. "So there's no way any mermaids are here?"

"I don't know of any."

"And to find Gemma I would need to speak with the Coral Circle?"

She shook her head. "It's not that simple. Each circle is controlled by a race, the royal line that formed it. And there's a rich tradition of closely-knit noble families, of course. It can seem like all races are confined to their own circles, but that's not the case. Some are more homogenous than others, but some are mixed, especially at the lower levels."

Throok grunted. "Even then, if you're speaking of the assassin, she'll belong to a secret society, not one of the official circles. The regular channels can't assist you."

I groaned. "So the kingdom doesn't know a lot about what happens outside it?"

"On and off," said Ceela. "What's troubling you?"

"Look, there's a deeper reason I'm here." I decided not to hold out on them. They had no reason to hurt me, and these were the two silvans in the world I trusted. "We've had strange rumblings topside. A killer sent by sisters in black. A push to out animists. Even some vampires doing dirty work outside the chain of command."

Ceela exchanged a puzzled look with her husband. "What are you talking about, Cisco?"

"There's someone in the Nether, a silvan or more likely a fiend, who has designs on Miami. They're playing around in my city and starting to piss me off. I figured if I was gonna get answers, I'd get them here."

Throok snarled. "Who are they?"

"Witches for a start. They cursed this man with a ritual. Snuffed out one of mine. They also consort with owls. I haven't been able pin down whether they're shape-shifters or not, but the owls are eerily intelligent. They have black feathers and acid blood."

The principesse frowned. "There are stories, of course, of witches consorting with owls, but acidic blood? A cabal of sisters in black? I know of no such fae."

"What about deep in the Margins?"

Ceela shook her head. "It would be known, Cisco. We carry the knowledge of countless long-lived generations. These are no Nether beings."

"They have to be somewhere." I gritted my teeth and scanned the distant grove, second-guessing losing my chance at answers.

"Orpheus is a trickster," spat Throok. "Perhaps he knows something of this."

"I wouldn't put it past him. He's been standoffish ever

since I arrived."

Ceela took a long breath. "You two, my favorite human and my favorite silvan, but neither will ever see Orpheus the way I do."

"He still loves you," grunted Throok. "That's all I need to know."

"I hate to bring this up," I said, "but people all over are whispering stuff about the deaths in his family."

Ceela blinked. "What stuff?"

"You know... Orpheus the lowly baron. His two brothers and father die, leaving him in charge of his circle."

"That's nonsense. The entire traveling party was wiped out except for one surviving centaur. I don't know what the Circle of Bone was up to deep in the Margins, but they were beset by a man-eater."

My eyes narrowed. "The same manticore that attacked me. I knew Orpheus was withholding something." She was momentarily taken aback by the information. "And what about the poisoning of his father? Word is he and Orpheus hated each other."

"That's unfair. Even humans must understand how family relationships can sour. Yes, Prospero never loved Orpheus as he loved the other two. That's why Prospero took his own life; his own poison, his own hand. He couldn't stand to live in a world without his two favorites, and couldn't bring himself to make amends with the one outcast."

I grumbled. The explanation made sense, in a way. It almost made me feel sorry for the duke. But there was still something I didn't like about him. "He looks creepy and wields a weapon made out of bone."

The principesse chuckled. "I don't blame either of you, after what happened. But you must understand the honor that drives fauns. The Circle of Bone appears cruel and grotesque on the surface, but as with everything else in faundom, it is a trick. Bone signifies death, but also support, and strength from within. Ever since joining the Table of Oak, Orpheus has proven he can be relied upon. He takes his charge seriously. You have nothing to fear from him."

Damn, it was hard to dispute Ceela when she came off all stately like that. Maybe there was something to the whole royal line after all. But if that was the case, it only muddied the waters I was wading in. I was miles away from finding any truths, mired only in gossip and rumor.

But for once, some good news was on the way. The medical staff approached from the stream.

Chapter 33

The team of nymphs was mostly women, and had expanded in size and variety since I'd last looked. Some were naked, but most had decorative flairs treading the line of decency. Sea shells, kelp, leaves, and sprigs. Kasper was still trying to figure out how it worked, and I didn't spoil it for him. The flourishes were part of their glamours, easily modified and removed. Still, even with the knowledge that they were illusions, the thorny vine covering a male nymph's junk made me squirm.

"Ah, here comes the medician," said Ceela.

The head nymph had aquamarine skin and was similarly equipped as the duchess, except she was much younger. I wondered at their relationship as we converged. She nodded to me but reported to Ceela.

"The blood is problematic, principesse."

"She's still not healed?" I asked.

"There are... complications."

"What kind of complications?"

Ceela placed a firm hand on my shoulder to calm me down. "What's her condition, Electra?"

The woman pouted. "She appears healthy on the surface, but she is indeed poisoned. The tainted blood is partly silvan in origin, but not entirely. Our normal methods are... encountering obstacles."

I ground my teeth as I checked the stream. Kasper was drinking a beer and getting some deep tissue work on his inner thigh. Milena still had a couple of attendants keeping her afloat. She was so relaxed she looked asleep in the water.

"They said she couldn't die," I insisted. "They said the coin of immortality... Will she live past tomorrow? An expert in pestilence told me that was it for her."

Electra offered a soothing smile. "I cannot say for certain whether or not she'll recover. We have attempted some purifications, but our most extreme treatments are being rebuffed. We threaten to worsen her condition."

I paced a few steps away and almost shouted a curse, but I stopped myself. I tried to placate my features and put on a mask of ease. For Milena, at least.

"How could this be?" asked Ceela.

"I don't know what to say, principesse. We can strengthen her body and ease her pain, but this form of blood magic is beyond us."

The satyr pressed her lips together in thought, but that wasn't good enough for me. I didn't mask my anger this time. "You guys are supposed to be the best healers in the Nether. What good are you?" It wasn't lost on me that I, too, specialized in blood magic yet could do nothing for

Milena's underlying condition.

The medician swallowed uncomfortably. "The best in the kingdom, yes. And I am relaying all that I know."

"It's okay," soothed Ceela. "No one's blaming you."

Throok crossed his arms and snorted in the background. Milena coughed once, almost stirring from her slumber. A few more nymphs crowded her. Kasper, oblivious, had his drink refilled while being hand-fed from a plate of picked grapes.

This whole thing was suddenly feeling like a waste of precious time. *Why did I think we could enjoy a wedding together for a few hours? We were spending leisure time with high society, surrounded by impeccable connections—fortune had even favored us with the coin of immortality. And for what? A few more hours.*

"Maybe..." started Ceela, "maybe the Amaranth Circle are the best healers in the kingdom, but not the entire Nether."

Electra was almost offended by the assertion. Ceela hurried to explain.

"I simply mean, there are masters of poison and masters of blood. I know of a queen who is master of both."

The blue nymph's eyes fluttered. "Principesse, you can't mean... She can't possibly—"

"Cure the woman?" asked the satyr pointedly. "She has the power."

"That may be, but she would just as likely kill the human. She has no love for them."

"Stop," I said brusquely. "We're not doing this. I want to

know who you're talking about right now."

Ceela smiled at my ornery demand. "Of course. It's just an idea, and it's admittedly a long shot, but a gorgon wanders the Margins."

"A gorgon. Like Medusa?"

She smirked. "You could say that."

My brow furrowed. "She's supposed to be dead. And besides that, wouldn't she just turn Milena to stone?"

Ceela chuckled. "You humans shouldn't believe every word of those legends. I thought wizards knew better. Perseus didn't behead Medusa, he bedded her."

My eyes were plastered open. "So the story of turning people to stone with a head in a bag is bogus?"

"It was an enchanted shield with her likeness. Gorgons are collectors, of a sort. They deal in relics. They likely inspired your stories of dragons hoarding treasure."

Electra took over. "The pertinent point is their healing ability. The principesse is correct: Gorgons know blood, and they know poison. They can rot away your insides or spring Pegasus to life. But it's too dangerous. Gorgons are not mere silvans or fiends. They aren't traders of relics or skilled medicians. They're closer to the Fates, touched by the gods. Human men look upon satyrs and fauns and nymphs with awe, they beseech them for blessings and offer worship, but silvans aren't gods." The woman took a heavy breath. "I cannot say the same for gorgons."

I scoffed at the face of it. Reverence in the presence of power was one thing, but I didn't put much stock in the various gods. Animists sourced their magic through many spirits that many believed to be divine. Over the years I'd learned terms like god and demon and even silvan and fiend were useless. We were what we were, and I wasn't about to be stymied from saving Milena because of a label.

"Tell me how I can find her," I said.

"It will be a trek," replied Ceela, "and the gorgon won't enter our kingdom. You'd need to take Milena with you."

"The high king would not approve of such an action," murmured the medician. "It risks indebting the Juniper Circle and the entire Table."

"This has nothing to do with you," I contested. "I'll keep you silvans out of it. This is about me and Milena."

"The humans would be venturing to their deaths."

"Again," I said, "that's on me."

Throok's nose ring rattled at his snort. "She isn't wrong, Cisco. Gorgons only act to achieve their own ends. They don't help you, you help *them*." He grunted. "I really *hate* gorgons."

"I get it, guys. But you two were willing to do anything it took for love, and so am I." My eyes drifted to Milena relaxing in the stream. "I'm not letting her die without a fight."

"It's settled then," announced Ceela with a rush of nervous excitement. "And I'll help you on your way."

I turned to them appreciatively. "You don't need to come with me."

"We can't," said Throok. "It brings ill-luck for us to abandon the folkmoot."

"Besides nullifying the wedding," said Ceela. "I'm afraid

you're on your own, Cisco. But I might be able to help you with the gorgon. Give me an hour."

The principesse turned back to the castle and left with her new groom. The crowd that had gathered in the distance went to follow them.

Electra swallowed uncomfortably. "An hour's not a lot of time, but we'll do our best to fortify Milena until then. If fortune favors her immortal for the time being, it is our honor to comply."

I thanked her as the nymphs returned to the stream.

I stood by myself a minute, digesting the events. The silvan healers couldn't help, but they did discover the blood Gemma had used wasn't silvan. Which explained the vial. The silvans also came up with a promising lead, albeit a dangerous one. Milena was still on the clock but there was a solution in sight. And if I needed to stop messing around with garden-variety entities and get a demigod on my side, so be it.

Passersby kept a healthy distance, curiosity giving in to peeks. They didn't know the details of our pressing business, but humans in the kingdom were notable enough. I didn't see any familiar faces though: Baron Ludwig, Lady Fenn, Eden, not even a stray angel. As I watched a passing faun, I contemplated Ceela's words about Orpheus.

There was a lot to distrust about the duke, and still she thought highly of him. Despite her youth, she didn't strike me as gullible. Quite the opposite actually. It made me consider bringing Orpheus into this plan.

But I just couldn't get there yet.

I wandered to the water's edge and crouched beside Kasper being serviced by a pair of women. "Hate to be the bearer of bad news, bro, but the festivities are reaching an end. At least for us."

The tattooed biker opened his eyes and spit out a half-eaten grape, tongue purplish-red. "What?" The sudden exclamation startled the nymph feeding him. She lowered her head and backed away in the water. "Milena's getting the help she needs. This is exactly where we should be."

The other nymph was sitting behind him, squishing his cheeks in and out as part of some newfangled face massage. My eyes strayed to the departing nymph as she turned, a bit of side boob covered by an autumn leaf, and then wet red hair plastered to her butt.

"I know this place seems like heaven, but it doesn't have all the answers. Milena's still in trouble, and the only way to save her is to quest back into the Margins."

Kasper snorted and coughed at the same time. He shook away the hands prying at his face and cleared his throat. "Well, that's one way to kill the mood."

I noticed the faun nearing the stream, still gawking. Milena was in her sexy corset and underwear, for which I'd need to thank Beaumont later, but apparently some were taking it for a show. The pack of nymphs around her was thicker than before. I caught the nymph that had been feeding Kasper whispering to another in a masquerade mask.

"The leaves," I murmured, catching sight of the lithe girl's breast coverings. "She's a dryad." I stood up, realizing she looked eerily similar to one that had visited our room. "Kasper, I think we have a—"

As I approached Milena's group, my gaze immediately darted to the mysterious masked woman. Strange flair for a not-so-demure nymph in the water. It was tough to see the rest of the girl's body through the gaggle, but she was more voluptuous than the sprightly girls. And her face may have been hidden, but her neck had darkened skin like someone had choked her out with burning blood magic.

I whipped up my jacket and drew the pistol. The gun barked.

Panic exploded from the gaggle of nymphs. Amid their fearful scramble, my gun stayed trained on my target, waiting for another shot.

"Cisco!" warned Kasper.

My hands were knocked down and the second shot went off into the ground. I leapt backward as a knife whizzed by my face.

The faun wasn't just a nosy onlooker, the dryad was in on it, and the masked nymph was really a mermaid. The coin of immortality was a setup.

Chapter 34

The nymphs screamed and scattered. Several huddled protectively around Electra and whisked her away. The faun came forward with a knife. I checked my hand. He'd cut me open, but I hadn't dropped the pistol.

"No way," I remarked in disbelief. "Did you really just bring a knife to a gun fight?"

He flipped the blade in his grip and lunged. I popped him with a couple of rounds and rolled aside in the grass. The silvan turned on me and growled. He sported a couple of new holes, but Trinh's pistol didn't have the stopping power of my MP7.

"Milena, get up! Kasper!"

The old man was already on his feet and pushing to the shallows. But he coughed again and gurgled, drooling dark-red ooze that stained the water.

"Broham..."

Kasper collapsed.

I turned the gun on the nymph at his side. "What did

you do?"

She sobbed hysterically. "I don't know!"

The blood in the water was opaque and gooey, with some chunks too. The grapes had been poisoned. It was the dryad. I lowered the gun and yelled, "Fix him." Before I could turn to Milena, the faun attacked me again.

Enough Mister Nice Guy. The Nether always had plenty of shadow to work with, but one thing I'd been too distracted to notice was that this brightly lit cavern had a whole ceiling of light sources coming down from multiple angles. It was almost as bad as twilight in here, which limited my options in the open.

But it didn't much matter 'cause I was itching for a fight.

The faun's knife came down on my armor tattoo. He retained his grip, but I pounded him in the chest with a bit of darkness. He stumbled as I wiped my left hand over my bloody arm and grabbed him by a curved horn. Magic immediately sizzled at the contact, but my blood protected me. I stomped my boot onto his hand, pinning the knife to the ground.

Weight hit my back and I almost toppled. Instead I used my grip on the faun to brace myself. The damned dryad was hanging on me, clawing at my eyes. But the real trick was her whisper. Her lips tickled my ear as she spoke, and my mind swayed. My muscles went lax and I began to lower to the ground.

I squeezed the grip of the pistol, fighting the lethargy. I pointed it backward at my waist and squeezed off two shots. The point-blank scream was music to my ears. The girl convulsed and kicked my back, and I was back in the zone. I lifted the gun past my ear and put a bullet into her forehead.

Even with my toughened body, the report made my ear ring. As the nymph fell away, I shook my head and absorbed a couple of awkward blows from the faun. I still pinned his arm with my boot, and he was trying to punch me loose. Good thing he wasn't a lefty. I jammed the gun into his mouth and pulled the trigger.

It clicked empty.

The faun grinned hungrily. "So much for the gun fight." He rammed his horns forward. With my arm keeping control, I shoved most of the blow aside. Unfortunately, I couldn't also use my arm to block. He shifted my center of balance and heaved me off his knife. I fell back. He swiped toward me. My hand came up from the ground, sawed-off aimed at his heart.

"You were saying?"

Fireshot ripped open his chest. The silvan thudded into a ruined heap beside me, his insides still searing.

I hopped to my feet powered by adrenaline. Then I nearly collapsed, lightheaded. But I was barely hurt, and Kasper was coughing out a lung on the river bank. Besides his attending nymph, who appeared to be offering true assistance, the others had fled. Milena was gone. A scarlet tail flashed as it receded up the river.

"Be there in a minute, broham," gagged the biker. "Go get her."

My boots twisted in the grass and launched in pursuit.

The stream wasn't very deep and the current was against

her, but there was no way I could outrun a swimming mermaid on foot. I found some spots to dive forward through shadow, though the opportunity didn't present itself enough. After over a minute of hauling ass in a suit, I skidded as the river widened at the foot of the waterfall.

Damn. The water was deeper here. If they were submerged, I couldn't see them through the white foam. I pulled the Intrinsics into my eyes, scanning for traces of magical energy. This was fresh water and didn't innately disturb my spellcraft. It still occluded my senses though.

I scrambled on the edge of the water, debating diving in. But a piece of magic caught my eye several yards from the embankment. I hurried to the rock wall, under the deafening sound of falling water, and picked up a gold coin. The coin of immortality. She'd dropped it here.

"Clever girl."

Gemma couldn't escape from here. This was a waterfall, with no way to climb up. So she'd swum to the end of the water and taken Milena onto land, following the wall. I pocketed the gold piece as horns blared in the distance.

This time they weren't ceremonial. The silvans were mustering the troops.

I followed the rock wall, searching the crevices for possible means of escape. First and foremost, though, I relied on speed. Gemma may have had a head start, but she couldn't drag a hostage over land faster than I could run. If she was ahead of me, I'd overtake her.

Even with the folkmoot going down, the silvans mobilized fast. A troop of fauns raced across the lawn. For now they seemed to be rushing to the river. My last-known position. I pressed ahead.

Were the fauns looking for Gemma or were they looking for me? Either way, I wasn't about to stop and file a report. This had Orpheus written all over it. A trickster, with fauns and dryads in his employ. I didn't understand how Ceela had such a blind spot for him, but it probably had to do with his service to the kingdom.

That was it for me. I'd had it with plots and politics. This was about them messing with my girl. I ran for another couple of minutes, the castle in view in the distance. I'd barely made any headway. This chamber of the Nether was so large it might take hours to do a full lap.

Which meant I was behind the eight ball. Gemma had mapped this place out beforehand, coming in with a plan and an escape route. I was running blind.

Noises ahead came at me fast. I shoved into a nook in the cavern wall and dipped into the shadows. Thirty seconds later, two fauns and a minotaur with drawn swords rushed by.

They were good. Immediately checking the perimeter, starting on the opposite end. With additional troops coming up the river, they were giving me the squeeze. Well, at least that's what their plan was.

Now I knew why they hated wizards so much.

I let them fade behind me, knowing I had maybe a minute or two before they realized I'd slipped them. Nothing to do but rush forward.

But as I ran, a thought nagged me. If Gemma was

running ahead with Milena in tow, the fauns would've intercepted them.

I'd missed something.

Maybe I'd sprinted by a secret path in the wall without seeing it. Maybe Gemma had purposely tossed the coin to throw me off and run the other way. I glanced around, still pressing ahead, feeling the weight of the possibilities slowing me down. The Nether was wild, winding, and almost impossible to decipher. I was starting to question myself. Milena could be anywhere.

And through it all, my thoughts crept to darker places, to darker plots. Maybe Gemma and Milena were ahead of me and the guards had allowed them to pass. Maybe this plot ran deeper than I imagined. I'd left Kasper behind, coughing up blood, and had no idea if he was safe.

I ran another minute, knowing it was useless. I'd lost her. I'd fucking lost her when she'd been right next to me. I stumbled forward, out of breath, and ducked behind foliage as I approached a bushy glade. There was a break in the wall. Finally, this chamber had an exit.

Except twenty guards stood at high alert facing the inside with weapons drawn. Minotaurs, fauns, satyrs, and centaurs, loaded for bear. They were expecting an escape attempt and were well defended against one. There was no way I could get through them quietly or by force. Not that many trained combatants at once.

At this point, Gemma was at least five or ten minutes ahead of me. By the time I figured out a way to get through the gate, even if it was possible to fight my way through, I would never be able to find them. And all that assumed she'd gone this direction to begin with.

But the contingent was too varied for me to think this was anything but a good sign. Gemma couldn't have bought them all off. Even Orpheus, running security for the Circle of Bone, didn't have sway over all of them, did he?

I sunk to the ground, losing hope. I had truly lost her.

Idle desperation taking over, I scanned the grounds, hoping Gemma had been rebuffed at the exit and detoured inward. My gaze settled on the grove of trees some ways down.

The Wishing Tree.

I didn't know who'd sent the note, but someone had known I was in danger. If they knew about the assassin, maybe they knew where she was going or who would harbor her.

It was a long shot, a risky one that wasted valuable minutes, but I didn't have any other plays.

Besides, the trio of guards that had sprinted past me were now doubling back. I couldn't stay here.

I weaved through the shadow from bush to bush, avoiding the attention of the guards while keeping a wish on my lips.

Chapter 35

Trees of various colors dotted the grove, spaced apart at even intervals with a well-maintained lawn between. It didn't leave a lot of room for hiding so I stuck close to each tree's trunk before moving to the next.

Bright pinks, purples, and oranges caught my eye first. As I moved closer I saw beyond the forest *and* the trees. Dozens of small sticks draped with paper, like kites, hung from one stately tree. This was a good enough marker in the absence of signposts.

The tree itself was unremarkable: a thick, patchwork trunk; long green leaves; and batches of cherries. While it wasn't nearly the most impressive specimen in the grove, the ceremonial decorations proved it held a mystical place in the hearts of the silvans.

I closed quickly, hugging the rough trunk and checking the perimeter. I was undiscovered. A nearby batch of black cherries appeared plump and luscious. I reached up and turned an orange paper hanging among them, reading the handwritten words "Forever Love." I spun to take them all in, spanning the colors of the rainbow, some out of reach caught in the branches, some hanging by string, some littering the shaded grass. Innumerable wishes made into physical form.

I guess I knew how the tree got its name.

My boot kicked over a thin clay pot among the roots, unstoppering it and spilling a clear liquid. I crouched and picked it up, saving some of the substance. I took it to my nose and smelled. Odorless. A few other offerings littered the base of the tree. A wood figurine, a paper flower. I closed the bottle and stepped more carefully, uncomfortable with treading on the hopes and dreams of others.

Meanwhile, my hopes and dreams were quickly dashing away. I'd missed my secret meeting. Whoever had written my note was long gone.

I straightened behind the tree trunk as silvans shouted in the distance. They were branching out, searching the grounds. With any luck they'd capture Gemma. While I was off the beaten path, so to speak, it wasn't a great place to stay out of sight. My best bet was to leave silvan influence or find a place with better cover. Maybe try to get word to Ceela.

As I peeked around the tree, my eyes strayed from the horizon to a mound of earth under the Wishing Tree. A pentagram was scraped around it, marring the perfect lawn. Signs of spellcraft.

With the guards snooping elsewhere, I inched away from the trunk and approached the mound. The pentagram was sloppy, traced in haste and without a reinforcing circle. I kneeled beside the ritual symbol. No wax or signs of candles or fires dotted the points of the star.

On the other hand, the amount of blood was staggering. Scarlet soaked the dirt and spotted the grass, messy and incomplete and overwhelming. This was amateur blood craft.

I leaned over the mound and scanned for Intrinsics. No strong traces. Not only that, there wasn't evidence of chalks or powders or bones.

This wasn't a ritual, this was bait. A sign—

A warning.

I suddenly realized the significance of a bloody mound of dirt. Something—or someone—was buried here.

"Milena!"

Confident there was nothing here that could harm me but uncaring for my safety all the same, I clawed my fingers into the soft dirt and frantically dug it away.

This wasn't genuine spellcraft. Gemma had done this to get my attention. If she'd hurt Milena I was going to annihilate her entire world.

Voices called in the distance. I was too exposed here but couldn't stop digging. I forced the soil away, desperate to find out if Milena was all right. I moved forward, straddling the mound and using both hands at once to shovel large chunks of earth away.

My fingertips caught on something. Hair. It was brown. I gasped audibly and dug at the dirt around the head. That mermaid bitch. She'd decapitated her and used the pentagram and blood to taunt me. She—

I stuttered as I brushed the soil away. The hair was too short. This was all wrong. In the face of hurried footfalls and shouts converging on me, I grabbed the head with both hands and heaved it up from the earth.

I was holding a dog head by its shaggy mane. It had been buried face down, snout scrunched deep, lifeless tongue lolling over menacing teeth.

Bait was right. This was no ordinary dog.

An arrow punched my shoulder, nearly knocking me off my feet. I vanished into shadow as two more projectiles whizzed through, one embedding into the rough trunk of the Wishing Tree.

"Surround him!" ordered the female faun who'd fired first.

I'd seen these bodyguards before, only it wasn't just them. Various silvan guards, mostly fauns and minotaurs, circled me. Swords, axes, and bows pointed my way, but all stood at a distance. At the ready but not advancing. I grimaced, waiting in the shadow of the Wishing Tree.

"You," came the nasally voice of Orpheus, "have a death wish, shadow charmer." The Duke of Bone broke through the line of guards.

I materialized with a grimace, dropping the dog head and checking the arrow in my shoulder. It hung limply, having barely broken my zombified skin. I made a show of tossing it to the ground as if it didn't hurt in the slightest. It did, though, and I wouldn't get that lucky with all of them.

"Necromancy," spat a nameless minotaur.

My hands were covered in dirt and blood, the latter mostly mine from the knife wound.

"No," I said, "I—"

"That's the head of the cerberus," piped one of the faun archers. The bodyguard who'd shown us to our room, Hera.

I swallowed. What was going on here? The only time I'd seen a three-headed dog was at the guard post with the minotaur the night before.

Orpheus snarled silently. "You were the one who took out my guards."

"Your who?"

One of the bull-men on the line growled in fury. "You dare kill a minotaur..."

I searched the eyes of the hostile guards. Not a friendly one in sight. Seven of them and Orpheus. It would be difficult but I had shadow. I could get out of here.

Except more soldiers were on the way. The prey was already in the trap. They were just coming to recover me.

"I saw them," I explained with a cool head. "Last night. That was the only time. I killed no one."

"You killed a faun and a dryad," spat another guard.

I rolled my eyes. "At the river. They attacked me."

"The nymphs claim you fired first."

Orpheus sneered and put his hand up for silence. Several reinforcements arrived, dashing my chances of escape. The Duke of Bone paced within the circle of guards and glowered at our surroundings. He reached up into the tree, picked a ripe cherry overhead, and sniffed it.

Seeing the picked fruit, I immediately connected the

dots. These were what Kasper had been eating. With their round shape and purplish color, I'd mistaken them for grapes.

The faun strolled to the base of the tree and hefted the clay pot, removing the stopper and taking a whiff.

"Night willow. You poisoned your own ally."

I scoffed. Holy shit. I blinked at my accusers, scrambling for an explanation of what was happening. Throok joined his compatriots and came to the forefront. I looked at him wordlessly.

"Was it a deflection?" asked Orpheus. "Fake a poisoning to give you an excuse to go on a rampage?"

"No. I didn't do that. Why would I?"

The duke turned to the groom. "He killed a minotaur."

Throok snorted loudly, shooting hot breath from his nose. He was pissed.

"It wasn't me. I swear."

"We caught you literally red-handed," barked Orpheus. "You still want to play coy? I advised the principesse against inviting the wizard. I warned you, Throok."

"It was you!" I growled. "You sent the dryads to me last night instead of getting us healers. You were the one conspicuously absent during the ceremony. Instead of sitting with the other nobles, you stepped out with your team and murdered the minotaur and cerberus."

Orpheus shook his head. "You fool, I was called away to investigate the dastardly act."

"Then it's your word against mine."

He snorted back hysterical laughter. "No right-minded

silvan will believe a human wizard over me."

Throok glanced between me and Orpheus. It hurt to see it, but even he wasn't sure what to believe.

"But the faun at the river," I protested. "The dryad with the poisoned cherries. They're tied to the Circle of Bone..."

Orpheus frowned. "You know nothing of silvan circles, human. The dryad and faun weren't mine."

I blinked. Instead of a harried denial, he'd spoken with cool composure. A statement of fact that was accepted by every one of the growing crowd of silvans holding a weapon.

And I remembered Ceela's words about how silvan circles weren't completely homogenous. Fauns weren't automatically attributed to Bone.

"What circles were they in?" I asked.

The duke sighed gruffly, wary to take part in a charade but answering all the same. "The nymph was Amaranth and the faun Juniper."

It was so random. And just like the clump of guards at the gate, it was too random to be coordinated. No, this wasn't a huge conspiracy, it was the act of an assassin and a few rogue contacts.

And I started to understand. The whole twisted thing.

It was obvious that this, right here, was exactly what Gemma had wanted. I didn't know why she'd killed the guards. Perhaps it was the only way she could get in. Or maybe it was the one part of her plan that went wrong. But they went missing and raised the suspicion of Orpheus, who was called out during the ceremony.

Then Gemma somehow made sure Milena received the

coin of immortality. Maybe her dryad from the Amaranth Circle had set it up. That achieved the objective of separating me from Milena and getting her into the water, part of the mermaid's easy escape route.

At the same time, Gemma also sent me the warning note to further pull me away from Milena. I would go one way while she went the other, and as icing on the cake, the site at the Wishing Tree expertly framed me for the murders of the two dead guards.

Gemma timed this move in conjunction with the ceremony, when everyone's attention was on the bride and groom. Nobody would see her fake magic circle, not until I'd been at the scene, essentially staking claim to it.

Except there had been another crink in the assassin's plan. Turns out, I was smart enough not to immediately blunder toward the Wishing Tree. I'd made the right choice not to play along, to ignore the note and stick to Milena. Only it didn't matter anyway. Sure, Gemma's plan blew up. The faun and dryad were outed and killed. But she'd still gotten away in the end. And I was still caught holding the head of the dead cerberus beside a good approximation of a blood ritual.

I put my hands in the air and spoke calmly. "This is ridiculous, guys. I couldn't have done it." My eyes lit up. "I have the note."

I reached in my pocket and the bowstrings tightened.

"Hold," growled Throok.

Orpheus glared at him, making me think the minotaur didn't have the proper authority to give such an order. Still, few silvans would so hastily ignore the desires of the Juniper principesse's new husband.

I nodded thanks to my friend and slowly slipped the napkin from my pocket.

Orpheus stomped over and snatched it from me. "It's blank."

My jaw dropped as he presented both sides to the crowd.

"More wizard tricks," he spat.

"No. I mentioned it to Ceela and Throok."

Orpheus raised his eyebrows and turned to the minotaur.

Throok frowned and grumbled, "You never actually showed us the message, Cisco."

I swallowed. That was true. And even if I'd tried, I had a feeling it would've already expired. Gemma had really covered all traces of her intervention. And now that I'd killed her two cohorts, there was nobody left to point the finger at her.

The duke used his heightened senses to carefully sniff the napkin. "Hmm. Whisper Bloom."

"What is that?" I asked.

"Spies use it to send secret messages that fade away." He grunted and canted his head. "This proves nothing."

"Come on!" I bellowed. "It proves I was set up. Gemma did this. She did the whole thing." I pointed at the burial mound. "I know you can't tell at first glance, but no self-respecting necromancer would be this sloppy. There's not even spellcraft here." I huffed. "And plenty of people saw me at the party. I'm guessing the guards disappeared around the time I was at the refreshments table, right when Gemma was sneaking in. And I wouldn't hurt Kasper."

Orpheus scowled. "He'll live. It gives you convenient cover."

"Because it's true." I splayed my hands to the air. "And what about Milena? This whole thing was about protecting her. She's the key to this, and she's missing. Why? Because Gemma got to her again."

I stared at the ranks of inconsolable silvans, all hungry for blood. The open question of the day was who was the one that was gonna do the bleeding?

Chapter 36

"I think we should hear him out," concluded Throok. "He may be a human, and he may be a wizard, but he's Cisco. I've only known him to be honorable."

Orpheus scoffed. "For all of five seconds." He put his hands on his furred hips. "But I agree the circumstances are suspicious."

The minotaur frowned and turned to his companions from the minotaur pit. "Come with me."

They marched a short way to the guarded gate I'd previously passed. I knew this because Orpheus and his fauns marched me right along with them. Under heavy guard, of course. Throok called the line of troops and a minotaur hurried to stand at attention before him.

Throok got right in his face. "How long have you been here?"

The guard shook at his tone. "Since the morning, sir."

"Did you at any time abandon your post?"

"No, on my honor."

Throok snorted. "Could anyone have come through the gate?"

The soldier looked at all of us before returning confident eyes back to Throok. "It's not possible in the slightest. Our orders are no ins or outs for the duration of the folkmoot."

Throok spoke further words in private. He dismissed the guard and returned to our group. "If he swears on his honor that none have passed, then none have passed."

Orpheus snickered at the minotaur's honor and questioned his own people. He asked a few, separately from each other, and dug for details. It seemed a legitimate attempt at weeding out subterfuge. Afterward, he came to the same conclusion as Throok.

"If this *was* the work of Gemma, she didn't use this gate to enter or exit."

"Well, we know that," I said. "She came in the passage we used last night on the other end of the castle, right? Where the minotaur and cerberus were stationed."

"If your theory holds up." The faun worked his jaw, obviously troubled. "We'll sort this out in the castle."

My protest died before I could formulate the words. Exiting the silvan border here did me little good if Gemma hadn't come this way. Then again, exiting here would at least get me out of silvan influence. But that would leave Kasper behind.

The entire contingent started back toward the folkmoot. Stubbornly defiant to the end, I stood my ground. The faun bodyguards were pretty forceful about shoving me with them. When I still didn't comply they grabbed me tight. I yanked my shoulder free of one faun's grip. He readied a backhand but Orpheus butted in.

"Enough!"

"We should put him in irons," suggested the soldier.

"I'm a guest here," I protested. "I won't let you get them on me."

He narrowed his eyes. It was a sticking point bound to lead to a skirmish, but I couldn't risk it. Cold iron negated my spellcraft. If I was bound I wouldn't be able to enter the shadow. It was too much of a disadvantage around too many people I didn't trust.

Orpheus considered me a long moment and finally scowled. "No irons. If he comes peaceably. Does that work for you, wizard?"

"I'll take what I can get. I wanna get to the bottom of this as much as you do."

He chortled. "We'll see."

We began the march, and Throok fell in line with him. "Thank you, Orpheus."

"I didn't do it for you. Or for the wizard. As her personal guest, the principesse asked me to extend him every courtesy of the kingdom. It's utter folly, but I'll do it for her."

Throok nodded but his eyes flashed anger. Unspoken in their exchange was the fact that Orpheus still loved Ceela. The duke, ever resentful, was making sure to stick it to the minotaur even while being helpful.

Throok trudged to my side, grumpy nature returning. "My people are with Kasper. I figured he could use some friendly faces."

"Thanks for that."

He sighed. "Is there anything you're not telling us, Cisco?"

Great. Even my friend had doubts. "Just that Gemma set me up. Look, I can't stay here long. I need to get out there after them. I need to save Milena."

The minotaur was quiet a moment as he stared ahead and came to a decision. "How can I help?"

"Ceela might open some doors. Also, I need to know how Gemma got out of here."

"On it."

His contingent of minotaurs broke away and hurried ahead. My relief at his speedy assistance slowly transformed to worry. Because now my allies were gone. I was alone with Orpheus and his men. For all I knew, the few minotaurs here were Circle of Bone troops.

My entourage kept a steady but slow pace, mostly because we kept half our attention on each other, making sure nobody suddenly made a move. Despite the throng of partygoers in the distance, this was a far cry from a fanciful Nether wedding.

It did get me wondering, though. While currently vulnerable to the Circle of Bone, I didn't think this was the trickster's style. Sending the manticore that had killed his brothers after me? Sure. Framing me for murder? Definitely. Once he had me in custody, though, I didn't think I'd wind up Epsteined. Especially when he hadn't forced the issue of the cuffs.

Thinking further on it, the duke had been unusually understanding, considering how the situation appeared. The silvans caught me in the middle of a cerberus blood ritual and were still willing to hear me out. That had to count for something. Orpheus was even the one who'd detected the substance used to write the secret note. He seemed genuinely in the dark about this.

I grunted and turned to study him.

"What is it, wizard?" he hissed, cheeks twitching in annoyance.

"This really isn't you, is it?"

"This mockery of a plan? Of course not. It has holes all over it."

I nodded. I didn't doubt enough supporting evidence would emerge to clear my name. Then again I didn't think the silvan kingdom charging me for murder was the ultimate goal. This was all a deflection, a way to keep me busy while Gemma escaped. For that purpose, it was hard to deny her trap had been wildly effective.

I leaned toward the duke so our conversation would remain private. "Do you know anything about the manticore that attacked me?"

He snickered dismissively. "What you really mean to ask is if I commanded it to kill my brothers."

I swallowed as I looked him in the eye.

The faun scoffed. "My family was on a routine diplomatic mission. One *I* was supposed to be leading until Prospero called me away at the last moment. My father thought it wiser to entrust the task to the golden boys." He glowered as he spoke, reliving bitter familial drama. "My brothers were caught in the wrong place at the wrong time. Their deaths, and my father's, are exactly what they appear to be. And woe be to any that had a hand in any of it."

The faun trembled with rage and his eyes went nearly black. I decided it best not to press the issue.

Chapter 37

"The human won't die on our watch," announced Duchess Ariadne.

A small crowd surrounded Kasper's bed. Orpheus and Hera behind me, with other fauns outside the room. Maura the minotaur stood watch, with two more of her crew also outside. I was pretty sure the fauns and minotaurs watched each other more than they watched me.

The duchess was here as the head of the Amaranth Circle, putting the ceremony behind her and wearing a loose robe. I thought it curious she was seeing to Kasper personally, but apparently this was an embarrassing event for the kingdom. Royal guests should not be wounded. The silvans were hoping to stave off an international incident.

The biker coughed. "I don't know what all the fuss is about. It takes more than a little indigestion to kill me."

"Night willow is more than a little indigestion," Ariadne chided, "and you very well may have died without our healing talents."

"Great," he rasped. "Can I get my lollipop and get out of here?"

She placed a hand on his chest as he pushed to sit up. Then Maura put her mitt down and Kasper couldn't budge. The old man stroked his beard and muttered to himself, eyes pleading with me to do something. I motioned my head to the fauns behind me. It took him a moment to understand the circumstances, but his face darkened in acknowledgment.

We weren't going anywhere.

Orpheus questioned the scribe, who was predictably difficult even after my prodding. But the story came out, exactly as I remembered it. It wasn't what the duke was hoping to hear. If I had been the problem, then he would've already had a handle on it. It was simpler that way. Humans come in, do bad, get caught. Instead Orpheus had a legitimate conspiracy on his hands, with the main perpetrator in the wind.

Duchess Ariadne cleared her throat. "While the human is out of the woods, so to speak, his pain will continue without our constant supervision."

Kasper tried to smile but it came out like a grimace. "Constant attention doesn't sound so bad," he rasped.

"What's worse, the minute we suspend treatment, his condition will worsen."

"I don't believe this," I said. "You can't heal him either?"

"Night willow can easily be negated, but the human requires a day of sunlight."

I almost shot back at her before realizing how simple the

cure was. But that would mean... "Kasper needs to leave the Nether."

Ariadne nodded. "From this point, it's as simple as that."

I crossed my arms and glanced at the Duke of Bone. "I'm assuming he's allowed to leave?"

Orpheus didn't answer. Kasper grunted and grabbed my arm, pulling me close.

"Broham, this was planned in advance."

I nodded, already knowing that much.

"Even the manticore couldn't scratch me." He pulled me closer, angrily grinding his jaw. "They couldn't get through my tattoos so they went inside my body."

Heavy hooves marched through the hall until Throok ducked into the room. He placed a hand on Maura's shoulder and thanked her vigilance as the blue medician from the river entered.

"Electra has something to say," announced the minotaur.

The whole room turned to the girl. She spoke with a shaky voice. "We uncovered suspicious behavior in the distribution of fortune cake. We believe Val directed the slices the humans received."

Orpheus frowned. "The dryad."

"That proves it," I said. "The note, the coin. It was all a setup."

The medician called to the door. "Nala?" The last nymph who'd been massaging Kasper in the river entered. "Tell them what you told me."

The girl swallowed. "The wizard fired his gun first." The fauns eyed me angrily, but Electra prodded her to continue.

The nymph cleared her throat nervously. "But Val supplied the poisoned cherries. And the faun had already drawn his knife."

Orpheus cursed and she flinched.

"I have word of a satyr couple who saw the pentagram at the Wishing Tree," continued Throok. "Before Cisco was there. My people are trying to locate them."

"It's not necessary," muttered the Duke of Bone. He waved his bodyguard away. "You can ease off."

"But sir..."

"The humans are free. Do you understand me?"

Hera bowed and backed away. Orpheus glared at Nala.

"Let's give them a moment, dear," said Ariadne, pulling the nymphs to a graceful exit. The few remaining in the room bitterly contemplated the next steps.

"There's one more thing," said Throok. "We found an underwater tunnel near the waterfall. I have people investigating."

Orpheus stepped to the door and addressed all three bodyguards. "Find where that tunnel leads. Now." They marched away.

"That's great news," I said, breathing a little easier. "I need to go after her."

The duke nodded. Kasper began to sit up. "I'll just get my clothes and be on my way."

Maura's arm put an end to that plan.

"Fine," he groused. "I'll go naked."

My tone hardened. "You heard the duchess. You're in no condition to go on a Nether hunt."

"Ridiculous. We let Milena down. *I* let *you* down. I need to—"

"Kasper, you're done. I can't worry about you while I'm going after Milena. I need you back topside."

"We'll get him there," said Orpheus.

The biker scoffed. "No offense, goat man, but I'd rather take my chances with the manticore."

Both men stared defiantly at each other.

I sighed and turned to the minotaur. "Throok, you've been a dependable friend throughout all this. Can you see to it that Kasper gets back safely?"

He solemnly shook his head. "Impossible. A bride and groom cannot leave the days-long folkmoot of their wedding. If they do, not only does it curse their futures together, it officially nullifies the union."

I chewed my lip. Stupid silvans and their stupid rules. I couldn't go and ask Throok to give up all that for us.

"I'll go," piped up Maura. "The bull and I have been wanting a trip. The human has proved his valor. We'll protect him with our lives."

"Is there any chance I can get a personal nurse from the Amaranth Circle too?" asked Kasper.

Maura snorted. "Sorry. I'm all you're gonna get."

The old man sighed loudly and poorly hid his appreciative smile.

"Then it's settled," I said, shaking Kasper's hand.

"One more thing, broham," he said in warning. "I think my mind was messed with. We're animists, so that junk doesn't work well against us, but who knows what state of mind Milena's in right now."

I gritted my teeth. The dryad had even managed to throw me for a loop momentarily, and it wasn't too long ago I watched Milena succumb to a vampire compulsion. If I ever got her out of this, I vowed to train up her mental fortifications.

"Make sure our people are safe topside," I said.

The folkmoot still raged on, and it was still light outside, or at least in the giant chamber making up the castle lawn. I'd seen the plant-based illumination dim during the ceremony, but it gave no indication of doing that as the night wore on.

A contingent of silvans stood at the gate near the waterfall. Not just the border guards, but a royal troop. Orpheus had given me directions and watched from a short distance away. Duchess Ariadne was in attendance. Even the high king himself was here to see me off.

I felt a bit awkward at being the center of so much attention. Surely they didn't need an armed escort to walk me out the gate. But then, trust was running low these days.

I gazed past the crowd in hopes of seeing my friends. Throok was elsewhere, readying Kasper for his journey. Neither would be coming this way. I was also disappointed to miss Ceela. My inquiries were rebuffed.

"Do not worry about the bride and groom," placated King Vesuvius. "Young lovers are not for us to ponder."

I licked my lips as I prepared to press ahead. "I'd hate to put them out, but I've been meaning to speak with you, Your Majesty. There are... worrying things going down in Miami, and maybe down here. I'd like to discuss the possibility of coming to an agreement of sorts. You know, a way to watch each other's backs."

"Ha ha ha!" laughed Vesuvius with a good-natured smile. "For a human, you're well versed in silvan ways."

I arched an eyebrow, unsure of his meaning, and he explained.

"A folkmoot like this is the perfect place to discuss an alliance. An agreement with a notable human such as yourself would bring my people pleasure. But this is something that would be days in the making, over the course of parties and meetings and barter." He took a long breath and frowned. "Methinks that dedication of time is something you can't currently afford."

"You're right. But I'm hoping we can talk soon."

"Of course. But while we're speaking, what worrying signs have you seen?"

I chewed my lip, wondering how far to push this now. "I'm not entirely sure, to be honest. I hope to have something definitive next time we talk."

He nodded as I backed away, checking the distance for any more visitors. This was it, then. We said our goodbyes and I turned for the gate. The guards let me pass without a word, and just like that I was in another chamber, another glade.

It was grassy, with wildlife. It was still the nice part of the Nether but it lacked the guests and joviality of the folkmoot. I approached the far wall, dotted with passages, and located the one Orpheus had directed me to. I popped a cartridge into my shotgun and dropped it into the shadow, making my way for the exit.

The rock passage shifted and closed ahead of me. I staggered backward and looked up at a giant man shaped from the rock.

"Wizard," called a girl's voice. Ceela. I turned and she approached with something in her hand. "I thought I told you not to leave without me."

She was a welcome sight, but my expression was strained given the reason for my departure. She stopped at my side.

"It's a great dishonor to leave a silvan wedding without offering a gift. It's as good as cursing the union."

I rolled my eyes. "Anyone ever tell you silvans you have too many rules?"

"They're not rules, Cisco, they're the way of things. Now hand over my gift or you're gonna have a very angry silvan complain to a very angry mountain giant."

I snickered and nervously scratched my neck. "Fine. You know, your silvan messenger liked my coffee so much I brought you a moka pot with some ground espresso. But I left it in the bag back in my room."

Her eyes glittered. "Subsistence. Very wise. I look forward to it. Although it won't do in this case. You need to hand me something now."

In the distance at the gate, I realized I had an audience. The royal troop.

"Uh, but I..."—the mountain giant grumbled—"suppose I can give you a second gift." I pouted and dug into my pockets, realizing I'd also left my normal clothes behind. I was still wearing the suit. The engagement ring was my possession of greatest value, still safely tucked into my jacket, but I had every intention of using that today. "I don't suppose you want a *Knight Rider* key chain?"

She stared daggers into me.

"Just kidding."

I dug into my belt pouch and pulled out a birthday candle. She wasn't impressed.

"This is one of those ones that you blow out and it lights up again. You know—"

"Cisco, can you get serious here?"

Sheesh, for a mostly ceremonial second gift, she was really giving me a hard time. It took me another minute of scrounging. "Ah, I got it. Here's a small bag of yopo seeds. These things are psychedelics. They can get pretty trippy but you won't lose your mind. Just start with one or two and go up from there."

"Ooh!" she purred, "I bet Throok would love these on our honeymoon!"

I sighed in relief.

The principesse then handed me a fold of leather. "And for you."

I untied a small ribbon and opened the wrap to reveal... a

pair of sunglasses. And these weren't just any sunglasses, but a mega-futuristic pair of Oakleys from the nineties. Matte gray grips, sharp angles, mirror lenses—the kind of thing teenager-me thought was super cool. These things were... a little tacky actually.

"Uh... thanks?"

Ceela smiled. "For when your path is too bright. Don't lose them. They were mine." She reached up to kiss my cheek. "I hope you find her, Cisco."

As the satyr turned to go, I considered asking for my yopo seeds back. But the sound of the mountain giant settling stole my attention. Luckily, the big guy was just clearing the passage and getting out of my way.

I held up a fist of solidarity and strolled into the tunnel.

Chapter 38

I leaned beside the shallow pool. The water was clear and still, and barely looked larger than an overgrown pothole. But it was bigger upon close inspection, leading sideways under the wall and likely into a larger underwater cave network.

This was where Gemma had escaped with Milena, and unless the mermaid had headed back into silvan territory, there was only one direction she could've gone from here.

I hurried down the tunnel, not a moment to spare. I figured I was an hour behind them. Depending how far they were going and how troublesome Milena proved, it was possible I could catch up. As long as there wasn't anymore swimming involved.

My jacket flapped behind me as I sprinted, eyes scanning the passage. The clumps of grass grew more sparse. I was entering the Margins.

I skidded at a small alcove in the dirt wall. A large stone in the ground served as a makeshift wall. I slipped behind it to find a pocket for people to hide in. The tamped soil appeared recently trod upon.

And then my eyes spotted blood. I traced my fingers through it and sniffed. The substance was sour and black. Silvan blood.

I couldn't be sure how long it had been here. I was used to silvan blood rapidly degrading, but that was topside. In the Nether, away from the harsh sun of the Earthly Steppe, their bodies decomposed at a slower rate. I wasn't versed in the intricacies and sciences of Nether creatures, but everything told me this was a recent passing and a fresh wound.

Perhaps I had hit Gemma with that first gunshot at the river.

The nymphs had been correct. I had fired first. It was afterward that the faun's knife had forced my second shot into the ground.

The amount of blood wasn't insubstantial. If I was lucky, Gemma was hurt. The mermaid would be slower on foot, especially if wounded.

I was close.

Renewed by the fortunate turn, I raced ahead, scanning the ground for a blood trail. Twice I encountered forked tunnels, and twice I let the blood lead the way. But it was drying up. The bleeding was being stemmed.

I rushed forward, willing luck to stay on my side just a little longer, when I entered a large round chamber similar to the one we'd passed through with the upirs. An interchange. Multiple passages headed out in a starburst pattern.

I scowled. With so little blood left and so many possible exits, it would take valuable time to get back on track. The silvan blood was too difficult to pick up from a distance, even with my shadow sight.

But I did spot a faint green glow, pulsing like a heartbeat.

I entered the passage and picked up Milena's snake charm necklace. The clay was completely black now, dried and warped, like it had been overcooked in an oven.

This wasn't good. Milena was supposed to have an extra day, but that was with Chevalier's magic. Without the charm staving off the pestilence, her condition was sure to degrade fast.

I didn't know if Milena had done this on purpose or by accident. I didn't know if it was another assassin trick to draw me away, like the coin. The only thing I was sure of was I needed to pick a tunnel, one passage out of ten, and that I needed to operate on a little faith.

I charged through the passage with the charm, feeling like I was close. Telling myself I had to be. Not seeing any more blood but making up for it with pure, focused speed. When the sound of light coughing echoed to my ears, I knew my persistence had paid off. I wound around the corner and found her huddled in the distance in the center of the tunnel.

"Milena!"

She shivered on the ground, feverish, without answering. I ran, needing her back in my arms, back under my protection. I called again as I closed on her, but she didn't look up. There was something wrong.

Ten feet away from her, I sensed it in my peripheral vision. I skidded backward, slipping into the rich shadow of the Nether, claws and teeth ripping by me.

My boots scraped lines in the dirt as I spun back into the world facing Gemma. She was in human form, wearing a tight wrap around her torso. A ripped length of Milena's skirt was tightly knotted around her thigh, lines of dried black blood painting her pale skin.

"Damn you!" she spat. "This hurts more than you know."

"I've been shot before. Besides, you're the one who told me to shoot first and ask questions later, right?"

She glowered and lunged at me with long claws. I batted them aside with my forearm and popped her in the jaw. Her claws went for my stomach. I faded into the shadow behind her and planted my boot into her spine, sending her face into the ground.

Gemma spun in the dirt, scowl broadening. "I hate you!"

"The feeling's more than mutual."

"You killed my sister, you bastard."

"And how many people hate you, in your line of work? How many people have you killed?" I stepped toward her and kneeled close. "How many families have your contracts split apart and destroyed?"

"I didn't do this for the contract."

I nodded solemnly. "Too bad, because then I could've bought you out."

"You'll never buy me," she hissed. "I'll come after you.

I'll come after her. I'll kill everyone you've ever loved."

Milena moaned. "Cisco..."

I turned my attention to her. She was crumpled in a pile, half delirious. While I was distracted, Gemma struck.

And was caught just inches from my face.

A twine of shadow stretched from her neck to the ground, taut like a leash. The mermaid reddened in rage as she forced all her might against it.

"It didn't need to go like this," I muttered, and I squeezed my fist tight. The shadow constricted around Gemma's throat.

I hurried to Milena, clutching her in my arms, trying to rouse her. She was charmed, under the mermaid's spell. As I dug through my belt pouch, Gemma dragged herself toward me, reaching with claws as she gasped for airless breaths. Even choking to death, her only goal was killing me.

I pushed the white powder into Milena's nose, having her breathe it in. She instantly recoiled and came to her senses, eyes stabilizing on my face. "Cisco!" We hugged tightly and she shuddered in my arms. "My insides hurt."

"Just hang in there."

I pulled the snake charm from my pocket. My palm came up holding a string and chunks of clay, dust spilling between my fingers. Our eyes met, both understanding the significance of the necklace's destruction.

"No," I snapped. "I won't let you—"

I pulled out my copper knife and slashed my palm open, incanting the blood into its purest form. I painted Milena's bare shoulder with it. I squeezed out more blood and cupped it to her mouth. As she slurped it up, Gemma wheezed in the dirt, convulsing as she turned blue.

"We'll figure something out," I said. "We'll..."

The twine of shadow choking Gemma snuffed out. I spun as the mermaid gasped back to life, sounding like something from a horror movie. I hadn't been the one that released her.

And then I realized too late as I was tackled and my entire world turned upside down.

Chapter 39

I came to, head woozy, hot breath on the scruff of my neck. My body dragged on the ground in a swaying motion. Weakly, I forced my eyes partway open. Locks of brown hair tickled my face. The breath was rank. I was being held like a mother cat holds her kitten, except this mama was a man-eater.

I fought the urge to tense so as to keep the illusion I was still asleep. I wasn't dead yet. That was a good start.

The ground was damp, the rocky walls slick with water. How long had I been out? This terrain was unfamiliar, farther in the Margins than I'd ever ventured. It must've been a new dominion.

I should've known Gemma was working with the manticore. Murmurs from somewhere out of sight confirmed she was working with more. Behind us. Were the gnolls in on this too? For a brief moment I hoped I'd been saved by the upirs. But I knew that was impossible.

The only people I could see were Gemma, limping

ahead, leading Milena. She looked healthier, thankfully. The protection medallion was gone but the last-minute blood magic had given her system a boost. It wouldn't last long.

My head lolled as I tested the manticore's bite. Her teeth were clamped tightly on my shirt and jacket collar. It was a bit restraining though left hope of escape. The shadow might not help but a quick cut of cloth would. Unfortunately, I'd dropped my ceremonial knife after being pounced on.

I couldn't be sure how bad the situation was without seeing who else was here. One thing I did know, however, was that I didn't want to get where they were taking us. As my arm dragged over the dirt, I discreetly turned my hand around and reached through the ground, into the shadow, fingers folding around the grip of my shotgun.

"You've done well," announced a scraping voice.

The manticore stopped. Gemma pulled Milena aside. I remained limp, frightened by the voice I'd heard before, the one that had commanded the man-eater not to kill me. This time it wasn't projected through maddening magic. It didn't scratch at my mind. Still, it was horrifying for an entirely different reason.

The woman was close.

I could easily make out the depths of the dark chamber. A sister in black stood very near, enveloped in shadow. She wore a twisted hat that ended in a point. From its wide brim hung a black shawl that covered her face, the whites of her teeth and eyes barely visible. Her flowing black dress was similarly see-through, with various skins and feathers hanging at her plump waist. The witch's arms were bare, off-color gray skin cold and mottled. There was something otherworldly about the eldritch figure, but also something very near and familiar. Grandmotherly. She definitely wasn't human or silvan. I was beginning to wonder if she wasn't a fiend either.

The manticore abruptly dropped me to the ground and settled on her haunches behind me. She growled in warning, making it clear she knew I was awake and hoping I tried something. I scowled and bided my time.

A voice rang out behind me.

"The human wizard, as agreed."

High King Vesuvius strolled ahead, eyes to the ground, and presented me with a wave of his arm.

"You traitor!" I spat.

No longer keeping up the charade of being asleep, I turned to take in the full contingent of guards who had seen me out of the silvan kingdom. Satyrs, fauns, even Orpheus. No wonder they'd made a big show of mounting up. They'd followed me.

The only good news was Ceela and Throok weren't among the backstabbers. Not even a minotaur among them, just in case. So they were keeping this from the bride and groom. They wanted to keep them out of it. Then again, what good was the principesse when it was her father who did the ruling?

"For what it's worth, Cisco, I'm sorry," said the king, still refusing to look at me. He chewed his lip and fought off a frown. "It is the fate of kings to make difficult choices."

"This isn't right."

"I agree. And I warned you that right and wrong don't come into consideration when acting for the benefit of a kingdom." His features hardened. "It won't be sacrificed for a human."

Still on the ground, I leaned toward him as if about to rise, but the manticore growled, calling me off. Vesuvius wasn't worth it. There were lots of assholes here. He only ended up one because he was too scared to go against the black witch.

She watched us, unmoving but not a statue, swaying and twitching and muttering in delight under her breath. My shadow vision picked up no traces of magic on her, which should've been impossible if she was really a witch. Either she was blocking me or she was something else... something external.

"I'll take it from here, Your Majesty," said Orpheus, hoofing forward with a bow. "No need for you to bother with these bungling humans."

The king hesitated a moment before nodding. He gathered up his contingent of fauns and satyrs and marched away, eyes avoiding mine. Chickenshit till the end. Orpheus remained with his three bodyguards.

"I see you've warmed to the untimely deaths of your elders," rasped the black sister knowingly. "It is as I said: power has its privileges."

Orpheus bit down. "I'm stronger than they ever were."

I glowered at him, conjuring every name in the book for

him in my mind but knowing they were all useless. I didn't doubt the Duke of Bone felt some measure of guilt for his part in this, but in the end he had settled for power and status. The same reasons he'd attempted to kidnap Ceela. His true colors were resoundingly clear. Rather than add to the already-considerable satisfaction evident on his face, I chose to ignore him, to treat him for what he was: an expendable pawn in a greater game.

The witch's head and hat swiveled to study her prizes. "Foolish younglings," she gloated. "You would do anything for love, even meet your doom." The woman was suddenly at Milena's side, shawled face close, inspecting her. I didn't know how she did it, but it wasn't spellcraft. Not any kind I'd ever seen. Milena shivered under her gaze.

"Don't look at her," I urged. "I'll get us out of here."

But she didn't answer, in a daze of the mermaid's making.

Gemma grinned. "This won't end well for either of you," she croaked.

I snickered at her difficulty in speaking. "How's that voice box healing up?"

Gemma scowled but didn't advance. She knew who was in charge here, and it wasn't her.

A whisper in my ear. "I am."

I recoiled from the witch crouching beside me. Had she read my thoughts? I put up every mental block I could and searched the shadows, trying to get a count of how many sisters I was up against.

But the one at my side was the same one that had been

here the whole time. An army of one. For now.

"This whole thing was a ruse," I grumbled. "You were never trying to kill Milena. You had her poisoned just to draw me into the Nether."

The hat dipped in a curt nod. The witch broke into a hungry grin, visible through the shawl. From this distance, I could see her patchy and scarred face. "Go on," she instructed, eyes flicking toward the man-eater.

I regarded the creature. "The manticore attacked Kasper and the vampires first. You sent her to knock out my support system. Take away my backup. When brawn didn't work, you turned once again to poison."

"A simpler strain," she admitted. "The girl's poison was a much more twisted concoction."

"What did you do to her?"

The witch cackled inwardly. "Death is a powerful tool, but a coarse one. It was her suffering that was paramount. As for your scribe, we arranged his return to the Earthly Steppe."

I gritted my teeth. I'd been played every step of the way. Every one of the witch's moves had the ultimate goal of isolating me from my friends and luring me here. And boy, did she have me now.

"So let her go," I chanced. "If I'm the one you want, let Milena return topside too, like Kasper. I won't try to escape."

The witch stood. "A noble plea. If I had a heart it would pain for what's to come. You see, the concoction in her bloodstream is incompatible with human life. She's going to die."

"No."

"Yes," snapped the woman. "And very soon. It's beyond even my abilities to save her."

"Because of your blood?" I asked. "What are you?"

The witch took a step back. "Does the clever wizard not yet understand? Have you been chasing us without knowing what we are?" She chortled, amused with her advantage.

I glared at Orpheus, standing quietly to the side. Unlike Vesuvius, his eyes bored holes into me, watching my every move. Two of his bodyguards flanked me just in case.

"Perhaps," mused the witch, "you have never encountered anything like us before. But you've heard the stories. *Oh, how you've heard the stories.*"

Gemma's eyes were bright and sparkly in the presence of the witch, the architect of her revenge. The mermaid held Milena tight, claws exposed. She was the weakest person in the chamber yet her actions scared me the most. She was easily capable of the simple twitch that would open Milena's throat, and there was no longer a reason for them to keep her alive.

This is what Gemma had wanted. Not only did she get to witness my destruction, but she got to rip my heart out first, killing Milena in front of me, making me feel what I made her feel for killing her assassin sister.

The black sister took in a long breath, drinking up the tense atmosphere like a fine wine, and watched me. "You wander your city like a lost child, throwing tantrums when you don't get your way. You believe you are good for the people, that they need you to protect them. You are blind to the greater machinations outside the steppes, of what shapes your world and the things to come." She paused pointedly, flatly. "You've bumbled into our plans."

"Manifesto bumbled into me," I snarled. "Why are you going around killing animists?"

The witch's voice spiked sharply. "You have stuck your nose where it doesn't belong."

I set my jaw. "You're the ones who don't belong. Not in my city."

"The city is no longer yours."

"My ass. Who do you think you are? Someone worse than vampires? Something older than giants?" I trembled at her fascination with me, at Gemma's worship of her, at Orpheus' cooperation. At Manifesto. Through cons, coercion, and curses, the black sisters had leveraged their will onto just about everybody. But how could they pull it off? What made them so powerful?

And then it hit me that Manifesto believed they were angels. It was the right ballpark but the wrong team.

"You're hellions," I spat. "This entire plot is being staged from the World Below."

The witch's eyes lit up. "So you *have* heard the stories." She appeared behind me. "The monsters in the night." Then on my other side. "The demons in your head."

"I don't believe in demons. That's just a word powerful men use to scare frightened ones. You can die, just like anybody else."

The witch pulled back, displeased with my attitude. My

lack of veneration despite learning what she was. "You will bend to my will, young one," she warned.

"Is that what this is about?"

"We can use you. Your influence on the Earth is not insubstantial. We'll give you a castle if you help us take the kingdom."

"You said he would die," hissed Gemma.

"Know your place, child," warned the witch, not even bothering to look at the silvan.

Gemma bit her lip, furious.

I heaved on the ground, knowing with every fiber of my being that I was in the presence of evil greater than any I'd ever encountered. The sister in black was mistaken—I *had* seen a hellion before. I did know something of their kind. But I knew nothing of the depths from whence they came. I was utterly ignorant of all the beings and desires and worlds that existed outside the steppes. And I had no doubt that, for the first time, I was good and truly in over my head.

"I'll work for you," I said. "But only on the condition that you cure Milena and return her topside. You let her live."

The black witch sighed. "What did I say about love and youth?" A grinding chuckle escaped her lips. She was enjoying this. "The girl cannot be cured. Besides, she's the one thing I did promise the assassin. We stiges are a crafty lot, but we pay our debts in full."

Stiges. I'd never heard the term before. Striga? Sorginak? I knew nothing about them.

"If you can't help me," I muttered, "then I can't help

you."

"Oh, young one, but this is how it works. We mine the ranks of silvans and fiends and humans and otherwise. We bend them to our will. And. They. Serve."

I grunted. "You don't know me too well."

"I could always curse you."

"You could try."

Her face twisted into a snarl. "YOU WILL SERVE."

I glanced to Orpheus, then to Milena. Felt the manticore breathing over me. The bodyguards too. And then I stared that bitch right in her warty face. "You can go to hell. Or home. Or whatever you call it."

The stige snorted, indignant at my insubordination. "So be it." She turned to Gemma. "Child, you may take your prize now."

The mermaid's eyes gleamed. She ripped Milena's head back by her hair and lifted jagged claws...

Chapter 40

With her neck exposed, I dove through the heavy shadow, past the manticore and faun guards. As quick as I was, I was helpless to do anything but watch.

But then Milena surprised everybody in the chamber.

She batted Gemma's arm upward and fell to her knees. She'd attempted a similar maneuver before, but she'd learned from the failure. Claws missed flesh and emptily ripped taut hair. Milena's other hand struck up and punched Gemma in the chest. The assassin choked, eyes wide, and stumbled backward.

Milena withdrew her arm to reveal my ceremonial bronze knife lodged in the mermaid's heart.

She'd been faking the daze. Not the whole time, but since I'd roused her with my powders. When the manticore subdued me and I'd dropped the knife. I didn't suspect Milena would secretly pick it up and wait for an opening with an MMA move, all while feigning a silvan charm.

As clever as it was, I didn't have time to admire the

deceit. The fauns swung at me.

I sidestepped into the shadow again, revealing myself at one's side and kicking him into the other. My arm stretched, sawed off in hand, barrel of fireshot trained on the black witch.

The trigger clicked but nothing happened.

The silvans ducked low, wary of the firearm as I cocked it and pulled again.

Nothing.

"Piece of..."

I cracked the barrel open and ejected the round, pulling another cartridge from the side saddle and slipping it in the chamber. The eldritch witch stood still, amused, as I once again aimed the weapon at her, clicking uselessly.

"Help me..." gasped Gemma, leaning against the wall and sliding to the ground. "Mistress..."

The witch's eyes never left me. "Your contract is settled. You're free to go."

The mermaid pulled the knife from her chest and dropped it. Blood welled from the wound. "But..."

A sharp intake of breath. "Unless you'd like to be dealt with yourself?"

The assassin's face crumbled at the black sister's horrifying pronouncement. She trembled, horror building as she realized her place in this. As she saw her mortality clarified.

The manticore, alert and on all fours, hissed at the silvan. Gemma, despondent, began crawling away.

"Not so fast," muttered Milena, rising to her feet and

reaching for the knife.

But after a single step, she wavered to the ground, ribs heaving in pain.

"Do you feel the end, child?" queried the witch, gnarled finger teasing the air, forcing Milena into a fit of coughing.

I snarled and formed a missile of shadow between my hands. It launched with spectacular fanfare, knocking the fauns aside just for being in its proximity. The full weight of it pounded into the black sister...

...And washed over her like a gentle breeze. The black shawl billowed sideways, flashing a horrifying visage baring its teeth.

"Do not presume to turn the darkness against me, young one."

I grunted and took a step toward her.

An agonizing screech roared at my side, ripping my forehead and nearly taking out an eye. Black feathers flittered down as the owl swooped away. I instinctively trained the shotgun on it and fired, but the firearm was still being suppressed.

Emboldened by the attack, the three faun bodyguards squared off with me. The owl veered and came around for another pass. I dropped the gun, dog collar on my arm bristling at the Intrinsics.

The Nether chamber exploded into spears of shadow.

Several struck the manticore in the head and chest. One on each of the bodyguards, doubling them over. I cracked the speedy owl too. Orpheus was sitting out so I left him alone for the moment, but the witch didn't get the same consideration. Five more spears stuck her from head to toe. I even snagged onto Gemma's ankle as she crawled away, locking her in place. And everything occurred in the blink of an eye.

The manticore yelped and hopped aside. The fauns grunted on the ground. The owl tumbled to the muddy ground at my feet. I lifted my boot and crushed its skull. The witch flinched at the sickening impact. She stood quiet, unaffected, but her eyelashes fluttered, amazed or impressed by the combination of strength and finesse.

"Please..." sobbed Gemma, desperately clawing the ground.

I scraped my sole in mud to wipe off the acidic blood before it did damage. I liked my boots.

"Listen up, lady," I growled. "I'm guessing you've heard the stories about *me* already, so I'll make this quick." Shadow drooped from my fist and folded over itself. "You mess with me and mine, and your lifespan gets greatly reduced."

I took a bold stride her way and another owl charged me. I slashed the air and an amethyst darksword sliced it in half, spraying blood onto the manticore. The beast roared.

"Every child you hurt will be a new needle I stick you with," hissed the sister in black.

I grinned and pointed the blade of focused energy at her.

The manticore scoffed and my spellcraft fizzled out. No shadows, no sword. She was furious, drips of black blood still smoking on her face. Her tail stump whipped tenderly.

"Watch it, kitty," I bristled, "or you're gonna get more

than declawed and having your tail docked."

"Let me devour him," snarled the man-eater. "He deserves no less."

"It's unnecessary," returned the witch. "He's powerless."

Milena coughed. She was still trying to crawl on the ground with the knife, still going after Gemma. The two women were frail and ragged but endlessly stubborn, each determined only to outlive the other.

It hurt me to see Milena like that, consumed by revenge in her final moments. I needed to stop this.

More owls screeched. The fauns and manticore backed away, wary of the blood spray about to ensue. Claws came at me fast.

I didn't have time for the sword, but my spears were immediate. They lashed out, striking and stretching, but they curled in on themselves like wisps of smoke and vanished.

I shot my forearm up, blue fire blazing as I defended against incoming talons. I bounced one away and slipped into the shadow to avoid another, but even my escape was interrupted. The manticore's magic nullification forced me back to physical. Claws grazed my back.

All the while the black sister tickled a finger up and down, embroiling Milena with pestilence. She dropped the knife and clutched her gut, convulsing on the ground.

"Enough of this!" I screamed, my entire body shaking, wracked with worry and guilt and unrelenting rage.

My arms trembled as I channeled the Intrinsics. Opiyel, the Shadow Dog, come to call. Black flames engulfed my arm, my back, rolling off me in waves, like my suit jacket was on fire. Slowly, deliberately, the shadow spilled down my arm like honey.

The manticore roared, straining in the face of my spellcraft. Her features went tight, focused. Disbelief gradually wore into her resolve.

I was resisting her nullification powers.

Owls shrieked. The fauns drew back into defensive stances. The man-eater lowered, ready to pounce.

"The Wings..." whispered the witch, staring at the growing forms on my back. "It is impossible."

A low hiss invaded the chamber, momentarily shaking my concentration. The manticore spun around. Serpentine scales whisked by in the darkness, disappearing before fully in sight.

The owls swooped. One, two, three. They thudded to the mud like bombs. Statues, frozen in poses of attack.

"No!" snapped the witch, head darting to the side. "You're bound not to interfere!"

A rattle went off, like bones jostling together. The manticore twirled to the cavern depths.

Power flashed at my side and Orpheus buried his bone hatchet between the man-eater's ribs. She bellowed as the three faun bodyguards converged, burying blades in her blood-red hide. She writhed in a collapsed heap.

"Fickle and flower," incanted Orpheus, "now is the hour." He grabbed the handle of his weapon and twisted it into the beast's heart. "Devourer of men, bane to all mothers—mine is the wrath for my father and brothers."

The hatchet flashed and he ripped the squealing manticore in half.

And then all hell broke loose. Or at least a part of it did.

Chapter 41

The witch let out a trilling shriek, so potent and deafening it brought everyone to their knees.

"You dare betray a witch of Stygia?"

Orpheus spat on the ground. "Did you think me a chess piece? A noble such as myself, your pawn?" The faun strode forward defiantly and brandished his bone hatchet. "No one eviscerates my royal family and survives."

The eldritch being lifted a palm and darkness crashed against the duke's enchanted weapon. The surge forced him back but he retained his footing. One of his bodyguards sprung into action, pouncing with a sword.

"No!" cried Orpheus.

The stige swiped her hand horizontally. Despite not physically contacting the faun, his goat head tumbled off his leaping body, horns digging into the mud.

"Behind me!" ordered the Duke of Bone. The remaining two bodyguards fell in line.

The witch spun to me. "And you, you bloviating sack of

blood and guts, of ramshackle magicks and grand delusions..." She appeared beside Milena. "You are nothing because of your love."

I gritted my teeth. "That's not true."

"She's your weakness."

"She's my strength."

The stige scowled, furious at my unrelenting certainty. She frittered her fingers in the air above Milena. "Then watch as your strength withers and dies."

Milena arched her spine and wailed. Her scream transformed to a racking cough, full of spittle and blood. Her eyes glazed over.

I'd seen death with my own eyes, countless times, and this was it for her. Milena was dying.

A bright light exploded down the passage. Gemma screamed.

I winced and shut my eyes, dispelling the shadow before the flash fully blinded me. The sound of hissing snakes surrounded us.

"Milena!"

As my vision swam, I reached out to her. My love, my world. Her breath slowed as she gurgled on the putrid fluid filling her lungs. Another blast of light hit us, knocking my head like a baseball bat. Milena's gasps of pain were immediately, maybe mercifully, cut short.

"No!"

I was bathed in my own shadow, quite possibly the only thing keeping me alive, but I hurt all over. Everything was too bright, as if I was approaching the sun.

The world slowed for a moment of clarity.

Glasses. For when your path is too bright.

I jammed my hand into the belt pouch and pulled the mirror shades onto my face. Immediately, the cavern came into perfect view. Not too bright, not too dark. The hissing, slithering snakes quieted, still there but more bearable, no longer whispers through my soul. Additional flashes bleached out all visible color, but only for seconds at a time before returning to normal. When it all ended, I found myself on the ground, hands in mud, panting heavily.

Orpheus stood tall, bravely defending his bodyguards with the boomerang hatchet out front. He was now a stone statue, like the bodyguards he'd attempted to save.

I frantically spun in place to find Milena, frozen in absolute misery, body solid rock. Beyond her, a short crawl away, were Gemma's petrified remains. I didn't see the witch. I didn't care. I scrambled and collapsed at Milena's side, tears exploding from my eyes.

A naked woman slithered into the cavern, hips swaying, breasts bobbing, neck twisting sensually. Her top half was entirely human except for the clump of golden snakes on her head. Eden in her true form.

The rest of her? Well, she had two legs, or at least her nude body split into separate thighs, but they were overgrown with green snakeskin and closed together, slithering as one. The snake body rested under her and folded behind, finally splitting off into what looked like two separate snakes, winding and coiling and filling the cavern floor. Among the tangled mass were what must've been other snakes. Pets, maybe.

"You can't interfere!" snarled the black sister. "You vowed as much."

Eden spoke, husky voice echoing now. "I vowed not to harm you or your sisters. There was nothing spoken of your strix consorts."

"Hag!" yelled the witch.

Eden cracked a smile. "Look who's talking."

I barely noticed the unfolding drama, uninterested in the shifting power dynamics. I no longer cared about anything because Milena was dead. The stige, the gorgon, they could both go to hell.

"You think yourself like the duke," charged the witch. "Playing along with Stygia until you wrangle the situation to your advantage."

Eden hiked a delicate shoulder. "I was your Damocles, working your poison at the point of a sword. That hardly makes me yours for life."

"Then you have gained nothing, foolish crone."

"You forget: I'm prophetic. The only one here who glimpses the future is me."

"What did you do to her?" I sobbed, still on my knees.

The gorgon paused at my side, full of sadness. "A thing of such beauty should not suffer so."

"But you killed her!" I screamed. "If it was your poison, you could've devised a cure!"

Eden's thin lips tightened. "No human can survive Stygian blood. My cooperation was necessary, not to kill her, but to give her the time she had. It was better that participation came from me rather than someone else."

"So you could keep a handle on things?"

"So I could protect you."

I groaned. "You could've stepped in ten minutes ago."

"I could not, Cisco." She gently lifted me by the shoulders and lowered herself so we were eye to eye. "I needed to see the Wings of Night. I needed to know your resolve. Past the hardened stoicism and careless bluster. I needed to witness the real you. The man who might weather the coming storm."

I spun away, uninterested in her motivations. What did any of it matter without Milena? What the hell had any of this been for?

The future? I didn't care about the future. Not anymore.

A jarring series of sniggers cut through my pain, discordant as they were disrespectful. My eyes flitted to the Stygian witch who had masqueraded behind the actions of so many these recent days.

"A sad play," she mocked behind the black veil. "A rueful result of a futile dream."

I locked onto her with all the rage of my being. "This was your doing."

She snorted. "I own it, failures and all. We still forced the gorgon underfoot. She cannot touch us. She cannot save your pitiful love. And she cannot stop the wrath I will now visit upon you."

I took a step toward the witch, voice coarse and heavy. "It's not her you should be worried about, stige."

More sniggers. "A stige I am, and so what? That word

should be hallowed to you. It reeks of timeless glory."

I stomped closer. "You're a bottom feeder, sucking up the excrement of a world you can't have."

She angered at that. "And you are worse: you're nothing but a human."

I took another step and my jacket exploded with roiling black flames. The witch recoiled as shadowy wings stretched from my back.

"The darkness cannot hurt me!" she crowed.

But her protests rang false, and her wild eyes told me the truth. She was afraid of me. Of a human bearing the Wings of Night.

Tethers of shadow lashed out and wrapped the stige's arms and legs. She grunted and snapped them away. I muddied the ground with spellcraft and lodged her in place. With an irritable force of will, she dispelled that too. But not before I lunged and wrapped my fingers around her chubby neck.

"Curse you!" she spat, attempting to knock me away.

My arms were seized with magic, some kind of foreign energy, but I didn't give in to the fear or pain. My thumbs squeezed the black shawl into her neck. Plump lips stretched against it as she struggled to speak.

"You... cannot..."

I put all my power into it, forcing the black sister to her knees, crushing the life out of her. I refused to hold back any longer.

Somehow, the eldritch witch screamed, all her rage and power focused on me, sound blasting my sunglasses and tie and hair like hundreds of locusts.

"YOU WILL PAY FOR THIS AFFRONT!" she boomed.

And then she vanished.

I staggered in place, hands left clutching a black shawl attached to an upturned hat.

But a whisper remained, just long enough for a lasting warning.

"Always remember," said the stige, "you are just mortal."

A rush of air escaped the cavern. My ears popped, the hairs on my neck settled. I didn't know how I knew but I was sure of it. The stige was no longer in the steppes.

"She's still alive," I muttered, empty. Gutted.

"Did you think it would be so easy?" posited the gorgon.

Chapter 42

I waited for a long minute, listless. There was nothing else to be done. I'd failed to save Milena. Giving an extra twist to the knife in my heart was my failure to accomplish something much more simple. The act of revenge.

Killing the stige wouldn't have fixed anything. She was one of many sisters in black. Their plans wouldn't change on my account. But at least I could've crucified the one who had engineered Milena's death.

Did I have it in me again? Another whole life serving nothing but vengeance?

I deflated quietly, unable to make sense of it all.

"Stygia is encroaching," warned Eden. "I sense we are living in a darkening dusk."

I scoffed, leaving my gaze on Milena's stone face. "What good are your prophecies if you played right into their hands?"

The gorgon was silent a moment, chastised by *her* failure. "The stiges blindsided us all. They're an aberration."

I finally turned to her, taking in the numerous stone fossils surrounding us. I had so many questions. Not because I wanted to do anything about it—this couldn't be fixed— but because I needed to make sense of it. I needed to know there was some purpose for it. That this tragedy had significance, even if my part was complete.

"You were the first to know," I said.

Eden nodded gravely. "But not the last. There are depths of the Nether that converge with Stygia. The witches aren't supposed to be able to pass through, but they managed it somehow. First, they get their hooks into my world, and then..."

"They come into mine." I worked my jaw, connecting the dots. Manifesto, certain members of the Obsidian March, the silvan circles. The Nether was already infested by a plague, and now it was spreading to Earth. "The owls..." I prodded.

"Strixes," explained Eden. "Stolen from Athena and corrupted."

I sighed, not as brushed up on Greek mythology as I should've been. I considered the golden snakes on her head. "I had no idea Medusa was a blonde."

Her eyes flashed. "If I didn't live thousands of years, I'd be insulted." Eden slithered close with a playful smirk. "I am the offspring of Medusa and Perseus."

I blinked. "A whole gorgon family."

"We're the daughters of the sea and the warders of evil." Her amused expression soured. "It's why Stygia needed us out of the way first."

"What exactly are you bound by?"

She placed a finger on my lips. "Quiet, dear human. That burden is not yours."

Eden pressed close, breath on my face, snakes folding into my hair. I was suddenly aware of her large breasts squeezed against my chest, stirring my blood. I straightened, uninterested in reciprocating her forward behavior. Eden's hand traced up my shoulder to my Oakleys. "The reflective lenses are clever, but hardly necessary for someone of your caliber."

My hand shot to the sunglasses before she could take them off.

She smiled, soothing me, and whispered, "Bolster yourself."

Then she pulled the glasses off. Eden's eyes met mine, inches away, and I was blasted with a powerful magnetism.

"Do you wish to save your love?" she asked.

"Yes," I breathed, vaguely aware of a snake crawling up my leg.

Eden grabbed my bronze knife and pointed to a small scar under her left breast. "A simple prick for a single drop of gorgon blood. Here resides the power to take life," she murmured, sliding the point to the other side without cutting her flesh. "And here the power to give it." The spot under her right breast was pristine. No scar.

"You can bring her back to life?" I asked desperately.

"She's not dead," said the gorgon. "I turned her to stone before the Stygian blood finished her off. She can be saved."

"Do it."

Eden pursed her lips. "There is a price for everything."

"I don't care about the price."

The gorgon appraised the knife. "This metal is not pure enough." She dropped it. "I need..." Her eyes lit up. "Silver."

I went straight to the stack of old quarters in my belt pouch.

"Not an alloy."

I released the quarters and dug through my bag, littering the ground with useless spell tokens. "The whistle." I lifted the string from my collar and presented the silver dog whistle to her.

She pouted. "Such an act of life should not touch something tainted by death magic."

I groaned, feeling like this was Ceela's gift exchange all over again. Then my mind settled. I turned to Milena's still body, took a long breath, and drew my mother's wedding ring from my jacket pocket.

Eden grinned at the sapphire in satisfaction. "Now *this* is pure. A symbol of devotion, a stone of love. I can work with this."

My heart was dashed as the gorgon crushed the ring in her hand. Golden power transformed it into a tiny spike the size of a nail. Eden set it against her ribs, about to prick the pristine skin, before whisking it away without completing the act.

"There is another matter," belabored the gorgon. She lifted me and slithered to a dark corner, sitting me down on a blanket of furs. I had no idea where it or the next item she grabbed came from. It was a handheld vanity mirror framed with shining black. "The Obsidian Mirror is yours. A gift."

I took it in my grip. It was heavy, much heavier than it should've been, but I didn't feel any presence of power. "I'm not the biggest fan of gifts from the Nether."

Eden laughed. "That's because we have no currency but barter. I demand payment."

I set the mirror beside us as she leaned into me. Over me. "What payment?"

A lithe shoulder innocently hiked in the air. "The silver ring is a worthy tool, but the arrangement must be consummated." She pressed me onto my back.

"No," I said.

Her thighs opened, scales fading into perfectly hairless olive skin, and the gorgon straddled me.

"I won't do this to her," I grunted.

"You're doing this *for* her." Fingernails clawed my chest as her other hand worked my pants open. "Look past the act. Do as Perseus did with my mother. It's the only way to give life."

Eden was beautiful, despite the snake wig. It went past her pristine complexion and large breasts and lithe body. It was the way she moved, the sway and grind of her hips. She could make any man hard on a whim. She eased onto me with a dusky moan and moved rhythmically.

"You must want it, Cisco."

Something was happening here. Something more than sex. My entire body tightened at her animal magnetism.

Shadows billowed from me as her eyes flashed. Her chest grew. Four breasts, then six. Eden rocked up and down, rows of nipples brushing my face, each with its own pair of arms grabbing, scratching, pulling.

I wrapped my arms around her back and pulled her into my face, forcing her body up and down as snakes slithered in the blanketing darkness. I gave in to the full pleasures and horrors, one and the same, and remembered something someone once told me about gorgons. They don't help you, you help them.

"Yes," purred Eden, slowing to an excruciating gait. "I give but I take. One kind of life for another." I couldn't stand it. It was unbearable. I pulled her hips into me. "I told you true, Cisco. A human cannot survive Stygian blood. Milena will have a new life now. Human no more."

"No..." I whispered.

Eden suddenly jerked her pelvis forward, arching her back and crying out as she quickened her pace. "Yes!"

My blood was boiling. I couldn't think, I couldn't do—I could only want. I shuddered as the words escaped my lips. "... Yes."

Chapter 43

I was roused from sleepful bliss, our bodies sharing warmth; tired, exhausted, but at peace. I opened my eyes slowly, reaccustoming to the dark in a bed of comfortable furs. Milena sighed in my arms.

I jolted upright, interrupting her rest. I cursed my thoughtlessness, but all guilt fled my mind as her large brown eyes fixed on me. "You're alive!"

"Barely," she breathed. "I'm so drained." She chuckled. "Like I just had the best sex of my life." Her eyes went wide and she peeked under the blanket. "I'm totally naked."

I laughed. I was naked too. I relaxed beside her and held her close. She sighed again, content, drawing the fur over our shoulders. "Did I die?" she asked with a trembling voice.

"I don't think so."

She frowned. "Did I have sex with a snake lady?"

I snorted. "You too? Um... I think we had a threesome with Medusa's daughter."

"Oh," she said pointedly. "That's kind of cool."

I kissed her passionately, flesh pressing into hers. We were naked and alone and I wanted her more than ever, but she was right. We were completely drained. And it wasn't lost on me that we were right where Eden had left us, in the creepy damp cavern so recently covered in snakes.

This perfect moment couldn't last.

"How much do you remember?" I asked.

"About Eden? Bits and pieces."

"Me too."

Milena bit her lip. "She liked to chat while she was doing it."

"Tell me about it."

"Not everything she said made sense." Milena took in a sharp breath of air, eyes going distant.

"Do you remember the stige?"

"Not much."

I whistled. "Mean piece of work. Imagine every witch from every horror movie you've ever seen mixed into one demonic grandmother. The whole thing with you was just a way of getting to me—"

I stopped when I noticed Milena's wet eyes, shimmering with tears.

"I'm sorry, baby. I won't make you relive the memories."

"No," she whimpered. "It's not that."

I watched her intently as she sniffled, trying to wear a brave face.

"We almost made it, didn't we?"

My brow furrowed. "What do you mean almost? We're

here."

"I mean a normal life. We got past the Covey and Connor Hatch. Past all the business that irrevocably scarred our lives. We were finally starting to look ahead."

My heart raced. Whatever was wrong I would fix. Whatever was in my power—

"I know about the ring, Cisco," she said softly, wistfully. "Your mother's ring, that you keep in your sock drawer, that mysteriously went missing two weeks ago."

I sputtered. "Yeah." I chuckled nervously.

"You were gonna ask me to marry you. But Eden destroyed the ring to draw the blood that saved my life."

My face went somber. "You know about that?" I cleared my throat. "The ring doesn't matter. Fuck material things. Our love isn't spellcraft in need of a token. It's you and me, together. It's what we have right here, right now."

She smiled sadly. "I don't have anything to give you anymore." She swallowed and owned up to it. "Eden told me. She said... she said I'm not human anymore. And I can feel it. Something is tying me to the Nether Steppe, like it's my home now."

My face was wracked with worry, but I forced a smile out. "I don't care about that."

"What if I do?" A tear fell down her cheek. "I can never carry your children."

I blinked in shock. I mean, that had been the furthest thing from my mind, but I'd be lying if I said it wasn't a blow. This was something real, something physical, but not like a ring. This was the personification of love and family.

Something we'd never even talked about, but nonetheless something we were robbed of.

She saw the crack in my face, the disappointment, and turned away. I pulled her toward me but she fought it.

"Milena, I swear to you that doesn't matter. The only thing I've ever wanted was to marry you. To spend my life with you."

"That's what you say now..."

I turned her face to me and shook my head firmly. "No. I don't need kids. I already have Fran."

Milena's face broke. "And what do I have?" She turned away and sobbed.

I leaned back, cursing myself for bringing Fran up. I'd been trying to comfort her, to assure her that I didn't care about the setback. Instead I'd only been thinking of myself. This pain was forever for both of us, but I was the only one with a safety parachute.

Instead of opening my dumb mouth, I caressed her shoulder. Why shouldn't she cry over this? I didn't know what it meant for her not to be human, but she still had her humanity. She was still the same woman I fell in love with.

Milena, if anything, was resilient. After a tragedy that claimed her past, she'd found a way to live every day to the fullest. To be carefree and happy and real in every way that mattered and some ways that didn't. It was that plucky drive that I knew would lift her from this malaise. She'd been hit very close to home, but Milena wouldn't give up.

And I would give her every damn thing she needed, even if it was a little time.

We comforted each other until she fell asleep again. It would've been nice to rest beside her, but I was wired. We needed to get out of this place.

This time, I was careful not to wake her. I slipped out of the furs and scooted over to a pile of neatly folded clothes. A silver whistle and spiked bracelet rested atop a polished vanity mirror. My other items, the copper knife, tokens, and even quarters were returned to the belt pouch. I slipped my clothes on, taking in the chamber. Once I was locked and loaded, I stood and paced the cavern.

The black hat and shawl were missing.

There were other changes. The strix statues remained but had been smashed to rubble, and the ones I'd killed had vanished without a trace of blood left behind. I couldn't say the same for the manticore. Its body lay in multiple pieces, skinned of its red coat. I frowned and considered the cold space.

A light cough echoed through the tunnel.

I pulled the shotgun into my hand and checked the breach, tip-toeing down the dark passage. My boots stepped past the stone mermaid who would trouble us no longer. I moved quietly and efficiently, leaving no time for a spy to escape, approaching a flickering light.

I rounded the corner and found Orpheus sitting on a large stone facing a fire, with his back to me. Two bodyguards, Hera and a man, stood a short distance away. The body and head of their fallen friend was wrapped in another fur blanket. Beside Orpheus sat a makeshift sack fashioned from manticore hide. Guessing from the mane of hair sticking out the top, inside was the man-eater's head.

"You can put your gun down," tempered the Duke of Bone. "We're not enemies."

"No?" I asked lightly, approaching but holding the shogun at my side.

"The manticore is dead. The Circle of Bone is avenged."

I stopped a few yards from him. "The stige was right about you? You were playing along the whole time?"

He sighed. "The Oak Table is the largest ruling body in the Nether. At its head is the Juniper Circle, a much smaller target. The stiges approached High King Vesuvius first, but the man couldn't keep a secret that large from a family of tricksters." Orpheus stoked the fire with his hatchet. "My father, Prospero, disagreed with the high king's edict. He sent my brothers on a missive to request help."

"A mission you were supposed to be on."

Orpheus turned to me with a curse. "The whole thing was my idea. But my father ultimately didn't entrust it to me. It was too important, he said." The faun grimaced inwardly, not wanting to speak ill of the dead. "We had no idea what would happen, but when it did we knew why. My father was overcome by the guilt of changing my plan, of being the one who'd sent his favorite sons and heirs to their deaths. He did indeed take his own life, wanting no more part of a world without them."

I peeked behind, making sure I didn't hear anything from Milena, and then dropped my sawed-off into the shadow and sat by the fire. "Your family's not avenged," I said. I nodded toward the bundle of skin and fur. "She was just a minion, forced underhand like the high king and the gorgon. Like you."

"Not like me," he countered. "I never had any intention of joining them. Vesuvius made his choice for the safety of the kingdom. I would rather die than give in, and die like my brothers and not my dad."

"That's good to hear, because the stiges have a long game, one that doesn't end here."

"End," grumbled Orpheus. "This has barely begun."

The faun stood and hefted the manticore head to his shoulder. I thought of Perseus carrying the head of Medusa, and how things aren't always what they seem. The duke trudged down the passage toward his comrades. I watched him go before calling out to him in the distance.

"Orpheus. Where were your brothers headed? Who were they going to for help?"

He paused and half-turned to face me. "A long shot. A specialist in Los Angeles who deals in matters of hell." He grunted. "She's nothing more than a thief, really. Her name is—"

"Don't bother," I said. "I know her name."

Orpheus snickered and disappeared down the tunnel.

Milena and I traveled lightly through yet another unfamiliar subterranean tunnel. It was the lackadaisical stroll of a couple who'd partied past dawn on South Beach and finally had to make it home. Even so, I remained alert to our surroundings. We no longer had stiges and manticores hunting us, but the Nether was still a very dangerous place.

"One thing I don't get," I said. "When you were under Gemma's charm, how did you have the presence of mind to drop your snake charm for me to find?"

She scoffed. "I didn't do that."

I blinked back surprise, which slowly turned to realization. "Of course. Gemma threw me off with the coin because she didn't want me to stop her escape, but she *did* want me to follow. She probably left as much blood around as she could spare, and ripped your charm off to lead me down the right path."

I had to hand it to Stygia: they put together a solid plan. At least until they came head-to-head with me. I nodded in satisfaction without acknowledging the part Eden or Orpheus played.

"Can we not talk about this right now?" she asked.

I wiped the smirk off my face. "Sure thing."

Milena was in a better mood now, considering, but there was no reason to pour salt on the wound. What she needed was sun and fresh air and friends. A vacation maybe. And then I decided to stop making assumptions.

"What do you need?" I asked earnestly.

Milena took in a long breath and put her hand in mine. "Can we just find the nearest rabbit hole and get out of here?"

"You know, if we do that we could end up anywhere."

"That's the idea."

We marched toward whatever the future brought us.

-Finn

If you're reading this, it means you demand more from your urban fantasy. Bullets and fireballs are a riot, but they're nothing without a layered cast of characters and realistic plot drivers. *Black Magic Outlaw* is my stab at a cut above the rest: non-stop action, true friends banding against impossible odds, and themes that hopefully make you put the book down and ponder, if even for only a minute.

My writing process demands quality control at every step of development. I hope you agree *Black Magic Outlaw* is the premium product I strive to make it. Unfortunately, doubling down on originality and quality in an on-demand world has drawbacks. It's simply not possible for me to get you a brand-new novel every month or two. The process takes time.

That's where you come in. If you want to be part of building a better book, consider one or all of the following shows of support. The best part? These displays of true fandom don't cost you a penny.

- Join the Outlaw Underground, our private Facebook group. (www.facebook.com/groups/dominofinnfans/)

- Leave an all-too-important review where you bought the book. Each one helps more than you know.

- Recommend this book to your friends. Link it on social media.

- Join my reader group newsletter, get a free Black Magic Outlaw story, and hear from me only when I have new releases or important news. You'll never miss another launch sale again. (dominofinn.com/newsletter/)

Simple, right? Five minutes of your time makes a world of difference to me and Cisco. Thank you for your heartfelt support. I'll keep writing as long as you keep reading.

- Domino Finn

Also by Domino Finn

BLACK MAGIC OUTLAW
Dead Man
Shadow Play
Heart Strings
Powder Trade
Fire Water
Death March
Blood Craft
Open Season

SUMMONER FOR HIRE
Tooth and Nail
Hell and High Water

<u>AFTERLIFE ONLINE</u>
Reboot
Black Hat
Trojan
Deadline

<u>Shade City</u>

<u>SYCAMORE MOON</u>
The Seventh Sons
The Blood of Brothers
The Green Children

About the Author

Domino Finn is an award-winning game industry veteran, a media rebel, and a grizzled author of urban fantasy and litRPG. His stories are equal parts spit, beer, and blood, and are notable for treating weighty issues with a supernatural veneer. If Domino has one rallying cry for the world, it's that fantasy is serious business.

Take a stand at DominoFinn.com

www.ingramcontent.com/pod-product-compliance
Lightning Source LLC
Chambersburg PA
CBHW051628180726
48284CB00006B/1639